Dangerous Devotion

Dangerous Devotion

CHRISTOPHER PORTWAY

LARGE PRINT

Oxford

First published in Great Britain 2006
by
Birlinn Limited

Published in Large Print 2007 by ISIS Publishing Ltd.,
7 Centremead, Osney Mead, Oxford OX2 0ES
by arrangement with
Birlinn Limited

British Library Cataloguing in Publication Data
Portway, Christopher
    Dangerous devotion. – Large print ed.
    (Isis reminiscence series)
    1. Portway, Christopher – Travel – Europe, Eastern
    2. British – Europe, Eastern
    3. Large type books
    4. Europe, Eastern – Social conditions – 20th
    century
    5. Communist countries – Social conditions – 20th
    century
    I. Title
    943.7'04'092

ISBN 978–0–7531–9434–8 (hb)
ISBN 978–0–7531–9435–5 (pb)

Printed and bound in Great Britain by
T. J. International Ltd., Padstow, Cornwall

To the memory of my wife, Anna,
who died of lung cancer, 29 July 2006

CHAPTER
ONE

It began to rain about mid-morning, spitting in my face like bursts of cold gunfire. The sky was low with grey cloud and it seemed to me, as the two of us walked between the tall featureless houses, that the whole of Kladno was closing in on us like a trap. In my hopelessness and frustration, the wind, the cold whip of rain and the dismal streets seemed to be combining against us. As we drew near the industrial sector of the town, I caught the smell and sound of a locomotive, shunting wagons within the compound of the steel works. The familiar odour was oddly hostile, its tang a warning of the danger we risked as strangers entering an unknown town.

Beside me, Gordon cursed the weather in his expressive London-Scottish brogue and I was comforted by the knowledge that we shared these sentiments. The hostility of the streets merged with heavy nausea — a sickness to be home, safe, away from the mess we had got ourselves into, away from Czechoslovakia, where we never knew who was a friend or a foe. I realised the war could drag on for months and that England was only a tiny speck of light a long way down the tunnel. If we stayed alive, though, we would make it back eventually, and the present alternative to our ridiculous evasion exercise was simply a return to the endless trudging, under German guard, along the roads of central Europe.

Being "on the run", at least we experienced a kind of freedom, albeit limited: nobody wanted us, most people were frightened of us, we had nothing to eat and nowhere to go. "Join the partisans!" had been our rallying cry at the time of our escape from German custody, but the partisans were nowhere to be found. I glanced over my shoulder at the receding suburbs of Kladno. No doubt the place had a heart of gold amongst the coal-dust and industrial grime, but it was the most uninviting-looking town I had ever seen. We skirted the grey slag heaps and veered off to the north, seeing small hope of succour among the lines of mean houses. In the shadow of a wall we held brief council until frozen into silence as a steel-helmeted German sentry appeared from out of the entrance to a military lorry park. He glared at us in distaste and we realised that our English *tête-à-tête* was taking place next to a sentry box. It just wasn't our day.

Clear of the town, hunger drove us to ask for food at an isolated cottage where our oft-repeated "Mam hlad" (I am hungry) eventually won us a glass of milk and a hunk of dry bread from a sympathetic but frightened householder. Increasingly, we hated ourselves for having to put these decent people at risk for aiding an escaped prisoner, but, other than resort to robbery, there was nothing else we could do.

Refreshed a little, we took to the fields and, by evening, were close to a village signposted as Smecno. Failing to break into one of its barns, we spent a miserable night in a damp ditch. The wet and squally weather continued into the morning and, to revive our cramped limbs, we left the ditch at dawn, maintaining the same direction across flat open countryside that seemed vaguely familiar. The worry that we were moving in a circle nagged us, but this depressing notion was at least countered by the appearance of a watery sun.

Entering a shallow valley, no more than a slight indentation of the terrain with the outskirts of a town draped about one side of it, we hurried on without much idea of where we were going. Now the world seemed peaceful, the war far away. The tinkle of harnesses and rumble of cart-wheels drifted over the abruptly still air. Along with the rain, the wind had died, intensifying the calm. A long dark wood, inexplicably ominous, stretched away to our left.

We headed warily towards a house on the very outskirts of the town. Its sturdy façade radiated the sense of reliability and security that we, as fugitives, had come to recognise as the sign of a "safe house". Someone called out from behind a row of poplars in front of the garden. Alert to danger, we initially ignored the summons, unsure if it was even meant for us. The shout was repeated, with a friendly intonation, and we recognised one of the words — "Anglicky" (English). So much for my conviction that we looked like Czech peasants. Warily, we turned to see a middle-aged bespectacled man standing at the gate, beckoning to us with nervous intensity. In the hope that he would cease broadcasting our nationality to anyone nearby, we approached.

"You are English prisoners of war," he said in poor German, grinning hugely, and I wasn't sure if it was a question or a statement of fact. Dressed in a dark suit, the man had the air of being someone of note in the local community. We were able to understand that he was inviting us into his house for refreshment.

Surprised at the lack of caution he exhibited, we followed him into a homely little kitchen, where we were treated to glasses of milk and a plate of mutton and potatoes which we wolfed down hungrily. During our meal, we were joined by the man's wife, a small grey-haired woman with kind eyes and a ready smile, who spoke no German. We attempted to explain our situation and asked for their advice. The man looked doubtful about us joining the partisans but intimated that he would see what he could do. He also hinted that he would be willing to hide us in the house until the end of the war, but we would have none of this, however tempting the idea of a home-from-home seemed. So instead, he proposed a hiding place some distance away, where we could remain for as long as we wished or until our membership of the partisans could be established. The man offered to have daily food brought to us by one of his daughters. We were immensely encouraged by his offer as we had no desire to remain in the house longer than necessary, endangering the family.

In the dusk, we were led away back into the valley to a rocky knoll about two kilometres distant, clear of the town, although close to an adjoining village at the base of the hillock. A long-unused quarry here contained a series of indents that were, in effect, narrow caves. Leaving us to select a suitable one in which to take up residence, the good man headed home, to return later with an armful of heavy, old blankets. Gordon and I set to work in the fading daylight, spreading these out just inside the mouth of the largest indent, where there was space for the two us to lie side by side, well out of sight of the nearest house in the village.

We settled down amongst the blankets, content. Given the reliability of the promises made to us, we saw no reason for not remaining in and around our bolt-hole until we had made contact with the local partisans, or even until the eventual arrival of the Allied armies. Wishful thinking, perhaps, but we were in need of some encouragement. Highly satisfied with this sudden change in our fortunes, we slept easier that night.

When I woke, it was broad daylight. Glancing around our shelter, I was shocked to see a girl standing at the mouth of the cave. She had seen me stir, but made no move away. A wicker basket containing provisions was clamped to the handlebars of her bicycle. One of the hand grips was pressing against her body, crinkling the dress she wore into shadow. Her eyes, big and bright and blue, did not waver. She stood motionless, seemingly untroubled by the risk she was incurring in helping the enemy of her country's occupiers. Beside me Gordon slept on.

My initial shock was replaced by an urgent concern for the girl's safety. I had known the enemy to impose horrible deaths on victims for far lesser transgressions of its rules. For a moment I was at a loss for something to say. The girl smiled, slightly embarrassed, as if she had accidentally entered a male dormitory. "Hello," I said eventually and then, as I remembered her father's statement that food would be delivered by one of his family, I added, "Are you sure it's safe for you to do this? Did anyone see or follow you?"

The girl shook her head, and I was again struck by her silence and calm. I knew she was not afraid.

"There is no danger." She spoke English with a composure that surprised me, as if meeting stray British soldiers deep in enemy-occupied territory was commonplace. "You have a good place to hide. Stay there and we'll do what we can to help." Her young, cool face looked upon me with reassurance.

Just as calmly, she watched Gordon as he awoke and struggled with his own initial surprise at her visit. Then she delved into her basket to bring out some bread and meat wrapped in a cloth. She passed these to us together with a flask. As she came close I caught the scent of her perfume. Her face flushed with a mixture of pleasure and shyness, making her beauty even more striking. She spoke again. "You are English, I know. Father has told me about you both. He seems to think you are his secret." The girl laughed lightly, her lips parted in a kind of challenge.

Both Gordon and I wriggled out of our blankets and, emerging from the cavity, rose cautiously to our feet. The girl's eyes did not falter. I half expected Gordon to jump fatuously to the defence of his Scottish ancestry, but he remained, for once, mute.

"You are very kind and very brave," I replied, "but please be careful. What you are doing is dangerous, very dangerous." She did not reply. Keen to listen to her lilting voice again, I asked, "What do you do?"

I was referring to her profession but she misunderstood. "I've been delivering cakes to the prisoners this last day or two. There are so many of them and the poor things are so hungry." Her eyes were fastened upon mine.

"Prisoners? What prisoners?" I enquired sharply, suddenly aware that there might be nearby compatriots, likewise on the run.

The girl stared in surprise. "The roads are full of them. They're making them march towards the west. The Germans sometimes allow us to give them a little food."

How out of touch we were becoming. It seemed like aeons ago that we too had been among the herds of captives evacuated away from the stalled Russian front in the east. The columns must still be going through. I felt a little foolish.

"How old are you?" Gordon asked with a soldier's directness.

"I'm 18." She turned her gaze to him and I resented it.

"Do you work in the town?" I asked. I desperately wanted her to stay and talk to us, despite the danger.

"I'm at college there, but I sometimes take time off."

"You speak very good English. How do you manage that?"

"Thank you," she replied with another heart-stopping smile. "I can only learn from books as the Germans don't allow it to be taught in the schools. I would like so much to visit England to improve my pronunciation. Perhaps one day it will be possible."

"Please do come!" I exclaimed with uncontrolled fervour. "You can stay at my home."

Again the smile. "Tell me more about yourselves tonight. My mother and father want you both to come and have a meal with us. Please come to the house when it's dark. You know the one."

"Will you be there?"

"Of course."

My pleasure at the prospect of seeing her again was enormous, as was my incredulity that she should want to continue this fragile acquaintanceship, despite the awful risk for the family. A strange excitement coursed through me.

"Have you any sisters?" asked the irrepressible Gordon.

The girl grinned. "Two," she told him and began to explain why they were both away from home.

I watched every movement of her lips, every change of expression on her face, mesmerised. She appeared younger than 18 but held herself erect like a soldier, full of self-assurance. As she bent over to adjust the basket on her bicycle, I noticed her legs were strong and smooth. The pallor of her neck in the weak sunshine contrasted delicately with the fall of her shiny dark hair.

"I must go now. People occasionally come this way," she said and I detected a note of reluctance in her voice, although it was perhaps merely my imagination. "But we will see each other again this evening," she added.

In silence we watched her go, a slight figure pushing her bicycle. I was convinced, even then, that meeting her had changed the course of my life.

CHAPTER
TWO

It is strange how, in war, one accepts the possibility of injury or death, but never capture. When I was taken prisoner by the 12th SS Panzer Division in the Normandy village of Maltot on 10 July 1944, I found the strange new circumstances hard to accept. That my soldiering days as a 19-year-old NCO with the Dorset Regiment were over — at least for the foreseeable future — took a while to sink in. For years we had been taught how to fight, kill and stay alive, lessons that had stayed with me as we battled painfully against a determined enemy in the treacherous Bocage countryside. Those weeks blurred into recollections of savagery: street-fighting among the ruins of towns and villages, clearing each house of its defenders by throwing grenades up the stairs or blazing away with our machine carbines in still-furnished rooms; the predawn stand-to in damp two-man slit trenches, dug as enemy artillery and mortar shells burst around us; the ominous and all-too-recognisable rattle of the unstoppable Tiger tanks advancing towards us in the morning mist; the man from my own platoon who, hit in the back by a phosphorous grenade, died slowly and terribly, screaming to be put out of his misery. I remembered vividly the swish of Spandau bullets scything through the corn as we advanced towards a target, with men dropping without a sound around me, and I recalled watching a Lancaster bomber spiralling earthwards; just three of its crew bailing out, and we on the ground shouting "Jump! Jump! Jump!" to those who never emerged. There were also more humorous moments: once, two senior SS officers, surrendering in the middle of the night behind the line, pointed out to me in perfect English that I had forgotten to insert a magazine in the "borrowed" German Schmeisser sub-machine carbine with which I was covering them.

I too was eventually captured after throwing myself into an empty ditch as a multi-gun barrage from our own artillery turned Maltot into a nightmare of flame and thunder. Other men had thrown themselves on top of me and it was, in effect, their bodies that protected me, their blood filtering down to me at the bottom of the pile. Emerging from this litter of human wreckage, I found myself looking down the muzzle of an SS sergeant's machine-pistol.

Beyond the hoary old injunction about revealing no more than name, rank and number in the event of capture I had received no advice on behaviour as a prisoner of war. Suddenly, I was on my own with no officer to tell me what to do. Escape, either back to the front line or home to Blighty seemed logical, but my fellow captives had no desire to participate in such madness. I have to admit that it took quite a time before the notion took serious hold on me.

Looking back, there were numerous missed escape opportunities during my first month of captivity, as we were shepherded eastwards across war-torn France and into Germany. I might well have got away by hacking through the floorboards of the dreadful prison train that jolted us, starving and mad with thirst, under a hot July sun for days on end, to the Polish border, all the time under constant rocket and machine-gun attack from our own air forces. At the Czechoslovakian border town of Tesin, I could have fled via the Stalag VIII "hospital" block, had I been quicker off the mark and successfully dodged the slow-witted *Unteroffizier* who was my escort. I learned from my failures, and a further attempt whilst aboard a slow-moving passenger train, bound for a working camp in Silesia, was almost successful. Alas, I was spotted climbing out of the toilet window and was dragged back by irate German soldiers.

A problem for the Germans was the ostensibly straightforward one of getting their prisoners out of the way of front-line operations when the roads were being strafed unceasingly by Allied aircraft. I lost count of the times we all — British captives and German captors — leapt for roadside cover from our eastbound trucks as rocket-firing Typhoons hurled themselves out of the sky. Our first holding camp was a French race-horse stable near Falaise, where we remained for some days. The further we travelled from the front the more unpleasant our treatment became. The quality of food deteriorated and at Alençon I fell ill with acute diarrhoea so that, for a week, I was unable to keep down the stale bread that was our sole diet. Things improved slightly at Chartres, where we spent a fortnight or so in spacious warehouses living and sleeping on a rat-infested, straw-covered floor under spasmodic air attack from the RAF.

Thereafter, our mode of transport changed from the back of lorries to the inside of railway freight wagons. At Limburg, inside the borders of Germany, we were brought to a stalag, Stammlager IXA, where I was to remain until the end of August. Here, we new arrivals were registered, washed (for the first time in weeks) and deloused. Any remaining belongings were removed from us. I became British POW No. 83023 and spent a barren week circuiting the well-guarded camp perimeter before we were put back on the trains again, travelling to the Czechoslovakian-Polish border under further spasmodic air attack.

Relatively speaking, the next stalag, VIIIB at Tesin, was bearable. The infinitesimal German rations were supplemented by irregular supplies of Red Cross food, and life settled down to no worse than stagnation. My first failed escape attempt from the camp resulted in my name being added to the commandant's list of "trouble-makers", to be removed to a working camp at the earliest opportunity. This is how I became a slave in a coalmine at Zabrze in Polish Silesia, its adjoining wire-surrounded compound designated as working camp E902.

Right from the start I found the occupation detestable. It would have been bad enough even had I been a highly paid coalminer in Britain, but having to work an unpaid eight- and sometimes ten-hour shift on an empty stomach for an enemy of my country was abhorrent. It was just my luck to land a job at the coalface on the lowest seam, nearly a kilometre (or so it seemed as we were dropped at stomach-churning high speed down the pit-head shaft) into the bowels of the earth. I worked a six-day, three-shift week lying on my back hacking at a ceiling inches above as the loosened chunks of coal fell into my face. Within very few weeks my ribs were protruding through my skin and every sore on my body had turned septic; I'd had enough. It was time to go home.

I found a like-minded comrade in Gordon Primrose of the Gordon Highlanders. A London-residing, tousle-haired Scot, he was a year or two older than me and we took to one another from the start of our acquaintanceship. His unit formed part of the 15th Scottish Division and he had been captured in the Normandy village of Bretteville. Unlike many of our compatriots in captivity, escape was uppermost in our minds; in fact it became virtually the sole subject of conversation. "We've got to get out of here!" he would exclaim in his rich brogue, and some mad-cap scheme would invariably follow. Our most feasible escape plan involved not only the unwitting co-operation of the RAF, the aircraft formations of which passed our way as regularly as clockwork, but also a pair of stolen wire-cutters, a homemade pulley device and a plank of wood, these last two items to be used for prising apart the concertina wire that lay, one double coil above the other, between the first and second fences of our prison compound.

The nub of our plan revolved around the overnight antics of the bomber fleets; their particular targets and route. Some nights they passed too far to the north or south, not close enough for all the camp lights to be doused, nor, if they were, far enough away for the searchlights in the guard-towers not to compensate by sweeping the fences with their inquisitive beams. Our plans depended entirely upon the extinguishing of all lights.

One particular night our prayers were answered. Not only did the waves of aircraft pass directly overhead, but they never stopped coming. And by the time the last wave thundered by, the first waves were coming back.

Emerging from the latrines, in which we had smuggled ourselves earlier, we crawled, dragging our tools, to the nearest segment of treble fencing. Lying on our bellies, hearts thumping, we cut the lower barbed-wire strands of the inner fence. There followed an interval as we spread-eagled ourselves — faces in the dirt — while a German sentry ambled by on the cinder path between the second and third fence. Waiting only until he was out of earshot, we prized apart the lower coils of concertina wire by hauling up the lower section of the upper coils using our simple pulley device and, at the same time, inserting the plank and pressing down the top of the lower concertinas. Spread-eagled again, but this time on the plank, we attacked the lower strands of the middle fence. Wriggling painfully through the resulting gap in the concertina wire, we reached the cinder track. Straightaway we attacked the outer fence, our hearts still in our mouths. We had very little time to spare before the return of the sentry on his rounds, but the cable-mesh was too tough for the cutters. At this point terror gave way to blind panic. The droning of aircraft was dying away and we knew that at any moment the lights would be switched on. Caught in the beam of a searchlight, we could be legitimately shot dead. Gordon saved the situation. With the strength that comes through desperation, he scaled the cable mesh at a point where it was affixed to a post doubling as a lamp standard. From atop the fence he reached down to pull me up after him and, as we balanced uncertainly on the swaying mesh, the lights came on. Dazzled by the sudden glare, we were transfixed for a moment, then, hesitating no longer, jumped into the allotment on the other side and dived for cover among rows of Brussels sprouts. A searchlight beam swept over us, its blue-tinged brilliance illuminating the vegetable patch, before passing on, leaving us in blessed darkness. No shouts or bursts of machine-gun fire issued from the guard towers.

Our immediate trials were not quite over. Creeping through the sprouts until out of range of the lights, we took to our heels and ran — straight into a battery of light anti-aircraft guns, which we had often heard thudding away ineffectively at Allied aircraft. With guttural commands — "Halt! Halt!" — ringing in our ears, we streaked away across an open meadow, miraculously escaping unharmed.

Having put several kilometres between us and the camp, we searched about for somewhere to sleep for what was left of the night. By daybreak our absence from both camp and work shift would be revealed and the security authorities alerted, if the artillery unit into which we had blundered had not already done so.

Although an industrial region, there was ample agricultural and wooded countryside between each grimy coalmining town that soiled this region of Silesia. We chanced upon a sizeable copse where, among the tangled undergrowth, we lay down side by side to rest. The night was cold and my jangled nerves prevented any possibility of sleep. Having cleared one hurdle, we now faced another. The closest Allied army of potential liberation was the Russian one, and reaching it had to be our objective. We were therefore faced with the daunting prospect of travelling hundreds of kilometres over alien territory equipped with no money, no identity papers, and very little food or command of the German language. In addition, our work clothes were conspicuously and ineradicably bestowed with big yellow Ks for *Kriegsgefangener* (prisoner of war) and our supplies were no more than a few of the more durable items saved from a Red Cross parcel.

It started to drizzle and I burrowed under Gordon, who had somehow managed to fall asleep. He awoke an hour later to berate me for keeping dry at his expense. A grey luminosity showed through the trees, and we rose from our damp resting place to make our way to the edge of the copse and into the eerie half-darkness of a waking world. To equip ourselves with supplies, we realised that we would have to resort to simple robbery.

Oddly, I didn't feel too dismayed by this, thinking that perhaps a short-lived life of crime would be fun. Gordon was even less conscious-stricken than I. It was almost as if he had been a professional burglar in his pre-military days although I was sure this was not the case. "The best time for the job is right now in the early dawn," he insisted, and although it had been I who had made most of the workable decisions in supporting our escape attempt, I was content for Gordon to lead the way in this new activity. It was late dawn by the time we had targeted a farmhouse which lay conveniently close to the copse. It was isolated and we were able to observe the occupants departing for work in the surrounding fields. A chained dog was barking incessantly, which suited our purpose admirably as we guessed its bark of real alarm would be ignored. Sauntering into the yard with an air — we hoped — of casual labourers looking for a job, we reached the door and found it unlocked, so ventured into an untidy kitchen-cum-living room. It was devoid of occupants except for a cat that fled when it saw us. Gordon unhesitatingly scooped up a pile of assorted garments, including a man's jacket, while I contented myself with a loaf of bread from the table. Another jacket hung from a hook behind the door and I grabbed this before dissuading my over-enthusiastic companion from nicking the family silver. Clasping our booty we withdrew to the woods, ignoring the paroxysms of enraged barking, to share out our spoils between us.

Then arraying ourselves in our new attire with, I regret to say, some levity, we threw our tell-tale working clothes into a ditch.

We had already experienced the foolishness of moving on foot by night, so resolved to make daytime use of minor roads and open fields, so long as we could maintain an easterly direction. We did possess a map of sorts, a sketch provided by a sympathetic miner, which indicated a line of urban centres through or near which we would have to pass en route to Cracow, the first major city of our intended route towards the Russian lines in Eastern Poland. At the time of these events, Silesia was part of the greater Germany, populated by Silesian people as well as ethnic Germans, all of whom we had to class as enemy. In Poland proper we hoped we might find help from the local populace.

Across the flatness of the landscape, the dreary towns and villages were easy to pick out. We felt obliged to enter one town if only for the purpose of finding out where we were and this we did, although not without some hesitation. The place was of depressing uniformity: rows of workers' houses, a few dingy shops and a deserted square. The exercise was not wasted, however, for at a road junction, a yellow signpost indicated the road to Chrzanow, which was on the route towards Cracow, and marked on our sketch map. Our bravado proved something else too. Although only a few people were about in the streets, those that were showed no interest in us. As we passed a crowded beer house, a gaggle of German soldiers spilled out onto the pavement in front of us. One of them, a corporal, asked

19

for a light for his cigarette and Gordon unhesitatingly obliged from our one and only box of matches, babbling away idiotically in Gaelic. The soldier didn't bat an eyelid. With occupied Europe awash with uprooted nationalities, any language, with the possible exception of English, passed muster, even if not understood. On the spur of the moment I nipped into the smoke-filled bar, removed the shoddiest cap from the crowded coat rack and returned. Now both of us could cover our give-away blond locks with headgear that was virtually a uniform in these parts.

Heartened by our reception — or lack of it — we made our way along the road towards Chrzanow, leaving the mean streets with undisguised relief. As we walked we chatted animatedly. Back in camp the universal subject of conversation, aside from our own escape plans, had revolved around food and the lack of it. There had been endless discussions about dishes each of us craved, and we had driven ourselves half mad with longing. Now, here within the hostility of our surroundings in enemy territory, we optimistically spoke of things we were going to do once we had made it back to Britain.

Reaching the bank of a stream outside the town, we bathed our feet in cold, rust-coloured water to relieve our heavily blistered heels. The road we were trying to follow now became erratic, running straight for a few kilometres and then taking a corkscrew route to serve half a dozen townships. Sometimes we walked along the road itself, scurrying back into the fields at the sound of approaching vehicles. In one such field we chanced upon the hot embers of a fire and we were able to bake potatoes gathered from a nearby clump. This was the one time we came upon food and the means of cooking it in the same place.

The autumn dusk arrived all too early and we cast about for shelter for the night. Within an hour we chose a cosy-looking barn. It was locked but we climbed in through an open window at the rear and found an inviting bed of clover-scented hay that shared the floor-space with sundry farm implements. Through cracks in the brick and timber wall we studied an adjoining farmhouse, noticing the thin plume of smoke issuing from its chimney. Eagerly we consumed the rest of the bread together with cold, burnt potato.

We slept well, disturbed only by the activities of the various types of wildlife in the hay, although these were far less unpleasant than the lice and bed-bugs that were the scourge back at camp. We woke early and lay listening uneasily to rough unintelligible voices, until we heard the rumble of a cart being driven away. Descending from our perch we found a heap of swedes, yellow and half-rotten, which we cut into portions and tried to eat. They were coarse, fibrous and made us unbearably thirsty. In disgust we flung the bits away.

The house revealed no further signs of life except for the wisp of smoke, so we prepared ourselves for a further forced entry. Adopting the bold approach of our last farmhouse raid, we made straight for the back door, gently pushed it open an inch or two, and listened. All was quiet, so we crept into another kitchen and, our ears strained for sounds from the yard or inner regions of the house, searched for food. I found a whole loaf and half a cake which I bundled into a sack brought from the barn for the purpose. Meanwhile, Gordon rummaged through a handbag he had found on a shelf. Sudden voices and approaching footsteps from within the house sent us into inglorious retreat, Gordon still clasping the handbag. We sped across the yard and away into the fields.

Once we were sure we were not being followed, we searched the bag and unearthed the equivalent of eight pounds in Reichsmarks. Burying everything except the money, we moved on, munching bread and feeling exceptionally pleased with ourselves. Even I was becoming inured to the profession of burglary.

On the second day we made better progress in spite of blisters and objecting calf-muscles but our general weakness from months of semi-starvation and neglect was apparent. Pauses for rests became more frequent and, as the day wore on, we found ourselves becoming increasingly light-headed and careless, walking straight through villages instead of detouring around them. Covered mounds by the roadside turned out to be potato clumps, so we dug several potatoes out, putting them in the sack with the idea of risking a fire or, as a last resort, eating them raw.

A lone barn provided a third night's lodging, this one stagnant and far from human habitation. The straw was musty and smelt of manure but was dry, so dry in fact that we used some as fuel for a fire, filling the place with smoke. The stuff made a poor heat source so we dined that evening on lukewarm potatoes as hard as unripe apples.

The ensuing days were ones of increasing pain and grief as we slowly reduced those kilometres to Chrzanow. Barns continued to provide shelter and were the single positive element of that excruciating walk, but further efforts to steal were lamentably futile. Urban shops held so little there was barely anything worth stealing or buying, and our one shop-lifting venture netted us only a couple of hard pears and a tin of spam. We did once catch a chicken, the wretched bird's squawkings being drowned out by a dog's barking. To celebrate this event we lit a fire amongst trees and toasted the limbs one by one until the smoke eventually drew a couple of boys to the fireside and we had to move on, stuffing half-cooked drumsticks into our pockets.

The buildings of Chrzanow appeared in the distance long before we reached the town. From there, Cracow, we estimated, would be at least another 50 kilometres, an interminable distance given the immense pain we were in.

"I'm not going another bloody inch," Gordon exclaimed at one point. "My feet are on fire, my stomach is aching and we don't really know where the hell we're going!" He really meant it. His feet were in a terrible state, much worse than mine, and he was right that we had only the vaguest of ideas about our route after Cracow. We could only continue onwards. Cracow had become a vital destination which we had designated as a major step towards the attainment of the Russian front line.

It was at this point that the train plan was reborn. We had discussed the idea of using passenger trains before our escape but had discarded it as too risky; virtually impossible in fact without any identity documents. But we had not delved so deeply into the concept of *freight* train travel; securing ourselves away in a railway wagon where no questions would be asked or papers demanded. This form of transit was fraught with difficulties, but as we got weaker and more demoralised, we decided it was worth risking the dangers for a speedier journey.

Chrzanow, we knew, was on a railway line which was part of a network that served Cracow. We were also aware that it was a junction, which meant that trains departing from the town could go in three directions, only one of which could serve our purpose. Snooping about in the freight yards, trying to decipher dispatch cards clamped to wagon-sides, would hardly pay dividends even if we weren't caught by militia or railway workers. The alternative was to locate a stretch of track outside the town where we could board a moving train. This would involve finding a suitably remote stretch of line heading uphill on curve, which would slow the train and foil the vigilance of the personnel already aboard it. Freight trains, we had learnt, often carried armed guards at the front and rear as a precaution against sabotage. Thus it was important for us that they remained ignorant of what we were proposing to do in the middle.

Again we took the road straight into town, this time intent upon locating the railway station and following the correct set of tracks out of the place. Our stomachs ached for food and rumbled audibly as we tramped the potholed tarmac but our spirits had risen with the prospect of new action. We plunged into a maze of streets, studded with intricately designed lamp standards, and wondered whether we dared enter a bakery and buy a loaf of bread. Citizens, muffled against the cold mist that heralded winter, scuttled along pavements made uneven by subsidence. A policeman directed desultory traffic at an intersection and a horse-drawn wagon full of soldiers clattered over ill-laid cobbles.

We found the station with no great difficulty. The freight yards adjoined it, the entrance, as half-expected, manned by workers' militia wearing armbands and carrying rifles. Any lingering ideas we had harboured of investigating such places faded.

We followed the eastbound line out of town, searching for the junction, but after several kilometres, we realised that the track must have split on the other side of the station. We were trailing a double track that kept firmly to a single route and we simply had to believe that this was, in fact, the line we wanted. It took two days to find a section of line that suited our purpose. For much of them we had walked beside the tracks, a never-ending spruce forest on both sides affording useful cover when needed. Two-coach local passenger trains and the occasional freight trains had us periodically scampering into the trees.

In this way, noting the speeds of eastbound trains, we came upon a curve of the line — not as sharp as we would have liked — as well as a slight gradient pitched in the right direction. Resting for a couple of hours to observe the performance of trains going both ways, we finally decided that this was the right place to try to board one of them. With a new course of action before us, Gordon had recovered his spirits, and though in pain, he tried not to show it beyond a pronounced limp. His earlier depression had lifted and his enthusiasm for the new project was stronger than my own.

A heavy-goods train jangled into view and we retreated into the tree cover, aware that the dusk was not dense enough to conceal us in the open. A tired-looking locomotive engulfed in a sweat of steam headed a long line of wagons that rattled and jerked against each other. We could see the driver and his mate leaning out of the cab and guessed that some obstruction ahead was causing a speed restriction. The pace of the train was perfect but it was going in the wrong direction. I cursed our luck, but then realised that the obstruction — if indeed there was one — might work for trains coming from the opposite direction too; those that had already been slowed but had not yet had time to pick up speed. We watched the brake van disappear into the murk.

Just before complete darkness, the sound of a train from the direction of Chrzanow lured us from our cover, hearts thumping against our ribs. Another large locomotive lumbered towards us, belching spark-infested brown smoke. We waited a few seconds to allow the engine to pass and then painfully sprinted for the track, confident that the darkness would be intense enough to hide our running figures. Crouching close against the passing high-sided steel coal wagons, we watched for hand-holds projecting from the mass looming above us as we ran, keeping pace with the train. I was also looking out for signal cables and other line-side impediments. Behind me I heard Gordon pounding at my heels, swearing with the exertion. A lever on the wagon I was pacing caught my eye and I lunged for it, clutching the cold metal and holding on. It dragged me along the ballast and I tried to swing my legs outwards, away from the menacing iron wheels of the train. My other hand soon fastened upon a hold. My feet dropped again, the toes of my boots bumping along the line, but with my two hands firmly anchored I was able to draw myself upwards. A red mist curtained my eyes as I fought to raise my body to the flank of the wagon, my right foot searching for a toe-hold above the wheels. And then it was all over as, with a final heave, I reached the couplings between two wagons.

Gordon, to my surprise, was already atop the high sides and was working his way along the rim to join me. To our dismay the interior of the wagon was bare of anything except a scattering of coal-begrimed sacks. We shook the coal dust out of some of the sodden bags and gingerly sat down on them. The train rolled on, making no attempt to pick up speed. It was pitch black outside now and the dancing sparks from the locomotive on the tracks were the only illumination, along with the occasional chinks of light from houses we passed. It was impossible to tell where we were.

Abruptly the train screeched to a halt, the wagon couplings reverberating. We covered ourselves in sacks in case of a search, listening to an exchange shouted over the wheezing of the train. After a prolonged banshee whistle, the train jerked into motion again, and began to move away, but in the *opposite* direction.

Gordon and I glanced at each other. We flung the sacks aside in a gesture of exasperation, our white faces smeared with coal dust. The train rolled on, still quite slowly, and we debated whether or not to bale out. After the effort taken to board it, we didn't want to admit that we had chosen the wrong train. "Maybe they're just shunting trucks onto another line," Gordon whispered.

"Or perhaps there's a junction this side of Chrzanow after all," I suggested. By the time we had exhausted the unlikely possibilities, the train had picked up speed, so we were forced to remain in the wagon, come what may.

A glow ahead intensified, indicating a return to Chrzanow, so we took cover once more, but the train kept a steady pace as we rattled across a confusion of points and crossovers and roared through the lit station, back out into the countryside again. Which line had we taken? Going at this pace, we would soon almost be back at the gates of the camp. Bleak despair engulfed us.

An hour passed and the train sped on. There was no sign of urban lights or pit workings. Maybe we *had* taken another line? Eventually, we blundered through one large town, but we were unable to make out its name.

It must have been in the very early hours that the train began to slow with ponderous deliberation. The faint outlines of houses drew nearer the tracks. We waited, clutching wet sacks, uncertain what action to take.

With a final hiss of steam we drew to a halt in a small siding. As the sky paled with the dawn, we made out a handful of early morning workers; indistinct figures whistling in the semi-darkness. Furtively we climbed out of the wagon and dropped to the ground. Looking around to ensure nobody was near, we ran to the fence that bordered the yard, clambered over it and melted into a deserted backstreet.

A lane led us away past several houses. Clear of the last one, we lay down, shivering and apprehensive, amongst a patch of undergrowth. Exhausted, we slept.

The cold woke us. Jumping about to restore our sluggish circulation, we considered how to retrace our steps. The landscape around us was flat agricultural terrain, similar to the area we had walked through before boarding the train. Clearly, we had been transported deeper than ever into enemy territory. Reasoning that there must be trains running in the opposite direction, we decided to risk boarding a passenger train, so that we would at least know where we were heading this time. We thought we had enough funds to finance such a journey if the neighbouring township had a station. That we had no identity papers was a distinctly negative point, as was loitering in a crowded station, but, steadily starving to death, we hardly cared. And so, once more, a method of evasion we had initially rejected at the planning stage had, all of a sudden, become infinitely appealing.

If we were going to travel in style we would have to appear a little less like fugitives on the run from the law. We tried to tidy ourselves up as best we could, removing the coal dust from our necks and faces with water from roadside puddles.

By mid-morning we had re-entered the township and located the station. On our way we had passed signposts indicating Breslau and Opole on their westward-pointing arms, so at least we had some idea where we were. At the station we were delighted to see that Cracow was a direct eastbound destination, and that a Cracow train was scheduled for less than an hour hence.

My knowledge of German was dismal, and Gordon's was even worse, although his Scottish accent, and a smattering of Gaelic, offered certain similar guttural overtones. We had practised our lines, repeating over and over again the German phrase we intended to use at the station ticket office window: "Eine Fahrkarte erste Klasse nach Krakau, bitte." (A first-class ticket to Cracow, please.) We chose to travel first class for two main reasons. Not only did "erste" trip more easily off the tongue than the German equivalents to "second" or "third" but also by travelling first class we hoped to raise a little more respect from a universally class-conscious authority. Furthermore, we were likely to meet fewer other passengers in the compartment.

Our timing was perfect, more by luck than judgement. In the company of a knot of commuters, we lined up at the ticket office with what hoped was an aura of nonchalance.

At the window, Gordon, always happy to air his atrocious German, cleared his throat, spoke the practised words and received a hard look from a Germanic lady behind the grill, as she pushed a ticket through to him. Swiftly I added "Ich auch" and proffered our entire bank roll, hoping it would be enough. In fact, we received a considerable amount of change which I pocketed gratefully. The next service was announced as a *Personenzug* (stopping train) to Strumen, wherever that was. It seemed to be the destination of everybody else, which was unfortunate, as it left us standing alone, highly visible on an empty platform; just the occurrence we had hoped to avoid. To hide our nervousness we strolled up and down it and came upon a stall that sold frankfurter-type sausages. With money in our pockets and less fear of airing our linguistic deficiencies, we purchased several sausages each.

Seldom has food had such an impact. The sausages could have been made of dog meat for all we cared; we were finally eating after days of hunger. We sat on a bench and munched away, oblivious to any eyes that may have fastened upon us. We reasoned that if we were going to be arrested we might as well have full stomachs.

An hour and a half went by and the station began to fill up again. Our train steamed in 70 minutes late; a four-coach affair classed, we noted, as a *Schnellzug* (fast train) which we hoped meant that it would not stop too often at wayside stations. Only half of one coach was reserved for first-class ticket holders and we settled ourselves side by side in one of the four empty compartments, adjacent to the corridor and facing the engine.

The train gathered speed along the single track. Small fields, woods and villages sped by. Gordon broke into a slightly hysterical laugh and I too felt strangely light-headed, this time, however, not from the pangs of hunger.

The door slid open and we stopped laughing. The ticket inspector, tubby but authoritative in his *Reichsbahn* uniform, stood in the opening staring at us questioningly, obviously imagining he had caught two passengers travelling in a higher class compartment than their tickets stipulated. His "Fahrkarten, bitte" was laced with sarcasm and he was plainly taken aback when shown the appropriate tickets. Slamming the door, he moved on, shaking his head.

Over the next hour we stopped at the larger stations but only a few people joined the train at each. Equally few alighted and thankfully none invaded our exalted section of the coach. We stopped for a longer period at a busier station, Oswięcim, and although soldiers — some displaying the double lightning strike of the SS on their sleeves — were much in evidence on the platforms we still did not appreciate the significance of the place we were later to realise was the German-named Auschwitz. Although more people joined the train here, we were still left in peace.

The ticket inspector padded down the corridor at intervals glaring disapprovingly through the glass as he went by but took no further action. I had to admit that our appearance and filthy attire could hardly allay suspicion. The train bowled on, rocking from side to side.

There was another prolonged halt back at a sizeable station on the main line, and here our luck ended. Two military officers, a naval lieutenant and a *Wehrmacht* captain, entered the compartment, stowed their briefcases on the rack and sat down opposite us. Not knowing what to do, we feigned sleep. With my eyes closed, I imagined the newcomers sizing up our very un-first-class appearance with a hard penetrating gaze. Just for a second I opened one eye and was caught. The smiling captain nodded, seemingly eager to chat.

I nodded back, whereupon he asked, in German, about our nationality. We were ready for such an enquiry and had decided beforehand our country of origin was to be Hungary, as few outsiders spoke or understood the language. I mumbled "Ungarisch" and hoped for the best. Gordon too had abruptly "awoken" and started chatting. The two Germans were handsome young fellows and reminded me somewhat of fresh-faced American college students.

"I've never been to Budapest, more's the pity. A lovely city I believe," observed the captain. I felt this needed more than a nod in reply so launched, in halting German, into a description of Bristol, having never, at that time, visited the Hungarian capital. Gordon added comments about Glasgow, which hardly helped. Our combined German was atrocious and words of English kept slipping into our speech. But the captain seemed satisfied.

The lieutenant entered the exchange. "What do you do?"

"We work in a hospital," I said quickly before Gordon could come up with something sardonic or implausible.

"In Cracow?"

I nodded, praying he wouldn't ask which hospital. We had hit upon that occupation because it was comfortably vague, suggested useful war-work and because *Krankenhaus* was a German word we knew. To account for our dirty clothes, I tried explaining that we had been working on a farm in the countryside over the weekend, but I struggled to find the right vocabulary, and soon realised that I didn't even know when the weekend had been. Gordon fortuitously interrupted. "Fahren Sie nach Krakau?" The two men nodded and mentioned some barracks or office of which we'd never heard but pretended we had.

Our feigned sleep had ensured we'd missed the location where we had made our ill-fated boarding of the freight train but I judged the city to be close. At all costs we'd have to leave the train before the main

Cracow station which would be a large *Hauptbahnhof* packed with police and Gestapo. I stared out of the window attempting to pick out tell-tale signs of an imminent conurbation but the terrain remained obstinately rural.

The captain rose to his feet, took down his briefcase and sat down again. Opening the case with a snapping of catches, he brought out a bunch of black grapes in the manner of a conjurer producing a rabbit from a top hat. Grapes were a rarity in wartime Germany, even for privileged German officers, and they were certainly a luxury for the likes of us. Breaking the bunch into four portions, he handed us each a clutch.

"Vielen Dank," gushed Gordon and I with unfettered enthusiasm, wondering what the two men would think if they had known they were feeding the enemy. Gordon began wolfing down his grapes, stalks and all, so I kicked him surreptitiously, trying to indicate that we should eat in a manner befitting of our first-class status.

"Fünf Minuten bis Krakau," remarked the lieutenant, thereby supplying the answer to what we wanted to know. Outside, houses began appearing with greater frequency.

I mumbled something about being late for work as an excuse to leave the compartment and, with Gordon at my heels, slid open the door. "Vielen Dank und Auf Wiedersehen," we enthused as we left, flashing our brightest smiles. We moved to the exit at the head of the coach, hoping nobody else would be in a hurry to alight. The corridor remained deserted, giving us a clear chance to jump off the train unobserved as soon as the speed slowed a little. The ticket inspector was, thankfully, nowhere in sight.

The brakes came on with a squeal and we felt the slowing motion of the train. I unfastened the door, leaning out of the window and scanning the ground for a smooth landing place. We knew passengers would start pouring from their compartments at any moment.

Gingerly I climbed down onto the first step, hanging on to the hand rail whilst restraining the door from swinging open too widely. The wind was fresh in my face. A few metres ahead, I saw a heap of clinker and cinders — the spot where locomotives had had their boilers raked out. "Here we go!" I whispered urgently to Gordon who was breathing down my neck, and we jumped.

I landed heavily with a crunch, Gordon virtually on top of me, and together we rolled away from the moving train. The clinker was sharp, scouring my hands and legs, even through my clothes. Hardly had we risen to our feet when we heard voices further down the track. A group of passengers from an adjacent coach had made a similar exit. I wondered what their reasons for doing so were; simple ticket-evasion perhaps, or, like us, loathe to enter heavily-watched railway stations. I remembered we were now in Poland proper.

We climbed over a substantial fence and found ourselves amidst rows of lorries. Under the cover of the cab of the nearest vehicle we took stock of our surroundings. It seemed we were in the middle of a military freight depot. Further down the line of lorries, soldiers were loading crated machinery onto flat trucks. We could only see one entry/exit point to the depot and it was blocked by more soldiers. The high timber fence, made from old railway sleepers, enclosed the yard on the other three sides and lay in full view, not only of the soldiers, but anyone at the windows of the houses overlooking it. For now, there was no way out. We made our way to a derelict wagon quite close to the wall and lay down under it to await nightfall or the departure of the working parties.

The wait lasted through the rest of the afternoon and into the night. More troops arrived, cheerful fellows in overalls, as well as a further convoy of lorries. A group of soldiers took time off for a smoke very close to our hideaway, forcing us to remain very still and quiet. With nightfall, arc lamps came on and the work resumed under artificial light. Cramped and cold, we continued waiting.

It must have been well after midnight when the work finally ceased. The troops departed, the main gate slammed shut and the depot was plunged into darkness. Stiffly we moved to the timber wall, helped each other to scale it and jumped down the other side onto a road. Neither a car nor a soul was to be seen or heard and the windows of the houses were dark. Even for so late an hour the emptiness was uncanny.

Proceeding cautiously along the deserted street we made our way towards where we thought the city centre lay, not quite certain what we were going to do when we got there. A delicious aroma of newly baked bread drifted out from a narrow alley, and we followed the smell to a small bakery. The door was locked and I toyed with the notion of knocking, revealing our identities and asking outright for succour, since we were amongst a generally sympathetic populace. But Gordon had more straightforward ideas.

Some of yesterday's bread was displayed behind a glass frame that formed an adjustable window. Picking up a rusted metal hinge lying in the gutter, Gordon attempted to prise the window open. With a tremendous crash of breaking glass, the whole frame disintegrated. We each grabbed a loaf and fled.

It was our bad luck again that a military foot patrol had chosen that moment to materialise from the end of the alley. Even had they not heard the noise of breaking glass, the sight of a couple of ruffians, sprinting down the middle of the road with loaves of bread in their hands, told its own story. A gruff authoritative voice shouted "Halt oder wir schiessen!" We stopped and turned, staring down the muzzles of three rifles and a Schmeisser. As devious as we had become, there was no way we were going to talk our way out of this one. Resignedly we raised our hands above our heads.

The soldiers, upon learning of our nationality, became exceedingly friendly. "You were lucky," they told us. "We have strict orders to shoot on sight anyone caught looting or breaking the curfew." Of course, the curfew! It suddenly explained the empty streets.

An indignant Polish baker appeared on the scene, ranting about his shattered window. A big man wearing a white flour-dusted apron, he took in the situation at a glance and invited all six of us back to the bakery.

There we were plied with as much fresh warm bread as we could stuff into our bellies. The patrol leader, a sergeant, encouraged us to eat all we could and then, almost sorrowfully, explained why.

Shamefaced, he told us that he had been ordered to hand over all curfew breakers to the Gestapo and there was nothing he could do about it. The man spoke a little English and was so sincere in his apologies that I felt sorry for him. "But I won't mention the robbery incident," he added. "They would shoot you for that."

Our pockets stuffed with still-steaming bread, we reached the centre of Cracow. As we tramped the cobblestone streets of the lovely old town, I dejectedly appraised the sum of our accomplishments. It had taken 10 days and more than 200 meandering kilometres to cover what was in effect just 80 kilometres towards potential liberation. The fact that we had been at large for all that time with no identity papers, only a few stolen clothes and just a little money had been merely luck. But we had, at least, avoided 10 days of slave labour down the hated coalmine. That alone had seemingly been worth the effort, although the immediate future looked none too bright. I was, however, still largely oblivious of quite how nightmarish our next few weeks would turn out to be.

CHAPTER
THREE

It was still night when we reached a tall building quite close to the cloistered Market Square of the city. We were led through a side door at the top of a flight of stone steps. A black-uniformed Gestapo clerk glared at us before signing a receipt and curtly dismissing our escort. The soldiers hastily scurried down the steps without a word. I would have given much to have followed them.

We were taken into a bare concrete-walled room and questioned thoroughly by a vile little man in civilian clothes, thin-framed spectacles perched on his nose. The thrust of his questioning was aimed at discovering the identity of Poles he was certain had helped us on our illicit travels. We answered truthfully that nobody had helped us. But this was not the answer wanted. Each time it was proffered he nodded to the pair of thugs who stood on either side of us. They promptly knocked us to the floor. As we lay there, mute and passive, we were kicked to our feet again with hefty blows to our chests from their heavy boots. The process was repeated until, presumably, our statements were believed. Our jackets had been removed and searched, our bread fragments discarded. The remaining

Reichsmarks they had found led to accusations of robbery. We falsely and stoutly denied this, saying that we had acquired the money from our camp guards. Again this was not believed and we were subject to further rib-breaking punishment. When it came to giving details of the camp from which we had escaped, we resolutely insisted, by pre-arrangement, that it had been Stalag VIIIB, which was a cushy number compared to working camp E902. In between bouts of being knocked down and picking ourselves up, our bare arms were burnt with lit cigarettes, which was incredibly painful. Twice I had to whisper urgent warnings to Gordon to keep as calm as possible. I knew his temper was such that he might have launched himself at our tormentors, which would probably have resulted in his death. I was very, very frightened.

It was full daybreak when we were led to a row of underground and windowless cells. That glimpse of daylight was the last we would see for some days. I blessed the patrol for insisting upon filling our bellies with bread as not a scrap of food was given to us during our time in the cells. With nothing to do, we passed the time by scratching rude epithets on the already epithet-daubed walls, trying to ignore the occasional screams from further down the corridor and the obscene stench of sweat and blood that permeated the block. Our cell measured about three square metres and contained no furniture whatsoever, not even a blanket to shade our eyes from the eternal glare of the single grid-protected lightbulb in the centre of the ceiling. My chest gave me considerable pain and I suspected that I had suffered fractured ribs.

We soon lost track of time; there was no day or night for us. It was a relief when the cell door was finally opened and we were hustled out. For a few blessed moments we were able to take great gulps of the fresh night air outside before we were forced into the back of a military truck. Our guard was a tall, blond SS man with a permanent sneer. He spoke to us in English, plainly taking pleasure in informing us that we were to be shot. The revelation hardly came as a shock given the method of our transfer from cell to truck as well as the pre-dawn timing. The fact that we had been condemned to death carried little impact. I felt no great dread. Gordon simply gave me a shrug and a resigned half-grin. Both of us were at a low ebb mentally and physically; our bodies ached and our acute hunger was unbearable. The hopelessness of the situation had completely sapped our morale, and we knew in any case that begging for our lives would be pointless.

The journey seemed endless. Surely the concealing forests through which we were passing were places where the deed could be done away from prying eyes? I asked why our execution could not be carried out at Gestapo headquarters and was told that it "would make the place untidy".

It was still only half light as we entered the gates of what appeared to be a sprawling barrack-like complex. Semi-darkness hid the final destination: a huge encampment with ranks of wooden huts stretching away in all directions. A feeling of immense evil pervaded the place. We were led to what I later found out to be the transit cage of the complex. At least our execution appeared not to be on the immediate agenda.

During the weeks of our incarceration in this place that smelt of death we were held in a sort of enlarged dog kennel, a chamber containing a treble wooden bunk. The top bed was devoid of boards, while the middle and lower ones comprised of no more than bed boards and a thin blanket. A battered tin was used as a toilet, emptied every day or so by a skeleton of a man attired in a shapeless pyjama-like garment. He was forbidden any form of communication with us and averted his eyes during his brief task of removing and returning the receptacle. Once a day we received a bowl of thin turnip soup, usually in the early afternoon, and very occasionally, a hunk of stale rye bread which we meticulously divided between us, lest one got a few crumbs more than the other. This, we were told by one of our SS jailers, was a special dispensation and not a regular part of the camp cuisine. I suppose we were expected to be thankful. When I asked him if I could see a doctor about my painful ribs, I was flatly refused.

For "exercise" we had the use of a few square metres of wire-netted exterior compound. Now and again rag-clad people shuffled past, their eyes downcast as if our presence was not to be noticed. Their gaunt faces were almost inhuman.

Once a week we were removed from our "kennel" and, under guard, taken between two rows of huts then across an open space to an ablution block. On these excursions the true horror of the place became apparent. The scenes were reminiscent of Dante's *Inferno*; in the open space was a litter of half-naked men and women, their gender barely discernible, sprawled across the ground. Amongst them, ignored, were forms covered in shrouds: people who were plainly dead or dying. Others, still alive, picked lice from their rags of striped pyjama-type clothing or simply sat, unmoving, in the weak sunshine. I stared, mesmerised by their faces, looking in vain for a vestige of human emotion, but there was nothing. The bestial treatment they had received had sucked all life out of them, leaving only skeletal husks. Their eyes, large and luminous in their skull-like heads, stared at nothing. Here and there completely naked corpses had been collected and piled up like bricks for collection and disposal. Their withered skin, sagging over protruding bones, was a strange sallow colour, which made them seem unreal, non-human.

I once saw a girl standing on her own. She looked at us without interest, another living skeleton, her face the same yellowing colour as the corpses. She had only a few tufts of hair left to cover her skull and it was impossible to judge her age. She, more than the others, personified for me the true horror of the camp.

The ablution chamber lay at one end of a single-storey, rectangular wooden building that formed part of an accommodation block, filled with rows of bunks. Rising almost to the ceiling, each set of bunks contained not one but up to three occupants, the majority seemingly too weak to move. Here and there strained faces and emaciated limbs emerged from filthy blankets. The stench was nauseating, all but unbearable; worse even than the foul smell of decaying corpses that permeated the whole camp. In Normandy I had looked upon mangled bodies lying among the debris of ruined villages as well as burnt, blackened corpses hanging out of destroyed tanks; the horror of these sights, I realised, was mild compared to the hellish scenes we now witnessed.

The washing facilities were simple; a line of taps released cold water that was momentarily refreshing as we dabbed our faces. In the centre of the block a row of open toilets stretched the length of the ablution section of the building. Few inmates were using them, most probably too weak to reach them in time, and so the passageway floor was covered in stinking excrement. Returning to our "kennel" after these harrowing trips was a relief.

With nothing to do all day the hours passed slowly, every moment haunted by what we had seen and what we, all too soon, might well be experiencing ourselves. We weren't certain why we were being kept separate from the other inmates, and we hoped that our status as British military prisoners of war was keeping us from greater harm.

The days extended to weeks and it must have been nearer a whole month before salvation arrived in the guise of two very frightened soldiers sent to collect us from a POW camp from which we had not escaped. They led us at speed from an office near the front gates of the complex to the railway station, a longish, painful walk, as we were so weak. Out of sight of the dreadful camp we practically hugged our new escorts, who were the first decent members of the human species we had looked upon for weeks.

Only as we waited on the station platform for a train did I recognise where we were: Oświęcim, the place that had featured in our evasion attempt and through which we had passed on the Cracow-bound *Schnellzug*. And only now did I begin to understand the significance of the name. This was confirmed by one of our new guards who told us we had been incarcerated in a camp, the name of which sounded, to us, like "Birkenau", part of the Auschwitz extermination complex.

It does not say much for German efficiency that it took the Stalag VIII administration three weeks after our arrival there to realise that Gordon and I were not authorised inmates of the camp. Taken before the commandant, we were sentenced to a fortnight of solitary confinement on bread and water, which we served in a Russian prisoner-of-war camp some distance away, near the town of Katowice. Even this was a soft option compared with what we had seen at the place called "Birkenau", and more palatable than hacking coal at the Zabrze mine. Additionally, our punishment rations were supplemented by further crusts of bread surreptitiously passed through the cell ventilation slits by the abominably maltreated Russian prisoners, a wonderful gesture that made me feel very humble indeed.

We were all too soon sent back to the despised working camp, where our notoriety earned us the exclusive grade of "dangerous character". Our working clothes and hard hats were liberally daubed with yellow distinguishing stripes that singled us out for the most unpleasant underground tasks. I obtained scanty revenge for the "gift" of a 16-hour shift on my 21st birthday by sabotaging the main conveyer belt of the relevant working level, which brought everything to a spectacular grinding halt. Had I been caught, this act would have certainly put me back into the very death camp I had so recently vacated. Christmas Day was a double shift for everybody and 1944 ended with the evacuation of Camp E902 and the participation of its occupants in what became known as the infamous "Death March".

Here arose perhaps the most horrific and brutal episode in the whole of World War Two, as the greatest migration in history pushed ahead of the steamroller advance of the Russian armies across the eastern lands. This titanic evacuation involved millions of civilian refugees, captives like ourselves, slave labourers, concentration camp inmates and broken units of the German *Wehrmacht* fleeing westwards. The tide of human misery stretched from Königsberg to Danzig and on through Pomerania, Prussia and Silesia to the banks of the River Oder. Along 400 kilometres of snow and ice-bound roads, the endless procession of desperate humanity stumbled, in enormous convoys, towards a river that was looked upon as the great divide beyond which, it was imagined, lay safety. In the coldest winter the region had experienced for decades, the roads became strewn with the stiffened bodies of those who froze, starved, or were beaten or shot to death by merciless SS troops.

The local population did not begin to flee until the Eastern front had been shattered and retreating formations of German rear echelons came racing through the towns and villages. Within days, thousand upon thousands of people, including those who had been evacuated from air-raid-stricken cities in Germany, had joined the enormous migration. In mid-January the front of the Second Army on the Narew River broke under the Russian assault. Inhabitants fled from the towns and villages which had been thrown overnight into the path of battle. Trekking groups formed, numbering up to 30,000 people, many of whom vanished without trace in the maelstrom and in temperatures dropping far below freezing.

Into this snowbound hell we were pitched, unprepared, unequipped and already half-starved, to become one tiny unit among the endless columns. Escape would have been easy, but death by freezing would have been the certain reward. Day after day, sometimes night after night, we trudged on, stopping occasionally in deserted farms where we fell onto hay or bare floors to sleep, often too exhausted to consume the meagre items of food that our guards could scrape together.

Man-hauled carts carried those who fell ill en route, but to ride these was little more than a short-cut to death in the freezing temperatures. I developed severe dysentery but somehow managed to keep walking. All too frequently, however, I was obliged to squat in the snow to answer the call of nature. I had to hurry nearer the front of the column in order to gain time to evacuate my bowels before the posse of SS squads at the rear could execute me, by bullet or bayonet, for delaying too long. Often I had not finished as they approached and was forced to haul up my trousers and rejoin the ranks, liquid excrement running down my legs.

Never in all my life have I experienced hunger as desperate as that which gnawed at my empty stomach during those hellish weeks on the road. My existence revolved entirely around acquiring food and staying alive in the intense cold. Occasional issues of soup allegedly made from boiled grass and rotting beet were issued when we halted at night in nearby farms and starving men fell upon the disgusting substance as if it were manna from heaven. But even these distributions came few and far between. We became so hungry that we would search farmyards for fragments of turnip that long-departed pigs had spurned, rooting for them in the mud. It was rumoured that men were eating cats, dogs and even rats, sometimes raw. My only reaction was disappointment in not being able to share their bounty. My companions were deteriorating into thin, wild-eyed creatures. I persuaded myself that this was not happening to me, until once, while resting in a barn, I caught sight of my reflection in a piece of shiny tin on the wall. Lowering my trousers and lifting my dirt-encrusted, lice-inhabited shirt, I studied my wasted, pin-like legs and the fractured ribs that protruded out of parchment-like skin. I had become a gaunt, filthy skeleton, but I still considered myself luckier than those who were in even worse physical condition and had suffered frostbite more painful than my own.

Sometimes we caught up with half-alive Russians in their tattered coats, with bloody bandages wrapped around festering wounds and rags tied around their frost-bitten feet. Time and time again we did our best to drag these wretched prisoners along with us to save them from execution, but were forced to leave them, one by one, to their fate.

Along the way I was to witness horror almost beyond human conception: Russians digging up long-buried corpses in graveyards and consuming, uncooked, the putrefied flesh; a squad of men beside the road disposing of a pile of Russian corpses stripped of every stitch of clothing, the spindly carcasses bearing teeth marks of comrades who had attempted to eat parts of them; a body roasting on a spit like a wild boar; a woman and child bayoneted for seemingly no reason. And, in a small concentration camp near the town of Racibórz, inmates deemed too weak to join the exodus being executed; in batches of about 50, lines of naked human beings, unrecognisable as man or woman, tottered like mechanical dolls before a bullet-scarred wall, there to stand in resigned silence until they were mown down by SS machine-gunners. If there was any flicker of emotion in those withered frames it must have been simple relief that their suffering was at an end.

Witnessing such scenes instilled in me a consuming hatred that I had never felt before. Revenge and

50

retribution were all my mind could focus on and I was not alone in my hatred. The anger of those in the column spread to become virtually audible in its intensity. I have no doubt we would have got completely out of control had we not been hastily moved by our guards from the scenes of massacre.

By the end of February the worst excesses of the hideous exodus were behind us and the survivors of the columns dragged themselves onto the soil of Czechoslovakia in their countless thousands. The snows had receded and we had entered a land whose populace looked upon us with infinite compassion. Our German supervisors saw a solution to the insurmountable supply problem and permitted Czech bread and soup, in restricted quantities, to be distributed as the columns ground westwards. Overnight accommodation in the larger Czech farms with their easily guarded and spacious barns became a more regular feature than before, and we were able to use the hay and straw inside them for warm and comfortable bedding.

With the improvement in conditions, Gordon and I began to reassess the practicalities of another escape. The daily marching stint of 15 to 20 kilometres remained a gruelling ordeal for our wasted bodies, its only heartening aspect being that every step was bringing us nearer to the Allied armies now within the western frontiers of Germany. We were also aware that our route would eventually lead out of Czechoslovakian territory into Germany, which would assuredly mean deterioration in our treatment. Thus the attraction of remaining in Czechoslovakia was strong.

The execution of another escape, however, was not going to be so easy. The guards had become more watchful and in the flat, open country of Bohemia there was little hope of making a dash from the column. This left the alternatives of escaping from or concealing ourselves within a farm. We decided to take one or other action as soon as the opportunity presented itself. At first, the circumstances required for both projects refused to materialise; either the Germans were too skilful with the placing of their guards or the props of concealment were too poor.

At last one day we arrived in a suitable barn. Within minutes, several hundred tired and irritable captive soldiers were making claims to bed-space. Gordon and I, with mounting excitement, resolved to dig our way deep into the core of the hay storage close to the outer wall of timber slats that allowed air to pass through. To undertake this task necessitated the help and trust of a third party and, in this, we were lucky to enlist the services of a Durham Light Infantry corporal. And so, the next morning, as soon as the others had descended to prepare for another day of marching, we burrowed deep into the hay.

We were in a perfect hide; deep enough, we hoped, to avoid the stabbing bayonets when the Germans came looking for us after we failed to show up to roll call before the day's march. All we had to do was to remain still and wait. As the interminable minutes passed, I became increasingly claustrophobic and convinced myself that I would suffocate if I didn't soon claw my way to the surface for fresh air. I desperately tried to restrain myself from moving and giving our hiding place away.

I tried to work out how long we had been buried, then I attempted to estimate the time it would take the German bayonet squad to arrive on the scene. With some 400 uncooperative prisoners to count it could take more than half an hour and then another 15 minutes or so as they checked and double-checked the five ranks of assembled men. The rigmarole of roll call never varied — even away from the established camps — prior to our departure from the farms at which we had spent the night. It would be far more likely that we had secreted ourselves somewhere amongst the barns than attempted a getaway from a closely guarded farmyard, so it would be the hay storage that they would search first. We knew their methods: first would come a yelling of warnings as they climbed aloft the stacks and then the hay would be systematically prodded by their slender, outdated bayonets. Other would-be evaders had sometimes failed to bury themselves deeply enough and had been lucky to escape injury as, realising the situation in time, they struggled their way to the surface before they were jabbed by the stabbing blades.

We simply had to believe that we were out of range of the lunging steel, although doubts began crowding my mind. My nose and mouth full of chaff, I wondered seriously if I might die from suffocation first. Then I remembered reputed cases where the Germans had sprayed haystacks like ours with machine gunfire and even set them on fire.

A drowning man is said to recreate his whole life in the moments before death; maybe the same applies to one on the verge of suffocation. As I lay waiting in the haystack, the events of the last few horrific months flashed past me in considerable detail until I heard the crash of the barn door being thrown open as the search for us began.

CHAPTER
FOUR

Disjointed voices filled the barn and we felt the hay storage vibrate as heavy boots scaled a ladder. A warning was shouted. Then the scything motion of jabbing bayonets began. We both squeezed ourselves into balls to make smaller targets of ourselves, preferring to be stabbed in the body rather than the head. Above and around us the long knives prodded deep and methodically.

At last came the faint sound as the men descended the ladder. The barn doors closed, indicating the departure of the search party, but we were taking no chances — we knew the ruse by which searchers would pretend to go away but quietly remain behind. We lay motionless, determined to stick things out for another hour or two even after the fading sound of multiple tramping feet outside told us of the departure of our former comrades.

In the event our caution was misplaced. We were on the point of scrambling to the surface when the barn doors crashed open again to herald the arrival of another batch of prisoners. We froze as numerous bodies mounted the ladder and spread themselves over the hay above our heads. Words drifted down to us, words which were not German or English. After listening closely we concluded they were Serbo-Croat. Our initial alarm was tempered with relief. At least Yugoslavs were allies; we had nothing to fear from them.

The heavily moustachioed Serbian sergeant was incredulous as we emerged, covered in hay. But within the hour he and his colleagues were feeding us morsels of their small German-issued rations and promising to re-bury us upon their departure. We spent the night in relative comfort and in the morning submerged ourselves once more, the Serbs enthusiastically piling hay on top of us. There was no need to go deep this time, just enough to allay the suspicion of any checking guard. There we waited until the noisy departure of our hosts, determined to delay our final getaway no longer than necessary.

Again we surfaced. All was eerily quiet within the familiar confines of the building as we descended to the ground and made our way to the open door. The farmyard too was deserted. The countryside, mottled with unmelted snow, was bathed in gentle sunlight.

Gordon was all in favour of making for Prague, which we estimated as being no more than 40 kilometres away, whereas I preferred sticking to more rural climes. We were firmly in agreement however about finishing the war with a Czech resistance group, which seemed to both of us a worthwhile pursuit. Up until this point I had been making most of the decisions, so I felt it was time to give my companion his way, although neither of us were sure what we would do once we reached the Czechoslovakian capital.

Our journey was not entirely without incident. Knocking, with reluctance, on the doors of remote houses, we obtained enough items of food to keep us going and, while crossing a road, were nearly run over by a speeding German military lorry. It braked violently, veered onto the verge and sped on again, the two soldier occupants cursing loudly.

What remained of our uniforms was, we imagined, barely recognisable, although our grubby tunics, our battledress trousers — the former covered by "liberated" civilian jackets — and the identity discs around our necks could save us from a firing squad in the event of recapture. We each wore thick pullovers, relics of the "Death March," that had been removed from some unidentified bodies.

Arriving at a barn where we hoped to spend the night, a farm labourer popped up from behind a tractor. To our consternation he straightaway identified us as British prisoners on the run but had no hesitation in taking us into his home for a hot meal. He even arranged for us to spend the night in the barn.

The urban spread of Prague reached out to us by the second afternoon. We followed the course of the River Vltava into the city, walking openly through the streets. The centre was mainly made up of drab office buildings and grimy historic edifices; the citizens, equally drab, hurried by taking no notice of us. There was little traffic, and most of it was military. Crowded trams clattered by at irregular intervals. The air smelt of low-octane petrol mixed with boiled cabbage. Like a couple of tourists, we gazed across the river, spanned by the lovely old Charles Bridge, and marvelled at the towers and spires of the Old Town on the further bank.

With dusk fast approaching and unsure whether a late-night curfew was imposed in the city, we selected a house that stood alone in a residential street, crossed our fingers and knocked at the door. The middle-aged lady who opened it gave no hint of surprise or alarm when we revealed our identities and requirements. We were ushered into the house without a word. In the gloom I jumped at the silent presence of a tall, soldierly looking man who stood in the background and who had, seemingly, vetted us before allowing his wife to let us in.

The meal with wine that followed was divine, as was the comfortable, soft-linened bed that the couple insisted on giving us for the night. As to joining the partisans, the man could only advise us to leave Prague which was, he told us, a hotbed of Gestapo agents and informers, and make our way westwards to the industrial region of Kladno, a reputed centre of resistance to the German occupation. Following the luxury of a cooked breakfast, we were supplied with thick sandwiches for the journey, and so took our leave of a nameless man and woman who had risked their lives to help two strangers.

Aided by a map he had given us, we followed the man's advice, clearing the suburbs of the city and moving across country in the direction he had indicated. Intending to ask for a glass of water at a village house, we knocked at a door, only to find it to be the local police station. Our hasty retreat must have surprised the policeman who opened it, although, no doubt, he would have been only too willing to help us had we not sprinted away.

With our eventual arrival at and departure from the dreary, drizzly suburbs of Kladno, I at last felt that I stood upon the threshold of something serene and wondrous that would help erase the horror of the past months. Our new-found sanctuary in a village quarry and the quiet beauty of a Czech girl seemed to promise the serenity I longed for.

The hours were leaden as we waited for the dusk. We stayed hiding in our quarry cavity until the daylight melted into shadow, then we made our way towards the girl's home for dinner. The house appeared larger than it had seemed the day before. I half hoped it would be the girl who would greet us, but her father opened the door. In the kitchen, the girl and her mother were busy with the preparation of the meal.

Again we dined lavishly — or at least as lavishly as the strict rationing in a Nazi-occupied country would allow — and for a blissful couple of hours the war and its consequences were forgotten. Every now and then I looked across the table at the girl — I knew better than to ask her name — who acted as an interpreter between us and her parents. As she struggled to find the appropriate English words, I watched her eyes fill with a sort of indecisive wonder. Amidst interruptions from Gordon I tried to tell her and her parents about my home, family and myself. I was aware that my monologue was making up for the details they dared not tell me about themselves in return. Gordon and I repeatedly attempted to express our gratitude for their help and kindness, but even as we spoke I felt an undercurrent of fear that had not been apparent when the girl's father had asked us into the house the day before. Everyone seemed to be listening out for the sudden heavy knock on the door.

The meal over, I asked the girl if we would see her again at the quarry. She made a tiny gesture of dismay. "I have to return to college tomorrow," she explained, adding with unflinching assurance, "But I will not forget you." She gave me a short, sad smile and I touched her hair briefly before we slipped out into the night.

Our outlaw existence in the quarry continued but, for me, a new and vital element was missing. The girl's parents brought us daily provisions but as grateful as I was for their help, I really only wanted to see their daughter again. Nothing materialised as far as joining the partisans was concerned so to counter our boredom and frustration, we decided to undertake a little resistance work ourselves, beginning with the sabotage of a single-track railway line, which lay beyond the nearby village. The escarpment of the hill behind the quarry led down to the track through allotments bordered by red-topped houses.

Perhaps fortunately for all concerned, the tools we had "borrowed" from a trackside hut failed to fit the bolt heads of the rail shoes so we shinned up a telephone pole and used pliers to bring down all the telephone wires. We put rocks in the crevices of points, and probably caused some delay to the train service. Heaven knows what else we would have got up to had we remained at large for longer than a week, our petty acts of sabotage putting at risk and inconvenience the local populace rather than the enemy.

It could have been those trailing telephone wires that finally put an end to our aimless existence in the quarry. One morning, we were woken up by two apologetic members of the local constabulary standing at the cavity mouth. They seemed to have known exactly where to find us. A small assembly of locals watched in sullen silence as we were escorted to the police vehicle on the road out of the village. I realised then that the presence of two *Anglicky* in their cave had been common knowledge. Our brief incarceration in the town jail was not a great ordeal. We shared a cell with an emaciated Russian soldier to whom we donated most of our prison rations, his need being assuredly greater than ours.

A few days later we were taken to the main square. As we stood at the roadside, people stared at us with more sympathy than curiosity. Eventually, a column of khaki-clad figures, which we recognised as yet another prisoner convoy, came into view. At its head strode a German officer. Our escort sprang to attention. The officer pointed a finger at the shuffling ranks behind him, we were given a push and once more we found ourselves amongst the nomads on the road to nowhere.

It was as if the last two weeks had never happened.

CHAPTER
FIVE

Our new compatriots were from camps in eastern Bohemia and Moravia that had only recently been evacuated. They had avoided the worst atrocities of the "Death March" and were reasonably fresh and well-organised. With them, Gordon and I began a new trek westwards. West of the Oder, and once inside the frontier of Germany proper, the great convoys had dissipated and split into smaller columns heading for different destinations.

As we marched I thought of the girl. People talk of love at first sight. Is this what I had felt when I saw her standing in the mouth of the cave? Repeatedly I chided myself for being an impressionable and sentimental fool, but the notion would not go away — nor, in my heart, did I want it to. Was it only my wishful thinking, or did she really seem to want to know me better? It was impossible to consider the whole situation with cold reason and I knew I had to see her again, if only to appease my torment. In the meantime, with a heavy heart, I lamented the fact that every step we took, although one nearer the Allied armies, was also one further away from her.

The new march came to an end in Bavaria, the German homeland, and in the town of Plattling we were put to work in a glue factory. It was an odious place to work, the chief ingredient of glue being bone, which, in the Greater Germany of 1945, was a commodity in plentiful supply. From glue manufacture we were switched to track maintenance in Plattling's railway junction, a transfer that was within an ace of ending our, so far, charmed lives. While we were pretending to shovel ballast in the heart of the rail complex, a tight formation of some 400 vapour-trailing USAF bombers rumbled across the sky. This was an initially heartening sight, but we realised abruptly, when marker smoke bombs were dropped, that Plattling was the intended target.

The first rain of bombs was actually falling as we dived beneath a heavy-duty locomotive attached to a flat truck bearing a quadruple-barrelled 20mm anti-aircraft unit. The young German flak crew, too frightened to fire a shot, joined us, shaking with terror. As the bombs fell I found myself comforting them, although terrified myself. The detonations were a deafening, thunderous confusion of noise. Clouds of debris followed, pelting the steel of our protecting locomotive.

Through the driving wheels, I watched the rail yard become an inferno of fire, smoke and huge explosions. The few minutes of bombing seemed an eternity; the silence that followed uncanny. We staggered, dazed, out of our shelter.

The air reeked of explosive; the rail complex had been totally destroyed. Where the junction had been, there were now huge mounds of earth topped with spiralling sections of track. A train containing a consignment of Red Cross food lay amongst the wreckage, chocolate bars sprinkled about the ruin of the rail yard. The rest of the town was devastated and stank of death. There were flames everywhere — red, green and yellow — some no more than serpent — like flickers between the jagged ruins, others rising steadily from roofs or licking around the edges of houses. There were also the burning dead and, worse, the burning wounded, who ran screaming out of the houses and collapsed, whimpering in agony.

We passed bodies that were mangled, crushed, mutilated and singed. Scraps of clothing still clung to them — an arm in a woollen sweater, a torso in a dotted dress, a leg in the remnants of brown corduroy trousers. In one street we found a nest of dead children lying in confusion: single hands and feet; trampled, hairless heads; twisted legs. A schoolbag and a basket sat incongruously intact among the burnt, black corpses.

With the departure of the attacking aircraft, rescue-service workers and camp inmates were formed into demolition squads and rescue parties to undertake what could be done for the surviving population. For five days we toiled unceasingly in the gutted town, unearthing victims, both alive and dead, from collapsed buildings, including an air-raid bunker that had received a direct hit. Along with a batch of Ukrainian prisoners, I was given the unpleasant task of removing the mangled bodies of scores of men, women and children who had been jammed tightly together when the blow had struck. We laid out the more complete corpses in long rows before, thankfully, being assigned to less sickening tasks.

The commandant of the camp, which adjoined the undamaged glue factory lying outside the town, encouraged the prisoners to remove some of the Red Cross parcels from the shattered train in order to lessen his provisioning problems. Shortly afterwards, it was revealed that, because of the eastward advance of the American Third Army, we were henceforth to continue the march — *eastwards* and away from the Americans. This announcement met with a howl of protest from his charges and resulted in a wild scramble during the last working shift before our departure to find means of transporting the precious food parcels. Gordon and I were singularly unlucky in this endeavour, having to make do with a sickly wheelbarrow. We had decided to attempt yet another escape, but even on the first kilometre of the new trek eastwards, our one-wheel vehicle laden with half a dozen parcels proved itself to be entirely unsuitable and on the verge of collapse.

We struggled along, kilometre after kilometre, being overtaken all the time by compatriots with more efficient carrying devices. But as desperate as we were to escape we were also loath to jettison any of our food. "Let's get the hell out of this!" Gordon groaned, echoing my own sentiments.

Luckily, it wasn't long before we saw our chance to slip away from the ranks. With the war in Europe plainly drawing to a close, we had noticed that the guards were more lax in their duties than had been the case earlier. However, we also knew that they would not let us simply walk away; there was still the odd fanatic among them who, given the opportunity, would shoot us. Shortly after leaving the small town of Leyling we saw our chance. Approaching a concrete water tower jutting out onto the road, a corner shielded one guard's line of vision behind us, while, for just a moment, another's was blocked by the marching column. To the rear of the tower was a large patch of bramble-choked undergrowth. We seized the opportunity and, together with the uncooperative barrow, threw ourselves into the brambles. Lying face downwards where we had fallen, the barrow up-ended, we lay still, and waited.

The nearest guard passed within a few feet but, his view now blocked by the tower, he failed to see us. We remained motionless while the rest of the column tramped by. It was already dusk when we ventured out to find a less thorny shelter. Back in potentially hostile territory, we could not expect assistance from the locals, although, at this stage of the war, the local population was probably no great danger to us either.

Our subsequent journey was almost farcical in its straightforwardness. Sleeping in the scenic and well-endowed wooded countryside of northern Bavaria and enjoying our ample food supplies, we progressed at no great pace towards where we presumed we might meet the advancing Americans. Walking straight through villages, ignoring the stolid inhabitants, we provoked little attention. In one village we spied a smart streamlined lined perambulator standing unattended outside a house, the owner having seemingly popped back inside for a moment. Fed up with our run-down wheelbarrow, we saw a great opportunity to acquire a better vehicle. In a flash we unloaded the boxes, but as we were about to put them into the pram, we discovered it was occupied by a sleeping baby. Hesitating only a second, we carefully transferred the still-sleeping infant and its bedding into the wheelbarrow and threw our own cargo into the pram. Then we — and our new acquisition — were off at full speed. My pang of guilt was momentary but I did wonder what the good *Hausfrau* thought when she discovered her nice chromium-plated baby-carriage had turned into a broken-down wheelbarrow!

In more open terrain we took to the grassy undulating countryside, although I was a little doubtful as to the durability of the fragile-looking wheels of the pram on the rougher ground. We continued on a vaguely north-westerly axis, convinced it would eventually lead to salvation. The drone of aero engines had become an incessant background to our journey and we were now seeing low-flying aircraft, easily distinguishable as American.

On a small country road we ran smack-bang into a German soldier, steel-helmeted and fully armed. As it was too late to avoid him, we could only brazen things out. In fact, he was charming, despite the fact that it was painfully obvious that we were British.

In good English he spoke vehemently of the unjustness of Hitler's regime and the futility of war. We enquired politely of the whereabouts of the Americans and received a full situation report. Seemingly, his unit had the unenviable task of holding up the American advance, he himself being part of a spotter team for an artillery battery hidden in a nearby wood. Not that they intended much resistance, he assured us, for what was the use? The Americans had far more artillery than they and would be able to blast them off the face of the earth. "Can't you hear it?" he asked, and then for the first time we realised the dull roar that we had dismissed as the sound of aircraft was, in fact, that of the guns of the American Third Army. "The area will be overrun in the next day or two," he told us, "so why not hide up and await your liberators?"

Thanking our benefactor, we moved off with the intention of making our way nearer the action — although not too near. The Bavarian scenery, bathed in mid-April sunshine, was idyllic but for the distant thunder of those guns. Birds chirped and spring buds were beginning to open, in total disregard of the war. The wooded grassland offered plenty of potential hiding places in which to await liberation.

By late that afternoon we had covered a respectable distance, occasionally waving ineffectively at the pilots of low-flying aircraft. The sudden appearance of more German troops in full battle kit as well as motorised vehicles of assorted types caused us some concern: not all enemy soldiers were likely to be so well-disposed towards us as our recent friend. But as we were looking around for a hiding place, a far more disturbing incident occurred.

Gordon was reloading the boxes into the pram after climbing over a fence when out of the clear blue sky came hurtling a groundhugging American Thunderbolt fighter-bomber. Although we had noticed it circling the valley, we had not registered the change in pitch of the engine note as it dived towards us. My yell to Gordon came after he had already dived away from the pram and spreadeagled himself close up against the fence. I did likewise on the other side of the fence. The swathe of 0.50-calibre shells from the multiple Browning cannons cleaved a long furrow of kicked-up turf that, at lightning speed, streaked towards the pram before the aircraft banked away steeply and disappeared westwards.

Although we were unhurt, the pram was a wreck; its wheels had been smashed and some of the parcels were punctured. We considered our next move. With our precious food supply already depleted it was no great feat to carry everything to the small wood which we were intending to make for anyway. The undergrowth was thick enough to screen us from sight, and it was there we put down roots to await developments.

During the few days we remained in this wooded island our Robinson Crusoe existence was enlivened briefly by a group of grey-clad figures who entered the top end of our sanctuary and, as if intending a final last-ditch defence attempt, set up a heavy Spandau machine-gun. Fortunately, there seemed to be a fault with the breech mechanism for we could see the crew struggling with the weapon, cursing loudly. And when a couple of mortar bombs exploded close by they obviously had second thoughts for, picking up the faulty gun, the trio retired in haste, joining other troops we could see withdrawing across the open landscape. In the distance we could make out convoys of German transport pouring eastwards along a road hidden from view.

A major problem we faced was a lack of liquid. Gordon had tried his hand at milking after we spotted a nearby herd of cows, using a Red Cross powdered milk can as a bucket. The beast appeared none too happy with his efforts but did allow a small amount of fresh milk to be extracted, much of it squirting in every direction except that of the tin.

Early one morning, a deathly hush fell over the landscape, uncanny in its intensity. The view from the wood showed no movement anywhere. A solitary farm-hand was milking the cows. He not only knew how to do it properly but was evidently not going to allow a small matter like a world war to interfere with his routine. Presumably he carried out this chore daily but we hadn't noticed him before, so walked over with all the empty tins we could find.

We were greeted with a stream of words in Bavarian dialect by the elderly cowherd who, seeing that we didn't understand him, gesticulated wildly towards the crest of a slight rise in the terrain with the words "Amerikanische panzer!" It seemed the American tanks were just over the rise. Incredulous, but unwilling to doubt this revelation we dashed off, forgetting our original milk-gathering mission, and, with pumping hearts, attained the top of the crest to behold the wonderful spectacle of half a dozen Sherman tanks, emblazoned with the white star of the Allied forces.

But our joy was short-lived as bursts of machine-gun fire once more had us grovelling in the dirt. A ludicrous exchange then took place as we shouted to our potential liberators in an attempt to explain that we were British soldiers. It was all too clear that the Americans had been caught out before by SS fanatics pretending to be Allied ex-prisoners.

A gruff Texan voice came across the void of no man's land. "Oh yeah? We've heard that before. This is an American sector; there are no Brits here." After a short pause, he continued. "Okay, if you are who you say you are, tell me, which baseball team is the current top scorer?"

"Haven't the faintest idea," I shouted back. "We're British, not Yanks."

"Okay then, Brit, what football team is top of the league in the UK?"

Unfortunately, I was just as ignorant of our own national game. Gordon piped up, "Tottenham Hotspur", which was the first team he could think of. There was a long pause.

Another voice finally called out. "You're so ignorant you must be Limeys. Raise your hands high above your heads and come forward slowly."

We stood up warily, our hands high above our heads, and walked slowly towards a multitude of levelled weapons. We were fugitives no longer.

★　★　★

At nearby military headquarters we divulged every scrap of information we could about enemy movements in the locality and even persuaded the local commander to allow us to join his outfit until the end of the hostilities rather than awaiting repatriation in rear echelons. So, soldiers once again, this time in American uniforms, we became auxiliary gunners of a half-track vehicle belonging to a mechanised infantry division of the United States Third Army under General Patton.

Those last weeks of warfare with a group of cheerful and generous Americans were very different from the savage fighting I had experienced in Normandy. Rolling ponderously forward with much noise and clatter under an umbrella of supporting aircraft, we advanced in the general direction of the Czechoslovakian frontier. Except for periodic pauses while aircraft and artillery dealt with pockets of fanatical enemy rearguards, there were no pitched battles or heroics on the part of the Americans; the heroics were exclusively reserved for the Germans.

The general cease-fire came in the second week of May when we were within 10 kilometres of the Czechoslovakian border. The unit was disengaged and ordered back for rest and refit. In a way I was sorry; I still had fanciful knight-in-shining-armour visions of liberating the beautiful, nameless Czech girl. Alas, it was not to be.

Instead, I accompanied our American colleagues to a base near the Danube town of Straubing where Gordon and I left them for Regensburg, since its airfield was reputed to be preparing for the evacuation by air of freed prisoners of war. We obtained a lift part of the way in a military police jeep and subsequently found an abandoned lorry which we coaxed into life, picking up a group of Hungarian refugees en route. In the outskirts of the battered town the steering shaft broke and we ended up nose-down in a bomb crater.

Eventually we made it to the much-bombed airfield, where a seething mass of released captives was awaiting transport to Britain. As the first aircraft were not expected for some days, Gordon and I drifted into town to find more comfortable accommodation. We imperiously commandeered a substantial house in the suburbs owned by a family called Schottenhammer, and allowed the family to remain there as long as they cooked the food we were able to forage.

Around the middle of May we boarded a Lancaster bomber stripped of its offensive weaponry and from the mid-gun-turret I watched the approaching white cliffs of Dover, teary-eyed. Although relieved to be free and returning home, and in spite of the dramatic events since we had briefly met, I still carried with me the image of a Czech girl who had captured my heart.

We landed at a Buckinghamshire airfield. After being questioned by medical, intelligence and military authorities, I set out on the final leg of the journey. And because of the petrol rationing in Britain I had to walk the last four miles home.

CHAPTER
SIX

I was no more successful as a businessman in the family firm than I had been as a soldier, but life in the picturesque village where my family lived had its compensations. The quiet, ordered, respectable existence washed away most of the recollections of the war, although the uglier episodes would always remain in the background. Most immediate and ineradicable in those post-war years were my happier memories of the girl, whose name, I was eventually to discover, was Anna.

It took literally years to locate and contact her. A war-devastated Europe lay between us, a place of ruin and despair where millions of broken families were struggling to be reunited. Although I had begun the near-impossible task of regaining contact whilst still a soldier in the British Army of the Rhine, part of the post-war four-power occupation of Germany, my efforts had been dampened by the thought that the girl might no longer hold any regard for me. But a breakthrough materialised from an unexpected quarter, long after my demobilisation and following world events that were to become known as the Cold War.

In February 1948 the savage politics of communism entangled Czechoslovakia in a new nightmare, along with Poland, Hungary and all of Eastern Europe, which fell into the harsh grip of a regime as ruthless as the one from which it had been so recently delivered.

Suddenly, out of the blue, I received a letter from another Czech girl, Vlasta, who, it transpired, was a school friend of the beautiful girl I had met near Kladno. Vlasta had managed to escape through the then still porous border into West Germany. She was being held in a displaced persons camp outside the town of Münster awaiting transfer to Australia, where her fiancé was waiting for her. Vlasta's letter intimated that, not realising that I was unable to contact her even when postal services throughout Europe resumed, Anna (and at last I was made aware of her name) had waited in vain for a letter from me and eventually presumed that I no longer wished to stay in contact with her. I immediately travelled to Münster to spend a few days in the camp with Vlasta, and learned from her that Anna's affection for me was as strong as mine for her. Owing to Vlasta's unauthorised defection from Czechoslovakia, her parents had been forbidden direct contact with their daughter, even after she had left Germany for Australia. Thus, on my return to Britain, I became a sort of two-way post box, receiving and passing on letters between parents and daughter. And now aware of Anna's name and address, I made up for lost time with a vengeance; a flurry of letters passed back and forth between us, as we gradually expressed our feelings of affection to one another.

Our exchange of letters slowly revealed snippets of knowledge about our respective lives. I learnt that Anna was a secretary in a state agency based in Prague, that she was studying to improve her knowledge of English (although this was forbidden by the authorities), that she had held me in her thoughts ever since our first meeting, that her parents were happy that she had succeeded in regaining contact with me (in spite of, again, the displeasure of the authorities) and a myriad other matters that helped me clarify and elaborate upon the image of Anna in my mind.

The new barrier of the so-called Iron Curtain that now lay between us, and which was becoming increasingly impregnable, mattered little to the strength of my love. A purely physical barrier between us meant little now that I knew for sure that Anna reciprocated my feelings. I had vowed to see her again, but with an edict from the communist regime expressly forbidding liaisons with foreign nationals it was now impossible for her to come to Britain, and equally as problematic for me to reach her as I was repeatedly refused entry visas from the Czechoslovakian embassy in London.

After being demobilised from the army, I had settled into the routine existence of a nine-to-five job. At my father's insistence I joined the Territorial Army, if for no other reason than to keep the peace at home, and eventually exchanged my sergeant's stripes for the pips of a commissioned officer.

It was well into the summer of 1951 before I was ready to initiate the course of action that I hoped would reunite Anna and me. For many months I had painstakingly delved into the secrets of the Czechoslovakian border defence system — its make-up, technicalities, weaknesses and the movements of its guardians. My repeated journeys into central Europe — chiefly Bavaria, which shared a common border with Czechoslovakia — incurred the annoyance of my father, who was also my managing director, but I was resolved to accomplish the tasks I had set myself. Travelling on foot, as well as on local trains and buses, I had set out to locate the offices and headquarters of various authorities and refugee centres who, I felt, might be persuaded to offer information that would allow me to successfully accomplish my mission. Thus my enquiries took me the length and breadth of a fast-recovering Western Europe to cross-examine refugees and escapees from the stricken lands, as well as West German border authorities, railway staff and intelligence services. Gradually I amassed a great deal of information to help me in my project, all the time keeping my plans secret from my parents, who would have unequivocally opposed them.

In the last week of September I set out to pit my wits and wage my own private war against the communist regime of Eastern Europe.

CHAPTER
SEVEN

As with all good military stratagems, I had prepared my offensive with a reconnaissance. The West German border with Czechoslovakia was 375 kilometres long; it was the line of the old border established between the kingdom of Bavaria and the Austro-Hungarian Empire in the time of Maria Theresa, re-surveyed and re-marked in the early 1930s. In the early 1950s, there was one rail and road crossing point, with very limited traffic. Since it had been erected, the Czechoslovakian border fence had undergone a number of changes of design and refinement but, unlike its East German counterpart to the north, the fence itself did not always follow the demarcation line between the two countries; in some places it lay up to five kilometres back from the border. In 1948 and early 1949 the obstacle had been no more than a single fence of barbed wire and cable construction overlooked by watch-towers equipped with searchlights and patrolled by armed guards with dogs. But such had been the subsequent epidemic of escapes, not only by Czechoslovakians but also by Poles and other East European nationalities through what was reputed to be an "easy border", that the barriers had been strengthened. Parallel to the "ploughed strip"

78

— a carefully tended furrow of soil intended to preserve the footprints of illegal border-crossers, a mined area had been laid, while the impenetrability of two additional fences had been intensified by an electrified element and gadgets that gave warning to the watchtowers of unauthorised interference with the wire.

Unsurprisingly, I had not planned to attempt a direct assault on the fence, at least not in the initial instance. First I decided to see what would happen if I remained on the one daily eastbound train — a portion of the Orient Express — that crossed the border to the town of Cheb, some 15 kilometres inside Czechoslovakia. At worst, I assumed, I would be thrown off somewhere, with no great harm done and some further useful information gained. If not, once through the German border formalities at the small station of Schirnding and the long pause at the demarcation line where, I learnt, the train was searched for "Western Imperialist spies", maybe there would be an opportunity to leave the coach and melt into the countryside as the train neared Cheb, or even once it had halted there, but before the border formalities began.

I had told no one of my plans apart from my horrified brother, with whom I had left the vague request to "*do* something" if he heard nothing from me after a fortnight. Even Anna was unaware of my plans, because I did not want to involve her if things went wrong.

Thus, towards the end of September 1951 I left home ostensibly on a social trip to Denmark. I carried a small rucksack, containing not much more than a strong pair of insulated wirecutters and some food. My passport, alas, was deficient in the vital stamps necessary to legally penetrate one of the most well-guarded borders in the world.

The border region east of Schirnding is composed of thin woods — pine, chestnut and birch — adjoining the single-track railway, and the woods are bordered by open meadows. I joined the Prague-bound section of the Orient Express at Nuremberg and at Schirnding the few remaining passengers alighted from the four coaches, leaving me as one of the few remaining on the train. As I had half expected, the pea-green-uniformed officer of the Bavarian Frontier Police, discovering that my passport held no Czechoslovakian visa, well-meaningly requested that I leave the coach. This I did, only to reboard it when he wasn't looking. Locking myself in the toilet, I awaited further events.

The train was coupled to a red-star adorned locomotive of Czechoslovakian Railways and another two coaches were removed. As the truncated express moved off, I emerged from my hiding place and returned to the compartment.

The woods, I noted, made reasonable walking terrain, not too thick to impede progress but dense enough to aid concealment. As the train slowed to a crawl at the approach of the border, the whole repressive apparatus of the Iron Curtain suddenly came into view. The trees had been cleared to allow for the treble fences, the ploughed strip and the expanse of mined terrain, which snaked together through the desolation of jagged stumps. On each side of the innocuous-looking furrow ran the walls of wire, with insulators like obscene white growths atop the posts. At intervals, watchtowers rose ominously over the structure. I gazed at it in awe.

The train halted ahead of this barrier and soldiers in overalls began the pantomime of searching in and under the coaches. No passports were asked for at this juncture and following a protracted wait we moved off again, with border guards riding the steps of the coaches to ensure no passenger disembarked illegally. That ruled out one of my schemes.

From a cutting we emerged onto a skein of tracks and drew into one of several roofless platforms connected by an iron footbridge. The station was nearly deserted; administrative buildings adjoined the furthermost platform.

Even before the train had ground to a halt I had the door open and, rucksack in hand, was making my way resolutely towards the bridge steps. I expected a shout from the nearest step-riding soldier but he must have been looking the other way. From atop the lattice structure I glimpsed uniformed officials leaving the administrative block, none exhibiting any sense of urgency. With a daily virtually empty train from the West the chore of passport inspection had perhaps become only a routine formality.

Ticket in hand — this was at least valid — I made my way to the platform nearest the station exit. A number of passengers were waiting for the Prague-bound portion of the express to reach the platform, where further coaches would be added. Given no more than a ticket control I could be through and away within seconds. But it was not to be. As I hesitated near the barrier, two policemen emerged from the shadows. Suspicious as well as indignant, they demanded to know why I had not waited for the attentions of the immigration authorities.

Once they had seen my passport, devoid of visa stamps, I was placed under arrest and locked in a small bare room that formed part of the SNB — Sbor Národni Bezpečnosti or State Police — presence in the station. Eventually my persecutors relented and, with my passport confiscated, I was allowed to spend some of my Czechoslovakian currency on soup in the station buffet. I chatted to a detachment of border guards, one of whom even stood me a beer. Upon learning that I too had been a soldier, they asked me to teach them British arms drills with the aid of their stubby machine-carbines, but an officer swiftly appeared on the scene to put an end to the lesson. Fortunately nobody wanted to inspect my rucksack; the wire-cutters could have provoked further unhealthy attentions.

Eight hours later, the Westbound express arrived and I was escorted aboard it. "Next time come with a visa," I was advised, not unkindly. My excursion had not been a complete failure, however, for I had collected further snippets of information.

The return to Schirnding was a carbon copy of what had gone before though in reverse order. Dusk had fallen by the time we drew level with the fence. Arc lamps bathed it in pulsating light, and I felt an icy pain in the pit of my stomach as I looked at its bulk. It was going to have to be the hard way after all.

My eyes became accustomed to the darkness soon after I left Schirnding station. Following the railway, I made my way eastwards along the single track, detouring away from it when I came upon a marker proclaiming the actual border. Continuing cautiously, I approached the brilliantly lit fences, choosing what I hoped was a midway point between two watchtowers. Crawling forward through the cover of the shattered tree-stumps, I eventually reached the base of the first structure. Then, spreadeagled on my back, I removed the wire-cutters from my rucksack and, firmly gripping their insulated handles, began cutting the lowest strand of the outer fence. Inevitably, recollections of breaking out of the Silesian prison camp with Gordon flashed through my mind.

I knew from my research that patrols came past every eight minutes, but I was uncertain as to when the last one had passed by before my arrival on the scene. Of course, I should have waited, knowing I would be shot immediately if they caught me between the wires, until the next one left, but I was over-eager to get the job done, I quickly snipped through three of the lowest strands — probably alerting the occupants of the nearest watchtower — and slid underneath the severed cables. Still on my back, I attacked the middle fence, sweating with terror.

Uncertain whether the lower strands of the fences were "live", I ensured nothing metallic touched my body as I squirmed through the gap I had made. This took me into the ploughed strip of no-man's-land, which I crossed, careful to leave no distinguishing imprints beyond an untidy trail of disturbed sand. Next came the deadly swathe of ground alleged to contain German-manufactured Teller mines. Here, I turned onto my stomach to inch forward like a swimmer on dry land, feeling for protruding detonators. My body was taut with adrenaline as I pictured the bloody results of impact; the explosive splattering my guts over the field, or blowing off my limbs. Halfway over the minefield I lost my nerve, rose to my feet and loped forward to the inner fence. I cut through the strands of wire with ease and slipped through the final barrier. Rising unsteadily to my feet again, I sped away from the harsh lights into the protection of the woods.

I ran through the intense darkness as the branches of pine trees whipped my face, the uneven ground tripping me as I floundered on, my heart pounding. I ran and ran, falling over and pulling myself up again, until at last I felt far enough away from the fence to slow to a walk, aware too that patrols were certain to be nearby. Never again, I told myself, would I undertake such a reckless mission.

I paused to catch my breath and bury the incriminating cutters. My watch told me it was a quarter to two; in another couple of hours dawn would begin to lighten the terrain, which meant I would see better but could also be seen. I struggled on as quietly as the carpet of crunching twigs would allow. Speed was still essential if I was to be clear of the restricted border zone by day-break.

I came across a track leading in the direction I wanted to go, but I veered away from it. Tracks could be watched. The woods thinned and I found myself among fields of corn stubble, my shoes making a swishing sound in the heavy silence. A train whistle indicated that I was still parallel to the railway line as intended, but I was now quite a distance from it. My plan was to bypass the town of Cheb, leaving it on my left, which meant I would hit the line again in due course as it curved south-eastwards towards Plzen. At a station somewhere along the line, I hoped to catch a local train to Plzen and, from there, to Prague.

Two hours of good unimpeded progress over unfenced, unhedged pastureland and stubble went by. The dawn illuminated the rough grass that had been scorched by the summer sun to a colour of dirty straw. Beyond, the land rose in a series of folds. On the lowest of these folds were white strips of land where corn had been harvested earlier in the year. It didn't look or feel like border country any more.

My impetuousness gave me away. I arrived at a bridge over a shallow river which I could have easily forded. Bridges of any description in or near border areas such as this should have set alarm bells ringing in my head and, indeed, I watched this one for any signs of movement but neither saw not heard anything. I decided to risk crossing it in order to save getting my feet wet.

At the end of the bridge, on the further bank, a soldier suddenly stepped out from behind the parapet, shouting "Stuj!" (Halt!) I took a step forward, not sure what to do, and four of his colleagues abruptly appeared out of the shadows, their automatic weapons aimed at my navel. Any vague notions of heroics were quickly discarded. Later, I found out that the demarcation line of the border swung towards the east near this bridge so that, although I had imagined that I was progressing away from the border I was, in fact, still in a restricted, even forbidden, zone.

The sarcastic patrol leader was irritated by the fact that I had caught his men looking the other way. "No one ever 'escapes' *into* the country," he intimated. "They all want to get out!" He showed his annoyance by poking the muzzle of his weapon up my backside as I snarled in pain and indignation.

I was taken to a series of local military and police headquarters, where I faced a barrage of questions, from beguilingly friendly enquiries to screamed ferocities. At one stark building I made the unenviable acquaintance of the SNB. Here the interrogation took place in a room devoid of decoration but for the statutory photographs of Joseph Stalin and Clement Gottwald (the then Czechoslovakian president). Incongruously, there was a bed. I sat down on it at the moment a rotund officer entered the room, and was immediately told to stand up. He asked a single question and, not receiving the desired answer, laid into me with the butt of his pistol. The first blow was aimed at my face, but, seeing it coming, I drew back my head quickly and almost concussed myself against the bare wall. In a daze I sat down again, only to be pistol-whipped up. All the while a silky smile played about the man's face. Eventually, unable to extract any satisfactory admission of guilt, he left. Except for illegal border-crossing I could think of no other crime I had committed. This was the only occasion during my arrest on Czechoslovakian soil that I was to meet with physical violence.

Only towards evening did I learn my immediate fate. I would be going to Cheb, the border town. I was optimistic enough to imagine prompt release once there. Guarded by two silent policemen, I was taken to the town on a two-coach diesel train. Cheb was a district centre and, as such, possessed a large police headquarters — and, as I was soon to learn, a prison. The latter was run by the SNB and was, in fact, a transit establishment for political detainees destined for the nearby Jáchymov uranium mines. My escorted walk from Cheb station was the last I would experience for many weeks but, climbing the steps of the main entrance to the barrack-like building complex, I still held hopes of catching the night train back to Nuremberg.

My rucksack was thoroughly searched and confiscated, along with everything in my pockets, including my passport and money. I was thankful I had disposed of the wire-cutters. Yet another interrogation occupied the whole evening. Everything I had already told everybody had to be told again and the slightest discrepancy became cause for more questions. My eyes kept closing with exhaustion and I was unbelievably hungry after the eventful last 24 hours. After a while I staged a strike, refusing to answer another question until they fed me. Eventually they brought me a stale bread roll and slice of sausage. Outside it grew dark; I began to think I wouldn't make the night train after all. Finally the questioning was over. I was led up three flights of stone stairs to a concrete-walled cell, where I collapsed into sleep, too tired even to acknowledge the greetings offered by the other inmates.

In the morning I was to discover my new world. It measured three by four metres and was about three and a half metres high, with a grilled window far up the outer wall. The electric light had burnt all night but I had slept too well to notice; indeed, I needed waking to participate in the stipulated chores. Blankets had to be folded and the floor swept with an old broom. The cell furnishings comprised of two treble-tier bunks with straw mattresses, a wooden table with three hard chairs, and a bucket for use as a toilet. A single low-wattage electric bulb hung from the ceiling. The iron door possessed a peephole through which the occasional official eye would peer at us. The only reading matter also served as toilet paper: the remains of a copy of the writings of Goethe in old-fashioned German print.

My companions were, initially, two Czechs and a Slovak who made me feel most welcome, each pleased to practise his limited English. The friendliest occupant of all was Bohuslav, a middleaged Czech schoolmaster with a 25-year prison sentence for, I later found out, daring to oppose communist doctrine in his school. His smile was infectious and he took me under his wing immediately. "You are the only English prisoner here so we are honoured," he told me. "I must therefore see you come to no harm."

For a time I continued to imagine that, at any moment, I would be released, but as days passed my hope died. Living became mere existence. Bohuslav kept my sanity intact, invariably raising my spirits when they had sunk to rock bottom.

So-called meals were the only high points of the day. Breakfast was a bowl of lukewarm liquid, optimistically called "coffee", accompanied by a hunk of bread. The bucket was to be used for its specific purpose prior to breakfast since it was permitted to be emptied, following the coffee issue, just once in 24 hours. Anyone using it at other times went to the bottom of the cell popularity scale.

From midday onwards — and a clock in the town maddeningly announced each plodding hour — we would start looking forward to lunch. It invariably arrived late and was heralded by a rattle of keys and the opening of the door, which was an event in itself. Cold and congealed potato soup was a permanent fixture on the menu. It was deposited outside the door to cool even more as we waited for the duty warder, who was never in a hurry, to bring it into the cell.

A former inmate had bequeathed to the cell a set of paper draughts that was in constant use, although afternoons were generally given over to pretence of sleep. Mostly, though, we were listening to the sounds of normality outside — the striking of the clock, the hoot of a train, the revving of a vehicle, the shout of a child. I invariably thought of Anna, torturing myself by imagining what might have been had I succeeded in reaching her home.

At dusk a new mood settled upon us as the door opened for the issue of the last meal of the day — usually more "coffee" and a strange sweet-tasting macaroni. Evening, and the end of another empty day, was always the best part of the routine. Inert on our bunks we chatted at length, Bohuslav ensuring I was never left out of the conversation because of my ignorance of the language. We turned in early, blankets pulled over our heads to hide the glare from the electric light.

I demanded my right to be put in touch with the British Embassy in Prague, in order to inform them of my whereabouts and plight but my efforts were ignored and incurred only the wrath of a brusque lieutenant of police who came to the cell. In another attempt I made two copies of a statement, one of which I dropped from the cell window in the hope that a sympathetic soul might pass it on to the embassy. The other I slipped to the barber who came to shave my hair. But one or both missives fell into alien hands for, a while later, the cell was invaded by a squad of irate soldiers who carried out a search during which I lost my precious pencil.

This was a grievous deprivation indeed, for scribbling in the borders of the diminishing Goethe tome was my one enjoyable activity. However, I was able to rectify this matter during the second of two interrogations in the weeks that followed. A hardfaced

SNB officer was my interrogator and, true to form, his questioning became increasingly ominous, accusing me of espionage. Once again, I was urged to be sensible and admit my "crime" so that leniency could be considered; moments later I was shouted at with accusations and dire threats of heavy punishment. All this was punctuated by the powerful glare of an anglepoise lamp thrust in my face — which gave me the opportunity to nick the man's pencil as it lay on the table. Later, our cell was searched, as I had anticipated it would be, but only half the pencil was recovered.

Bohuslav too was taken to the administration block and my heart was in my mouth until he was returned. The other Czech, a heavy, bespectacled man called Jan, and the Slovak were also removed one day but both failed to come back. Thus for a time Bohuslav and I had the cell to ourselves before an excitable Hungarian named Kux and an East German joined us. Our fluctuating numbers confused the cooks and we were sometimes able to manipulate an increase in rations when the food orderly demanded our number through the closed door. Occasionally we were rumbled and received no meal at all.

My thoughts during the long, empty hours never ceased centring upon Anna. I was glad she knew nothing of my present whereabouts, as this would only have added to her misery. I sometimes felt she was with me in the cell and that we lay together on my rough bunk bed; at night I sometimes imagined seeing fragments of her reflection in the glass of the electric light. Occasionally I also turned my mind to my parents who would be wondering what had become of me. I had not mentioned Anna to Bohuslav or any of my fellow inmates; there seemed to be an unwritten law that our "crimes" and reasons for them were never discussed and it was some time before I gained even an inkling of the why the others had been incarcerated. Nor had I explained the true reason for illegally entering Czechoslovakian territory to my captors, although, of course, the authorities were later to associate me with the girl who had been receiving my letters and who was currently under surveillance by the SNB.

One November day all the guards were changed because it was said the original set were becoming too matey with their charges. Certainly most of them had been well-disposed towards me for, as an Englishman I was a rare specimen; a cuckoo in the nest. Another influx of prisoners increased the cell occupancy to the maximum of six, one of them a Czech who had been caught trying to flee to the West. He had been badly beaten and his face was a mask of congealed blood but for days he received no medical attention, nor was he allowed to wash.

After my first interrogation, I had notched up a new charge of smuggling since I had not declared my few pathetic belongings, now appropriated from me by the state, at the border. This crime and the others, I was told, would be clarified at my trial, which took place a month after the second interrogation. It was a complete farce. To reach the People's Courthouse involved a very welcome walk in the open air — the first time I had been outside for a quarter of a year. Very few trial participants, other than uniformed border guards and police, were present. The judge wore civilian attire and sat facing me me in a high-backed chair positioned beneath the national emblem and a red star.

Nothing that followed seemed quite real. One of the other civilians present turned out to be a lawyer acting on my behalf, his table-top awash with documents. He occasionally rose to speak between lengthy pronouncements from the judge (who also seemed to be acting as jury) and though I had been assigned an interpreter, the man's English was so poor I was unable to understand a word of what was going on. With my stubby beard and matted hair I must have looked something of a hardened criminal deserving punishment.

Once or twice I had to reply to innocuous questions concerning my life and occupation using my few words of German. Thereafter I completely lost the thread of the proceedings mainly on account of a generous slice of homemade cake that my armed military escort was surreptitiously attempting to pass me below the lip of the dock. I was brought back to reality for a moment to plead "not guilty" to whatever it was for which I was being charged. I was pleased to note the judge at least didn't don a black cap for the final judgement. His summing-up speech went on for an eternity and I was hardly surprised to learn I had been found guilty of all my alleged crimes. Each one was listed — attempted espionage, smuggling, illegal border crossing, even insulting the People's Army (since I had been rather rude to the patrol leader who had painfully prodded my buttocks with his gun when I had first been arrested) — along with the resulting penalties. All of these added up to a total jail sentence of 104 years. And since my prison was a staging post before transfer to the uranium mines, my future looked decidedly unhealthy.

But the judge continued. It appeared that the British government had finally learnt of my apprehension and had reacted strenuously, mainly on account of the Czechoslovakian regime's failure to report the fact that I was in custody. So now, as an act of socialist clemency, I was to be removed from Czechoslovakian territory; expelled as an enemy of the people, never to be allowed to return. I was hugely relieved, but sadness also clouded the news. How was I now ever going to see Anna again?

I was welcomed back to the cell with a barrage of questions from my fellow occupants and the news of my impending release became cause for much rejoicing. I could detect the strain in Bohuslav's voice at the prospect of my leaving but it was typical of this courageous man that he refused to let it interfere with the joy he felt for me. Even the guards came to congratulate me on my good fortune.

But another week was to pass before I was finally released. I was shaved, cleaned up and given back the return portion of my rail ticket (but nothing else) before being driven to the border where, at an unofficial crossing point, my escorting warriors pointed westwards saying "Nemecko" (Germany). I walked on alone across the thick snow.

94

A little later, would you believe it, I was arrested by the Bavarian Frontier Police for illegally entering the Federal Republic! Christmas was near so maybe it was the Yuletide spirit that meant they released me after less than 36 hours, having at least fed me properly.

Back in Britain I had to face more music: the annoyance and concern of my parents, the displeasure of the Foreign Office for causing a rupture of diplomatic relations, and an edict from the Czechoslovakian authorities confirming my status of *persona non grata* in that country.

It was the last decree that hurt me the most. My mission to reach Anna was in greater ruin than ever before, but I was determined to continue my private war against the communist regimes of Eastern Europe. I vowed to return, illegally and via other republics bordering the Czechoslovakian state, if necessary. I had lost the first battle but was resolved to keep fighting, whatever the cost.

CHAPTER
EIGHT

My months of imprisonment had played havoc with our communications, Anna's letters to me being, by force of circumstances, unanswered. And with the imposition of Czechoslovakian censorship, together with letters being inexplicably "lost in transit", it could only be a matter of time before our fragile line of communication was severed.

A sheaf of letters from her awaited my return home and I read them eagerly in the order they had been written. She had grown more and more concerned at my silence. In the last letter, she had written that, while she could understand me ending our relationship given the hopeless odds set against us, she wished that I would at least *tell* her the worst. In my reply I told her, simply and with a minimum of explanation, of the reasons for the broken contract, gently chiding her for underestimating my pig-headed stubbornness. Now that I had been branded as an "enemy of the people", I knew our letters would all too soon come under the scrutiny of the SNB, if they hadn't already. I could only hope that my explanation would reach her, and without repercussions for her safety.

Partly for this reason, I had to act fast to plan to meet her face to face, at the Czechoslovakian border if it could not be at her home. A plan by which I would use the name and passport of a school friend who bore a slight resemblance to myself fell through when even *his* entry visa application was turned down. So I decided to follow a well-trodden — and risky — path. Hadn't I already managed to reach Cheb more or less unchallenged on the daily Orient Express train? If my earlier unscheduled and unorthodox arrival had not altered the pattern of control or hardened the restrictive measures of both Bavarian and Czechoslovakian authorities, then that way still lay open.

I chose the Easter weekend of 1952 — the following year — for the repeat attempt. With a four-day holiday and my still apprehensive parents under the impression I was visiting friends in Buckinghamshire, I left for Nuremberg and the border. In an earlier letter containing a code which Anna and I had managed to devise between us, I indicated a necessity for her to be at Cheb railway station on Easter Saturday. I could only hope the missive would get through and that she would understand the hidden message.

Everything went, almost eerily, according to plan. I was again politely requested for my own good to alight from the train by the Bavarian frontier police at Schirnding, on account of not having sufficient documentation to satisfy the Czechoslovakian immigration authority. I had once more slunk back onto the coach when the guards were engaged elsewhere. An hour later, the almost empty train, delayed by

Czechoslovakian border guards for the customary search, drew into Cheb station.

My mind was a turmoil of expectations and emotions as I scanned the familiar platform. All at once I caught sight of a lone figure in a dark coat standing beneath the iron footbridge. I knew immediately it was Anna, although seven years had passed since our very first meeting. I wondered if she had experienced difficulties reaching a platform which served a train from the West. As it shuddered to a halt our eyes met and I flung open the coach door. Seconds later we stood together on the platform.

For a few seconds I was speechless, greeting her simply by pressing my hand gently on her arm. "Hello," I said eventually and inadequately. "Glad you were able to meet me." Suddenly all the phrases and words I had planned for this, our first intimate conversation, fled from my mind. I looked at her in wonder. All I could take in was the pale shape of her face upturned towards my own. The surprise of seeing her there was as tender and beautiful and fresh as if we had met for the first time.

"Was it difficult — the journey?" she asked concernedly and the sound of her voice transported me back seven years to that unforgettable day in 1945. All I had seen of her since then had been photographs, but now a warm, living Anna stood before me and I was lost in disbelief.

"No, it was quite easy . . ." I found myself starting to explain the unimportant details and lapsed into silence.

"But us, what about us?" I burst out. "We've got to find ways of seeing each other more often."

I leaned towards her, putting one arm around her waist, and felt her smooth cheek against my own. There was such a lot I wanted to talk to her about, but this was not the place. I held her, full of happiness because she was warm and mine and because, although Czech, she was close to my own world: the world of being young and on the edge of danger. As I held her, I looked across to the station buildings, half expecting the intruding officials, but pleased they were being so slow about it. I thought of the pleasant English countryside now scented with spring blossom and how, one way or another, I would make Anna part of it, with the Cold War and all this surreptitious border-crossing business a far-off, laughable memory. It seemed unreal now, holding her to me, her face cool against my own weariness. I turned my head, placed my lips against her throat and kissed her. Suddenly it was all I wanted; to hold her there on the platform, under the iron bridge, not caring about time or things to say.

"You're tired," she said. She lifted her face. Her voice held a great tenderness.

"A little," I admitted. I waited a few moments and kissed her full on the mouth. Her lips were warm and soft, unprotesting and unevasive. She broke away only out of breathlessness and I laughed self-consciously, abruptly aware of the fact that we were no longer alone. Down the steps of the bridge clattered half a dozen members of the expected interference.

"The vultures are descending," I observed quietly and unwound myself from Anna.

An officer of the border guard was the first to reach us. He seemed puzzled.

"You're supposed to remain on the train," he said in German. He turned to Anna and a fierce exchange of Czech ensued. She interrupted the flow to explain.

"He says I'm not supposed to be on this platform or talking to you."

The group of officials went through my visa-less passport, handing it from one to the other as if for verification.

"There's no entry visa here. Why have you come?"

"To see my girl," I replied.

The senior member of the posse glared at me as if I was joking.

"She'll have to go back to Prague immediately and you've no right to be in this country at all. Come with me, both of you. And no talking." He spat out the staccato instructions.

I already knew the way to his office in the administrative section of the station. More border policemen were lounging about the poky room and pungent tobacco smoke rose in dense clouds to the ceiling. Our entry aroused considerable interest but, brushing aside the enquiries of his subordinates, the officer sat down behind a desk and, from his little edifice of power, began to pump Anna for explanations.

She gave as good as she got, or at least that was my impression watching the tilt of her chin as she answered the questions and defended her rights. The officer appeared unsure of himself and this was confirmed by his subsequent need to place a telephone call to some nameless headquarters in Prague. To restore his lost authority, he then gave me a dressing down for the indiscretion of carrying out an illegal tryst with a citizen of the Czechoslovak Socialist Republic. Our individual statements were typed out on an old Remington machine and Anna was removed from the room. The formalities completed, I managed to persuade the officer to give me a few more minutes with Anna. At first he refused point-blank but gradually he relented. At heart he was a reasonable man.

"You can have the few minutes before her train leaves for Prague," he conceded, and led me out of the office.

The Orient Express still waited. It had moved to another platform and eight more coaches had been added to it. These were filling up with citizens en route to the Czechoslovakian capital and towns along the way. Ignoring the armed soldier who was my escort, I walked along the train staring in at the windows. Most of the second-class coaches were full and there was an overflow of passengers in the corridors. She was in the fifth coach. Another soldier stood ostentatiously outside her window. Ignoring him too, I rapped on the glass and swiftly Anna left her seat to emerge on the platform, smiling happily.

"I've come to say goodbye," I explained.

Her smile faded slightly. "A long way to come for so short a time together," she said. There was a note of great pathos in her voice.

"I'd go to the ends of the earth for the same short time," I replied.

As I stood there on the platform, holding her close once more, I knew that leaving her would be the hardest thing I had ever known. I kissed her again and again, my sense of frustration and anger growing until I knew that she too could bear it no longer.

Suddenly everything we had been longing to say came out in a flush of words: all the plans, hopes and intentions we had written to each other about, and which we knew in our hearts might never be, we shared in those few ecstatic minutes together on Platform 1. The people in the crowded train corridor, who had learnt of the renegade Englishman in their midst, crowded about in friendly encouragement and sympathy. Stolidly ignoring everyone, Anna and I spoke our last words together.

"You'll wait for me, Anna darling?" I pleaded in a choking voice.

She saw my misery and whispered, "Perhaps one day . . ." Her words tailed away as she buried her face in my coat.

A whistle blew. To the delight of the crowd I took Anna in my arms and kissed her passionately. The soldiers, together with the officer who had joined us, shuffled their feet.

The whistle was for another train, but the time of departure for the express had come. Once more Anna buried her face in my shoulder to hide her tears and I felt both the trembling of her body and a sickness in my throat. Stroking her hair I murmured, "I'll come back, darling, whatever they do to me."

Her voice, muffled, was almost inaudible.

"Yes, dearest one, come back. Please come back."

Another whistle shrilled and there was a banging of doors. Anna slipped back into the train. Through my tears, I watched it slide out of the station.

For the rest of the day and throughout the night I was held in detention before being placed aboard the next westbound Orient Express.

A total of 14 minutes together with one's girlfriend might seem poor return for a journey well in excess of 1,600 kilometres but to me it was well worth the effort and the risks involved. A romance on paper is doomed to eventual extinction without an occasional physical encounter, however brief and unsatisfactory the circumstances.

Although we had discussed the subject of our becoming husband and wife in our correspondence, I was aware that I had not actually put the question to Anna. I realised that we might be more successful in our battle to be together if we were officially engaged to be married. After all, "girlfriend" has a far less permanent ring to it than "fiancée". Yet simply to write the question and obtain a written reply would have been uneventful as well as unromantic. No, I decided that the occasion should be marked in the time-honoured fashion, as is the right of lovers everywhere.

Over the following 12 months we had to rely upon our letters getting through, our continuing written exchanges enhanced by those 14 joyous minutes of borrowed time. To keep my sanity, I delved enthusiastically into hopeless schemes of rescue that at least funnelled the desperate yearnings of a distraught mind into doing *something*. My parents were of no help whatsoever and I kept my emotions hidden from them. On one occasion I asked my father to make a personal representation at the Czechoslovakian Embassy in London on my behalf but he declined on the grounds that it might tarnish his standing with the local community. My mother had other reasons for being unhelpful. In her mind *she* was the only woman I needed to be devoted to.

It was now 1953 and another Easter weekend had come round. With the news of the death of Joseph Stalin offering a tiny glimmer of hope in a troubled world, I set out again on a familiar train ride.

For my well-meaning but inconvenient frontier police at Schirnding I had evolved a new tactic. By locking myself in the through-coach toilet of the Orient Express and placing a specially-printed "*Kaput*" ["Out of Order"] notice on the door, I was able to evade their attentions.

At the border nothing had changed. The repressive apparatus of the multiple fences still stood stark and terrible in the fickle sunshine. I wondered how I had managed to pluck up the courage to cut my way through such a daunting barrier two years earlier. Again I was almost the only passenger in the single coach of the train and I kept a low profile, pretending to doze, in case my all-too-familiar features should be recognised.

104

As we approached Cheb station, I frantically scoured the platform for the girl I had come to ask to be my wife. But the concourse was empty and not a soul was in evidence except for a soldier by the water tower and a group of railway men at the head of the furthest platform. My heart was pounding wildly and despair raged within me. A host of explanations surged into my mind as I leapt onto the platform, the still-moving train carrying me towards the footbridge. The latest message had failed to reach her. She had been prevented from getting to the station. I had given her the wrong date. She had not been able to understand my disguised instructions. Then suddenly a figure stepped forward from the shadows and I was in Anna's arms.

I held her close while a cascade of emotions swept through me: relief, joy, triumph and pride. Kissing her hard on the mouth, I closed my eyes to preserve the moment for eternity.

Breathlessly I broke the embrace. "Did you have any trouble getting here?" I asked anxiously, aware that we were about to embark upon the same initial exchanges as those of a year ago. Were we destined for a lifetime of clandestine meetings and enquiries as to how we had managed them?

"No, did you?" She looked at me with wide, worried eyes.

"None at all. Not yet anyway," I replied, glancing warily towards the administrative buildings across the tracks. "But listen, darling, in a minute those vultures will be onto us. There's something I want to say and give you first. It's the reason I came."

While I fumbled in my pocket, my eyes rested lightly on the girl before me. She had changed since last time. Her dark hair flowed down around her shoulders and her face was more aware, confident, adult. Her eyes were rimmed by dark lines and I knew the reason; the bastards were already starting to get at her. I knew too that Anna, as never before, was for me.

"There's no time for pretty words — and anyway I'm not much good at that sort of thing — but you understand I love you and want you to be my wife and — well, I've brought our engagement ring, if you'll accept it." The words tumbled out of me as I tried both to gaze into her eyes and watch for the approach of the authorities. Then, forgetting the threat, I looked her straight in the face and added, "You will marry me, won't you?"

Anna smiled and with the slightest turn of her head put her mouth against my face, saying nothing but telling me, in that brief and tender moment, all I wanted to know. The smile on her lips deepened and her eyes were moist. She held up the third finger of her left hand and nodded her head, still unable to trust herself to speak as I placed the ring on it.

I flung myself into her arms again and kissed her long and forcefully. Still no official had put in an appearance. "Let's go," I said, leading her towards the steps of the bridge.

I suppose it was a hopeless quest but the notion of again leaving the station unobserved had lain at the back of my mind. We nearly made it, but not quite. The policeman at the station exit, his stare directed at me, laid a hand on my shoulder as the group of passengers flowing around us thinned and dissolved.

Taken to the familiar administrative building, we found ourselves before the same officer that had been on duty the previous year. Recognition was instantaneous and mutual.

"You *again*!" he bellowed. "I presume you do have permission *this* time, but you can't just wander out of the station." He held out his hand for my passport.

Even when its shortcomings were again revealed, he was really quite pleasant about things. I told him I'd come to see my fiancée.

"How long have you been engaged?"

"About eight minutes," I said.

This time the officer allowed us to be alone together for another ten. He glanced at his watch. "She must return to Prague on the express. I'm sorry."

Once more under escort we walked to the train. The soldier with us insisted that Anna board the coach. I stood by her window and through the glass I made out her features, cloudy and very white. I could hear her breathing very quickly, with small gasps of pain, and I saw she was trying to talk to me at the same time.

A passenger helped her lower the window further and we were able to touch one another and whisper our last words so that nobody could hear.

"Now we're an engaged couple," I declared brightly, "they'll relent, just you see. Never fear. I won't give up now."

Anna, recognising the need for mutual support, attempted to drown her own misery in a flurry of practicalities. "Despite the ban on marriages with foreigners I'll go and see the authorities in Prague. And I'll leave my job so that my usefulness to the state is no more, and . . ."

The whistle of the train ended the torture of our feigned jubilation. At the moment I wanted more than anything in the world to put my arms around her, for I saw she was crying and I could do nothing about it. In the long seconds before the train eased away from the platform I realised she was crying not just for herself, or for the sadness of the moment. She was crying for something that I would never understand without her, and now did understand because of her; she was crying for the agony of all that was happening in the world. Our hands were dragged apart as the train moved away and I was left staring after a receding coach, with Anna's small arm forlornly waving from it.

Locked in a small unlit room adjoining the police office, I waited for my enforced return home. Spurred on by despair, I was already planning the next move. A shower of rain had fallen and through the barred window the empty platforms were dazzling in the late afternoon sun.

CHAPTER
NINE

In the land behind the wire they came for Anna one early summer morning. It was barely three months after our engagement and she was in the orchard of her home in the small town of Slaný, picking cherries. A man and a woman, stern-faced and resolute, appeared at the foot of her ladder. She looked down at the couple and smiled.

"Would you like some cherries?"

There was no return smile. "We don't want cherries. We want you," replied the man threateningly. "We're from the SNB."

Anna climbed slowly to the ground. "You want me now?" she asked.

"Now."

"May I go and get my coat?"

"Yes, but don't tell anyone who we are, you understand? Say we're from the employment office if you have to say anything." The man was emphatic.

Anna ran into the house. Her mother was in the kitchen preparing the midday meal. "Afraid I'll be a bit late for lunch," she told the slight, grey-haired lady fussing over the stove. "The SNB are here. They want me to go with them." She wasn't going to tell lies to her mother for them.

"Where are they taking you?" her mother asked anxiously, the careworn face paling slightly.

Anna shrugged. "Their office, I presume. Don't suppose it'll be for long." She spoke unconcernedly, trying to hide her own alarm.

Donning her coat, she returned to the couple in the orchard and, with them, went out through the garden. At the gate they were met by Miluska, Anna's eldest sister, returning from a morning's shopping.

"Where are you going?" she enquired gaily, glancing curiously at Anna's grim-faced escorts.

"I don't know," was the reply as they hurried along the street, leaving Miluska perplexed, staring after them.

The woman spoke for the first time. "Why didn't you do as you were told?" she demanded in a hard voice.

Anna remained silent.

The man was short and bulky, dressed in a belted raincoat and squashed black hat. The woman was young but joyless; her jacket and skirt were as severe as her tight hairstyle.

A black Tatra saloon waited around the corner. A second man sat, relaxed, behind the wheel. Anna was told to sit between her escorts on the back seat.

Slaný SNB headquarters was on the other side of town, a discreet building in the outer suburbs. It took only ten minutes to drive there. When they arrived, Anna was taken to an office on the ground floor. Its four dirty walls were stained with what might have been

110

blood, but was probably just damp, and the only decoration was a framed portrait of the country's new president, Antonín Zápotocký. The door was closed behind her.

Captain Josef Koudelka,[1] district head of the SNB, sat behind a plain table bare except for two telephones. He had a bald head and a pink face and his prominent eyes sparkled, but not with mirth. Tyrannies everywhere — if they have a hope of establishing themselves — must be able to draw on a steady supply of such men. On orders from above, he would carry out any duty required of him without permitting personal taste to interfere with the strict and loyal discharge of his obligations. When ordered, he could even be polite, sometimes almost gentle.

Like his minions, Captain Koudelka wore plain clothes. Oddly, it made him the more sinister, for the ordinariness of his attire was in disquieting contrast with the far from ordinary appearance of the room: the stained walls, the high, small, barred window, and the over-strengthened door.

Today Koudelka had a pleasurable task — a simple interview with, and preliminary investigation of, a pretty girl. It would not be so onerous a task to show his gentle side. He looked over at Anna seated opposite him and smirked.

"Comrade Krupičková, we are sorry to have inconvenienced you like this. It won't take long but we must have some answers to a few questions. It's a

---

[1] Not his real name.

matter of state security, you understand. Would you please tell us about your contacts with your friends?"

Anna showed bewilderment. "I'm not sure what you mean."

"Just tell us about your friends."

"What do you want to know about them?"

"Who are they?"

Shrugging her shoulders, Anna replied that she had many friends: school friends, colleagues in the Prague office where she had worked as a secretary and translator, neighbours, friends of her parents . . .

"Have you friends abroad?" Koudelka cut in.

Making no immediate reply, Anna considered the implication of the question. Then she said, "As perhaps you know, I was at school with Vlasta Pučková before she left for Australia."

The captain smiled, softly, deprecatingly.

"No, I don't mean her."

There was a prolonged silence in the room.

"Why did you visit the British Embassy in Prague the other day?" The question came like a shot from a gun and the smile faded.

Another pause ensured.

"They asked to see me." Anna replied eventually. She knew she was evading the issue.

"Why?"

"Because of another friend of mine, an Englishman."

"Have you many friends in West Europe?"

"Not many."

"How many?"

"I once knew a Dutchman who studied in Prague. He returned to Holland and for a time we kept in touch. Is there anything wrong with that?"

It was the captain's turn to evade the question but asked another.

"Are you still in contact with him?"

"No."

"But you are with the Englishman?"

Anna saw no point in denying the fact.

"You have applied to the authorities to marry this Englishman, in spite of our governmental restriction on foreign marriages?"

"Yes."

"Why?"

"Because I'm fond of him." She muted the degree of affection, conscious of the fact they were discussing personal relationships, a subject she thought was no business of his.

Koudelka returned to the matter of the embassy visit.

"What did they have to say?"

"Not much. They wanted to know the situation and whether I really wanted to marry a British national."

"And do you?"

"Yes."

"Isn't it more the glamour of living abroad, especially in the West?"

Anna shook her head.

"Was the embassy helpful?"

She allowed a melancholy smile to flit across her face. They had not been at all helpful. Instead they had displayed outright suspicion, even antagonism, for reasons she was unable to fathom.

"Not very."

"So you are setting your cap at this faraway Englishman when you've got the opportunity to marry one of the most prosperous and eligible bachelors in Prague. Any other girl of your age would jump at the chance you're getting. Why, he even owns a house in the capital."

Anna was nonplussed. So they knew about Martin, who had been after her for years. But she didn't love Martin, or even like him much.

"I suppose it's for the love of this Englishman that you've given up your job?" he continued, once more startling Anna with his knowledge of her affairs. His tone turned "love" and "Englishman" into dirty words.

"My parents are old and I have to help them at home," she explained defensively, guessing that he was aware of the real reason — that to be unemployed by the state gave her more chance of being allowed to leave it.

"Quite so." Koudelka brought the tip of his thick fingers together, and leaned back until the chair squeaked in protest. "Quite so," he repeated sarcastically.

Smiling again with gentle reproach, he went on, "It may well be true that you've done nothing against the New Czechoslovakia, Comrade, but," and the eyes were mildly rebuking, "neither are you doing anything for it." He signalled an end to the interview with the words, "I advise you to be careful, young woman, very careful.

114

And say nothing, nothing about this talk of ours to anyone, do you understand?" His prominent eyes narrowed to steely gimlets.

After the sinister, depressing room and its occupant, the fresh air was a balm, and Anna was glad they expected her to walk home. Maybe next time she was summoned to the SNB, or, if not then, another time, they would not be letting her go home at all.

CHAPTER
TEN

I like to think that I was the first post-war Western visitor to enter Yugoslavia when that country, silently struggling to rid itself of Soviet domination, opened its doors to the initially hesitant tourists from Western Europe in the summer of 1953. With the opening of its borders, I predicted that other countries of the Eastern Bloc might follow suit.

At any rate, it seemed a good idea to go and investigate the phenomenon of an open communist country. Committed to no other activity for a summer holiday, I set out in my compact, eight-horsepower Morris saloon on a voyage of discovery. Yugoslavia had no common border with Czechoslovakia, but the itinerary I had set myself included, on my way home, transit through neighbouring Austria, which *did* possess a common border with that country. This fact gave rise to a scheme for another attempted tryst with Anna.

Having delivered her application to marry me to the cold impersonal offices of the Czechoslovakian Ministry of the Interior in Prague, there was nothing else for Anna to do but wait. As she had given up her job in the state import-export agency in Prague, the waiting was, without the distractions of her work, even more onerous. However, most of my letters to her got through and now she began receiving almost daily picture postcards from me as I journeyed through southern Europe. One of them, postmarked Zagreb, contained a hidden message concerning the proposed meeting 14 days hence.

My arrival at the Yugoslav border post had been cause for celebration. If I was not the very first Western European tourist to cross it, at least I was the first from Britain to do so, and a swarthy official, whose knowledge of my language was limited to the two words "yes please", admired my passport, stamped it delicately and offered me afternoon *slivovice* in lieu of tea. We toasted everybody and everything, went through a litany of "yes pleases" and, with much handshaking and back-slapping, I was permitted to be on my way.

My stay in Yugoslavia that summer was no more than a dalliance. My tour around the country was littered with irreverent incidents, my modest vehicle was a subject of deep admiration and envy, and my hotel accommodation — even of the multi-star variety — was ridiculously cheap because the state tourist agency had not the faintest idea of Western hotel prices — though they were soon to learn.

The evil-smelling, low-octane state petrol and the roasting sun meant I had to keep all windows of the car open and I soon became well-acquainted with dust and potholes. The locals who stopped me for lifts did little to help my progress, but did provide entertainment; one ample matron, requiring a lift to the next village, was happily car-sick all the way. Policemen periodically

117

brought me to a halt for no other reason than to marvel at my wheeled symbol of capitalist opulence.

At Gospić I ran out of petrol, a fatal occurrence in 1953 Yugoslavia, where filling stations were as rare as diamonds. "Go to the railway station," I was told. The railway station, it transpired, had taken over from the church as the source of wisdom and knowledge. So, emptying my last reserve can of petrol into the tank, I headed for the station.

There was no petrol there either. A solution to the problem, however, lay with one Marco Rankovic, station-master extraordinaire. Because I was an Englishman — and he would do *anything* for an Englishman — he would arrange to stop the Istanbul-Trieste "Benzene Special" due to pass through two hours hence. In the meantime: "Come, a little refreshment . . ." The train was, of course, late and we were both suffering from a surfeit of *slivovice* when the tanker wagons drew in to the accompaniment of indignant blasts from the locomotive, objecting to the red signal.

In a daze from both petrol and *slivovice* fumes, I drew the car up to a wagon where we flooded everything, including the tank and spare cans, in a deluge of fuel. We sweetened the locomotive crew with more *slivovice* as the sea of spirit, in which the car stood, evaporated safely. Vaguely I enquired about payment and my new friends laughed heartily. Contemptuously they indicated northwards. The Italians would pay for it, wouldn't they?

118

Between Zadar and Dubrovnik I took to the steamship service, which offered alternative discomforts to dust, petrol fumes and potholes. There were no refinements such as cabins or bunks; passengers just staked a claim to a space on deck and held it against all comers. As I morosely surveyed a carpet of prostrate humanity, I wondered why space had been left vacant in front of a closed door and discovered the reason the hard way when it was opened onto me soon after I sat down. Suffering mild concussion, I was treated to a tirade on nautical procedure from the chief engineer until, upon realising I was British, he promptly switched to abject apology and forcibly closed up a line of bodies to make room for me out of harm's way.

Sibenik, Roman Split and a shoal of romantic-looking islands had provided picturesque diversion during the day but a crisis enlivened the early morning following a wretched night. Clouds of steam issuing periodically from the engine room suddenly turned to heavy bursts of black and oily smoke. The sight of it was extremely alarming and the stench appalling.

The crew ran about preparing to launch lifeboats but, with the coast so close, the passengers exhibited little concern. The ship itself began zigzagging crazily on account, presumably, of the half-suffocated captain not being able to see where he was going. The ship faltered towards the shore trailing a grimy scarf of pollution and entered the harbour of Dubrovnik where, just short of our berth, the engine finally expired and the vessel stopped, smoking and motionless, on the sheltered water.

In spite of the historic charm, the massive walls and cloistered streets of this fabulous city of Emperor Maximilian, my return to dry land and some sort of normality was an anticlimax. Before, I had been alone but content, with every stranger I met becoming my friend. But now, based at a luxury hotel, the Argentina, even among fellow foreigners I felt despondently lonely. The swimming was idyllic and the hotel cuisine fit for a king, but these were not enough for happiness. The nightly ritual of an exquisite dinner on a bougainvillea-splashed terrace became an ordeal. At my table the ready-laid place setting and the empty chair opposite mocked my solitude. I longed for Anna to be sitting there with me.

On the third evening, with my last plum brandy, I silently toasted my resolve to see her again. I left next morning, initially by bus, and the open road became a delight simply because it led to her.

The route to Maribor, by way of Varaždin and Pluj, could, even then, be described as a road. Between the potholes occasional traces of tarmac were discernible. At the Yugoslav-Austrian frontier, a few kilometres north of Maribor, I was questioned about my financial status.

"How much Yugoslav money have you?" I was asked by a boorish official.

"Two thousand dinars," I replied, remembering the restriction imposed upon the amount of dinars permitted out of the country. I also remembered the 5,000-dinar note in my wallet.

"Only 1,000 dinars is allowed out of the People's Federated Republic," I was told. "Goods to the value of your remaining dinars may be purchased at the kiosk." Enthusiasm for Englishmen was not so noticeable here.

Thus, not without reluctance, I bade farewell to Yugoslavia and, driving a car laden with the kiosk's entire stock of homemade cheese — the only item for which I could find the slightest use — I entered neutral Austria. The customs check here, at least so far as I was concerned, was non-existent — possibly on account of the ripeness of the cheese.

The state of the Austrian roads was a treat after the Yugoslav ones and for the first time for hundreds of kilometres the speedometer needle crept passed the 30 mph mark. Via Graz and some handsome, hilly countryside I reached the Semmering Pass where, off the road, I pitched camp in a recently harvested cornfield. I could have reached Vienna by nightfall had I wanted to, but an inconvenience existed in Austria at that time which needed contemplation.

Following the defeat of Germany in the Second World War, Austria had also been accorded four-power occupation. Except for token forces, the Western powers had long since removed their troops and restrictions, but the Soviets still held the eastern half of the country in their grip, with Vienna — like Berlin — a multipower capital to the east. As with the then German Democratic Republic — East Germany — there were only two permitted routes for Western traffic across the Soviet zone of the country, these running on an east-west axis between Graz and Linz and the Austrian capital. I held the necessary document enabling me to continue to Vienna but not to head from south to north to Linz, where I wanted to go. Thus I would have to make a detour through Vienna, making the journey some 500 kilometres instead of the direct road of less than 300. However, while in Vienna I should be able to obtain another document permitting me to drive the trans-Soviet zone highway to Linz. From where I rested now the Russian zonal border lay just down the road and delays, it was alleged, were frequent.

I cooked myself a meal, of which Yugoslav cheese formed the chief ingredient, and pondered my scheme to attempt the next foray onto Czechoslovakian territory. Anna and I intended meeting at the Czechoslovakian border township of Horní Dvořiště, directly opposite the Austrian border town of Summerau, on the railway line between Linz and Ćeské Budejovice.

The operation was to be of similar ilk to those I had put into motion at Cheb on the much more sensitive West German-Czechoslovakian border. I had already informed Anna in cryptic fashion by letter from home, as well as by postcard from Zagreb, of my intention to arrive at the station of Horní Dvořiště on a certain day. From Vienna or Linz I intended sending her further notification of my estimated time of arrival. With a "softer" border there between the Soviet zone of Austria and communist Czechoslovakia, I foresaw no difficulties for her, the snag on my side being only that I would have to cross Soviet-occupied territory between Linz and the Czechoslovakian border. Even the risk of this could be discounted were I to be in possession of further documentation.

There was no delay at the zonal border. On the British side a corporal of the Royal Signals warned me about the hazards I was certain to meet ahead; his Russian counterpart, 50 metres on, offered a smile, a salute and a wave, sending me straight through the barrier without even a glance at my entry document. Except for occasional military lorries, signposts bearing place names in both German and Russian Cyrillic script, a general lack of paint in the villages and a proliferation of political slogans, there was little outward evidence of the occupation. At Wiener Neustadt I took a wrong turning and drove 10 kilometres off course into forbidden terrain, but no carloads of KGB followed in hot pursuit. It boded well for the unauthorised crossing of Soviet territory between Linz and the Czechoslovakian border that I planned to make, if necessary.

I spent a full 24 hours in the Austrian capital and put every one of them to best possible use. I had little time to experience the pleasures of this magnificent city, although I soon became aware of the gentle *Gemütlichkeit* for which it is renowned. In the Auhofstrasse I ran into an acquaintance of mine who, with his wife, entertained me to dinner, over which I earnestly pumped them for information about conditions in the Soviet zone, particularly around the border area. The Zenks were a willing source of information but had no personal experience of the situation beyond Freistadt, which lay south of Summerau. I chalked up another failure when it came to acquiring permission to traverse the restricted road to Linz, but learnt that on the zonal border on Vienna's outskirts inspection of documents was haphazard. I thus resolved to go without permission and put my trust in luck. From a post office in the Hietzing district I sent a telegram to Anna.

I left next morning. The A1 Vienna-Linz-Salzburg motorway today offers a smooth if featureless drive, but no such refinement existed then. At the Enns Bridge was the Soviet checkpoint and, close by, I parked the car and approached on foot the checkpoint itself to take note of the procedures. From a discreet distance I watched a pair of Russian military policemen, assisted by Austrian state troopers, examining each driver's documentary card, which I didn't have. However, I noticed that only those of every third car or so were being checked. One in three: a sort of Russian roulette. I returned to the car, keeping tabs on the numbers of cars already at the checkpoint and joined the queue at a point where, mathematically, I should reach the checkpoint just after the car in front of me had been checked. In the event, either my arithmetic was at fault or else the policeman changed his tactics, for the car behind me was the one checked. But it didn't matter: I had been lucky and I was through.

The clocks of Linz were striking midday as my Morris nosed its way into the busy streets. Austria's third city is an important railway junction and river port on the Danube, which here formed the zonal boundary. Once across the bridge from the suburb of Uhrfahr I could breathe easily again.

After booking into a hotel in the shadow of the towering Gothic cathedral, I was unloading the car when a cyclist drew up beside me and, in a friendly Sheffield accent, introduced himself: "Hello, how are you? You're British, I see — I'm Norman Shaw — working in a local garage ... enjoying myself immensely: no closing times here ... Come and have a beer."

The staccato invitation was most welcome. With another of my attempted border meetings with Anna due the following day I was only too glad of the company of a compatriot to help keep me calm. Over mugs of *Dunkelbier* and enormous ham rolls, we chatted. Norman was a most useful informant, having lived in Linz for some months, and I took to him at once. Small in stature, slightly younger than myself, completely unreserved, he proved to be one of those people that can be relied upon to help with anything. Although he spoke of his many Austrian friends, I guessed that he suffered from loneliness, for his pleasure at coming across me was joyously evident. I told him snippets of my intentions and his enthusiasm for the project brimmed over. He even had to be dissuaded from accompanying me to the Czechoslovakian border. Instead, he offered to look after the car in case, as he put it, "something happened" to me.

Together we spent the afternoon touring the city, calling at the railway station to purchase a ticket and confirm the departure time of my early-morning train to Summerau. In the evening Norman gathered together some of his vivacious Austrian friends in a back-street *Bierhaus* and, for a few carefree hours, in the company of the hard-drinking Fritz, a vivacious blonde named Hilda and a host of further characters, I forgot my anxiety. Tobacco smoke rose in blue spirals to the ceiling, accordion music and laughter vibrated around the tables, and beer flowed copiously.

While we were sipping black coffee and discussing the next port of call — for we had in mind an all-night session and I wasn't particularly enamoured of my modest hotel anyway — I slipped away to collect reserves of cash from my baggage back at the hotel, less than a kilometre distant.

The night was cold; the stars close in the clear air. I turned down a cobbled street to take as direct as possible a route to the hotel, using the indistinct spire of the cathedral as a guide. There were no houses nearby; only dim silent warehouses and, flanked by another bridge, the gaunt skeleton of the lattice steel pylon carrying the electric current for the railway. Somewhere a clock struck one, and two more church bells provided ill-tuned echoes. The narrow streets were empty.

I heard a car approaching from behind and moved to the pavement. I turned the corner and recognised the street of my hotel. It stood on the right-hand side of the road, so before crossing I waited for the car to go by, but it didn't. I glanced over my shoulder. A large saloon with its lights turned off was crawling slowly in my wake. The warm glow of the party spirit quickly gave way to a cold recollection of multi-power-controlled Vienna, city of intrigue. No doubt Linz too was crawling with intelligence operatives. I moved on again, chiding myself for an over-vivid imagination, then stopped once more. The car, closer now, stopped too.

I spun round and the vehicle accelerated to draw level with me. I was about to make a run for it, when a man inside the car spoke.

In a broad American accent, he said, "Are you Mr Portway?"

"Why?" I asked defensively.

The car door opened but the man in the front passenger seat made no move to get out. The driver, indistinguishable in the gloom, remained at the wheel. His passenger put his hand into his breast pocket and I backed away towards the protective darkness. Both men were wearing shoulder holsters.

He spoke again. "Take it easy. This is who we are," he said, handing me a cellophane-covered card. I took it warily and strained to read the lettering. With difficulty I made out the words "United States Central Intelligence Agency". Although I was less concerned now, my suspicions remained.

"What do you want?" I asked. Out of the corner of my eye I saw the driver flick a lighter for his cigar, the small flame illuminating a vivid-coloured checked shirt. This was reassuring; surely no selfrespecting Soviet agent would be seen dead in a garment like that.

127

"We want a few words with you, if you don't mind," came the answer. "Come and sit in the car; it's warmer." He turned and opened the rear door.

Hesitantly, I climbed into the back seat. The man in the passenger seat came round to join me and the driver swivelled to face us.

"We understand you are intending to catch a train to Summerau tomorrow morning." He glanced at his wristwatch, "No, sorry, *this* morning." The ghost of a smile creased the lean face as he looked at me for confirmation.

It wasn't their business, but I saw no reason to deny it. I nodded.

"You know it's in the Russkie zone?" he went on.

"Yes."

"We have no authority to stop you, but we advise you very strongly not to go."

Resentment boiled within me just as it had at Cheb. Everybody was in on the act to deny me the basic right of being with the girl I loved. I decided to ignore the advice.

"Much as I appreciate the concern of the United States," I answered primly, "I cannot — will not — cancel my arrangements."

I saw their looks of concern and wondered how it was that America now should be involved in my problems. To explain my uncooperative attitude I started to tell them the reasons for my proposed journey.

The driver spoke for the first time: "We know."

His remark confused me. I tried to work out from which of the various possible sources the information could have been gained. In addition to my last letter from England which cryptically alluded to my plans, there had been my similarly worded postcard from Zagreb and, of course, the communication from Vienna. Even so, if that telegram had been the give-away, the Americans must have acted pretty fast.

"No use me asking how you know, I suppose?"

"No." It was their turn to be cagey.

"Then may I ask *why* you are trying to stop me going? What risks am I running other than being in the Russian zone without permission? After all, nothing happened on my way here from Vienna."

"It wouldn't," I was told, "it's an international highway. You have the right to drive along it. But, believe us, you'll be in big trouble if you try what you intend to do."

I spent nearly half an hour in the car and the conversation became tedious. The Americans worked every gambit to prevent my proposed excursion and, equally relentlessly, I declared my determination to go.

"Well, it's your funeral," was the driver's last word on the subject. I didn't much care for his choice of expression. "Like a lift back to your party?"

I assented gladly. I could use a drink.

"By the way," the American beside me said, "I'm Hank and that's Joe." He indicated the driver. With their warnings issued and duty presumably done, the two men became affable and the atmosphere was less tense. Joe turned the car and sped me back to the

Bierhaus. I invited them in but they declined. Only as I watched the red rear lights of the car disappearing into the night did it occur to me that they must have been tailing me since I left the place or even before that — otherwise how did they know I was there in the first instance? I shivered as I re-entered the warm fug of the pub.

The party was still in progress, although Norman was wondering why I had taken so long to reach my hotel and return. I told him the reason, explaining too that I'd never even got to my hotel.

When I finally did make it back to my room, there was only time for a cat-nap before I packed and left at five o'clock. A clear sky promised a fine day as I hurried along the still-empty streets towards the station. I looked behind me every now and then, unable to rid myself of the experiences of the night, although everything looked so much less threatening in the daylight. Near the station there were more people, hurrying to work. I was hurrying too, urged on by the thought of seeing Anna again within a matter of hours.

Linz Central Station was a modern, airy building. Having already purchased my ticket, I made my way straight to the buffet for breakfast of a *Wurst* sandwich and a steaming cup of coffee, as I had plenty of time before my train left.

Suddenly I choked into my coffee. I had spotted the two Americans standing on the other side of the open grille doors of the adjacent platform. They were talking to a railway official and seemed not to have seen me. The plan for Norman to drive away in my car on his

130

way to work, and thus act as a decoy for anyone interested in my movements, had not worked. It hadn't been a very serious ploy anyway; no more than a way of satisfying Norman's good-natured desire to be involved in the operation.

I finished my breakfast as leisurely as I could and meandered onto the station concourse, taking care not to be observed by Hank and Joe. When no station staff members were looking my way, I crossed the tracks to the departure platform. The Summerau train was in and a few passengers were selecting their seats. It was a slow *Personenzug*, stopping at all stations along the route. I checked my watch. Fourteen minutes before the train left.

Selecting a seat in a second-class coach facing the engine, I waited. I had not been able to buy a ticket right through to Horní Dvořiště or anywhere beyond Austrian territory, but I didn't think this would prevent me reaching the Czechoslovakian border station. And since the border here was communist on both sides — Czechoslovakian and Soviet-Austrian — there was unlikely to be an intermediate security stop between the two border stations. Nor would the restrictions be so tight or, I hoped, the station officials so vigilant. I glanced again at my watch. Eight minutes to go.

Four more minutes passed before a trio of faces appeared at the window. Two of them I recognised. "Good morning, Chris," said Hank. In daylight his colourful shirt was startling.

"Good morning to you," I replied brightly. "Couldn't you sleep either?" Ignoring the taunt, Hank introduced me to the third member of the posse. He was older, wore a light raincoat and did not look at all American.

"This is Inspector Salzbach of the Austrian Police. We have news for you."

"Oh yes," I countered, without enthusiasm, nodding to the policeman.

Hank continued. "The inspector's district includes that of Summerau and the frontier. His men at Summerau reported a couple of hours ago that two members of the Soviet Security Police are waiting there for the expected arrival of a British national. All right, it might be someone else but I don't know what Summerau's got to draw trainloads of Limeys there so early in the morning." He looked at me quizzically.

I still refused to be deterred from my mission. It was wholly too incredible that the intelligence organisations of the two major powers should be mobilised to catch one little man going to visit his girl.

"And what the Russkies know it can be assumed the Czechs know too. No doubt they've been alerted on their side of the wire," Hank added.

I felt a slither of ice in my bowels. Anna would be at Horní Dvořiště by now. Could anything unpleasant happen to her? I knew damn well it could.

"How do I know you're not making all this up?"

It was the inspector who supplied the answer by producing a cable reply form and showing it to me. The writing was in German but I could understand some of the words and the missive held an air of authenticity. I

132

still hesitated. Yet only a fool would make up a flimsy story like that if they wanted to be believed, and these men were no fools.

Joe noticed my hesitation. He shot another bolt.

"Last night you asked us how we knew about you and the girl," he said quietly. "In Vienna you sent her a telegram, didn't you, and a postcard — a *postcard* — from Zagreb? You gave everybody plenty of warning of your intentions."

A whistle blew and doors slammed ready for the train to depart. I grabbed my bag and leapt back onto the platform.

"Thanks a lot," I murmured to the two smiling Americans. I decided I rather liked them.

They, in turn, must have noticed my crestfallen look. "Come and have a *real* breakfast," they suggested. The policeman gave a salute and departed.

Back in the station buffet we had waffles, fried eggs, ham and maple syrup, and, since Americans don't require a reason for anything, champagne.

They might have had something to celebrate but I hadn't. They would never have stopped me had I remained adamant about ignoring their well-intended advice and stayed on the train. And even if I *had* got into trouble at the border at least I would have fulfilled my obligation to Anna. But it was too late now to blame either them or myself.

Hank seemed to sense what I was thinking. "We weren't sure yesterday," he explained. "We only knew for certain this morning."

I asked how they knew but was not given an answer. "We have to protect our sources of information", was all they would say.

I thought despondently of Anna waiting wide-eyed on a strange, hostile border-station platform for me, ashamed that I had let her down.

For three further days I remained in Linz before returning home. Already I was planning fresh assaults.

My summons to the War Office was brief and to the point. The typed instruction read simply: "There is a matter upon which you can help. Please be good enough to confirm that you are able to report to the above office." It gave a date and time. The signature was illegible but the sender held the rank of major. His department was MI 11, which I understood to be concerned with counterespionage.

The anonymous major turned out to be equally anonymous in appearance. He was quite young, wore a Brigade of Guards tie and a well-cut suit. He said he expected I knew why they had asked me there and I replied that I had not the faintest idea. He showed me a file in a folder marked "Secret and confidential."

"This is on you," he said and I thought I detected a reprimand.

"Is that *all* mine?" I exclaimed with perhaps a shade too much enthusiasm.

"It's not a matter of pride," I was tartly informed.

The gist of the ensuing conversation was that, through my activities, I was putting myself and the girl in grave danger. That in itself didn't appear to matter to him. But what *did* matter was the fact that I had become a highly likely candidate for blackmail and in my capacity as commissioned officer in Her Majesty's Territorial Army this was of special concern.

"I'll resign if that's any help," I assured him brightly, wondering what secret weaponry in my TA unit of outdated anti-aircraft artillery the USSR would want to pressurise me into revealing. But it seemed I wasn't required to resign; the TA was extremely short of officers at the time.

My movements of late had been of unaccountable interest to MI 11. I was told every detail of my itinerary in both Yugoslavia and Austria; even to the post office in Zagreb from which I'd sent that damned postcard. As the major's toneless voice flowed on, the hairs on the back of my neck rose in awe. The discourse eventually drew to a close. "We are warning you," he said finally, without a smile.

Only later did I discover that Anna never received my telegram from Vienna. The Zagreb picture-postcard, however, did reach her and she spent a whole day and a half hanging around the station at Horní Dvořiště not knowing which train I'd be arriving on. Everyone — Czech, Russian, American and British — appeared to be enjoying my innocuous correspondence. Everyone, too, was making very certain that I never again reached my fiancée.

CHAPTER
ELEVEN

My parents, relatives and friends continually encouraged me to search for a more accessible marriage partner, but to no avail. "It's hopeless," I was told kindly and sometimes not so kindly, "give it up and find a nice English rose instead."

The most forceful inducement to do so came when Anna's application to marry me was rejected. I was angry that a regime could refuse the simple right of its citizens to choose whom they married. It was bad enough their being forbidden to cross its frontiers, but this meddling in the private lives of those who chose to find happiness outside them was the very basis of slavery.

In spite of my disappointment and anger the outlook to me was quite clear. I loved Anna; she loved me. We had contracted to become husband and wife and to share our lives. The fact that she was harder to get than other girls made not the slightest difference. And if the state — together with my own "well-wishers" for that matter — reckoned they could douse the romance, they could think again. Nevertheless, all these rejections and negative opinions together with the hopelessness of the situation were steadily wearing me down.

Only once, however, did my resolve seriously falter when, out of the blue, another woman briefly entered my life. Her name was Saimi. She was Finnish and very attractive. My mother had hired her to help with the housework. I remembered clearly the moment I first set eyes upon her. I had returned from annual Territorial Army camp and had just taken a bath when, from the open window, I saw her crossing the yard at the back of the house. "Hi, Saimi!" I shouted. As I waved, the towel I was wearing around my waist slipped to my thighs.

Thereafter, my free weekends were occupied with driving her to the East Anglian coast and countryside where we swam, sunbathed, laughed and frolicked. Despite my guilty conscience, I was openly smitten with her, not only because of her good looks, but also because of her charm and kindness. In return, she displayed considerable affection for me although, to her eternal credit, this was conditional on the fact that my priorities lay with the girl I had asked to be my wife. Only if this commitment ended would we allow our relationship to endure and prosper.

We saw a great deal of each other and the affair — if you can call it that — smouldered on even after my mother, having noticed the situation, sent Saimi to act as an au pair for my brother and his wife living four miles away. But, aside from a necessity to invent reasons for going out on evenings and at weekends, we were still able to meet (my regular duties as a Territorial officer greatly helped with this deception).

But my love for and commitment to Anna did not fade; always the image of her waiting patiently rose before me and her ineffably sad reply to my letter offering release from our engagement nearly broke my heart. Saimi, of course, fully aware of my dilemma, never allowed our affection to become too serious. And when her time with my brother's family expired she accepted a similar position with a French family in Paris, thus allowing our friendship to fade away.

And so my devotion to and correspondence with Anna continued. The simple code we had devised to beat the prying eyes of those who were randomly reading our letters seemed to be working. Several of our exchanges, involving what the regime would normally consider to be of a sensitive nature, and therefore deemed worthy of censorship, had got through, although this might have been by pure luck.

I continued to plan new incursions into the communist badlands. The ease of moving around newly opened Yugoslavia and the far-from-watertight restrictions I had found in Soviet-occupied Austria set my sights upon the other People's Republics neighbouring Czechoslovakia; Hungary, Eastern Germany, Poland and even the Soviet Union itself all offered distinct promise. Simply applying for an entry visa as a potential tourist would not work; these countries were not taking a leaf out of the Yugoslav book *that* fast. But given a bona fide reason for an entry visa, and so long as my crime sheet had not spread beyond Czechoslovakian borders, I held strong hopes of gaining legal entry to at least some of them.

In the autumn of 1954 an advertisement in a trade newspaper caught my eye. It was an announcement of the forthcoming reopening, after a 16-year interval, of the international trade fair at Leipzig, East Germany. There lay a key that might unlock another small door towards reaching Anna, and this time it was the enemy who was offering it.

The successful acquisition of a visa for the GDR, the German Democratic Republic (in German, the *Deutsche Demokratishe Republik* or DDR) as the East German communist regime chose to title their portion of the country, was by no means an easy task. Of all the states of the Eastern Bloc, the GDR remained one of the most ruthlessly efficient at repression. And although in 1954 the USSR permitted the GDR to become a "sovereign" state and join the newly formed Warsaw Pact, the Soviet Union continued to manage most of its affairs, especially those in the realm of state security.

Therefore it was to the Soviet Embassy in London that I had to address my application to attend the fair. With the aid of a letter of intent on my firm's notepaper presenting myself as a prominent businessman eager to sell products to the Eastern Bloc, I was able to obtain a special card issued by the fair's London agency. This, I was assured, would entitle me to a Soviet-issued visa allowing me to visit Leipzig over the period of the exhibition. In the event it did not. First I had to go through a charade of an exchange of letters with the East German State Import/Export Corporation detailing the products of my company and giving an explanation of how vital they were for the advancement of trade between my country and theirs and, more to the point, how necessary it was that I myself should be present at the fair. Finally I was granted a seven-day visa, together with a bonus offer of a reduced fare on the East German State Railway. I was the earliest British businessman to apply to attend this first post-war edition of a once highly regarded trade exhibition.

The Soviet visa, sent to me duly stamped into my passport, was a joy to behold, with a purple blaze of CCCP Russian hieroglyphics and rows of tax stamps across it like medal ribbons on the breast of a general. That, surely, would impress and confound the most diligent minion of East German authority. The fact that a translation of the visa's validity, enclosed with the passport, stated that it covered no more than the city of Leipzig and its immediate environs worried me little. So long as no Russian official looked hard at its wording, I felt sure there would be few difficulties as I travelled across the country.

Furthermore, the GDR shared a common border with Czechoslovakia in the south. In our coded exchanges Anna had made clear — as if I hadn't guessed — that there was little hope of her being allowed to visit the fair herself. No longer employed, she could hardly find an excuse of a commercial nature to attend a trade event of any description, particularly one outside her own country. In addition, now that she was being watched by the SNB, she would have been prevented from coming to Leipzig anyway. However, if she couldn't come to me, now was another opportunity for me to make my way to her.

In our exchanges I told of my intention of attending the fair, suggested a meeting place outside the main gates in case a miracle allowed her to attend, and, more realistically, gave the date I hoped to reach the Czechoslovakian border station of Děčín four days after my arrival at Leipzig.

On the German side, Bad Schandau was the corresponding border town and, according to my research, there were no stops for security checks in between. My plan, similar to the earlier one I had carried out, was to make my way to Dresden and board the Berlin-Prague Express, conceal myself in the toilet and arrive, unmolested, at Děčín. Only then would my lack of visa be detected, but at least I'd be with Anna for however short a period, and that was all that mattered to me. The scheme was similar to those I had employed on the Bavarian-Czechoslovakian border earlier, but the border between the two communist-allied countries was likely to be a "soft" one so that, should the railway scheme fail, a journey on foot through the woods would not be beyond the bounds of possibility. In support of these two projects I had, again, carried out considerable research.

As with the East-West Czechoslovakian border-crossing attempt, I had built up a dossier of information on conditions and security measures in the GDR border areas based on close examination of newspapers, periodicals and intelligent digests as well as letters from West German friends and conversations with acquaintances who had driven through the country or who had, at one time, holidayed in the picturesque wooded landscape of "Saxon Switzerland" through which my route would pass. But the most significant data collected related to the River Elbe itself, which flowed through the region. My source was a nameless individual in a Wapping pub who revealed the fact that the crews of barges that regularly crossed between the two countries could be prevailed upon to carry the odd stowaway in either direction.

The four days I felt it expedient to spend in Leipzig pretending to show interest in the exhibits at the fair would not be wasted. I had no doubt that some of the citizens and visitors there would be willing to talk to me to help me further.

A London travel agent accredited to the fair booked my return rail journey to Leipzig — the return ticket was a stipulation of the East German regime — and reserved me lodging for four nights. So sparse was accommodation in the city at the time that guests were being offered beds through a private home boarding scheme which suited me well, for I had no desire to come under the scrutiny of hotel staff probably acting as agents for the SD (*Sicherheitsdienst*) or other intelligence services.

Perhaps the hardest task of all was obtaining leave of absence from my firm. Initially I had managed to keep secret my plans to attend the fair, but having a father who was also my managing director made this impossible for long. He was, as expected, firmly against the idea, mainly on account of the reputation of the company. Consequently, I left Britain to the displeasure of both parents and my manager.

★　★　★

Leipzig would make a strong contender in a contest between the most attractive of historic German cities. The Old Town possesses not only the splendid Gothic *Rathaus* (City Hall) but also Auerbach's sixteenth-century *Hof* (courtyard) in the Madlerpassage, together with a labyrinth of narrow streets interconnected by other covered courtyards and alleys. Goethe, who studied there, called Leipzig "Paris in Miniature", although much of its heart was destroyed by bombs in World War II. Bach spent 27 years of the most productive years of his life there, Wagner was born and worked there, Mendelssohn also spent some of his working life there, and Robert Schumann attended its university. Leipzig was, and still is, something of cultural honeypot.

My journey to the city had not been entirely uneventful. At Helmstadt, the main West German exit point to the DDR, I purchased some East German marks at a favourable rate only to have them confiscated 100 metres on by GDR currency officials. At Magdeburg, where I changed trains, I chose a later connection to give me time to look around the city and observe a slice of life in the communist utopia of the other Germany. I didn't much like what I saw. In the Federal Republic (West Germany) a war ruin was fast becoming a rarity, but in Magdeburg that warm sunny afternoon I found myself back in the Germany of 1946, a country of fire-ravaged ruin, uniform drabness and despair. I was glad to return to my train, a local that halted for an interminable time at a still-wrecked Halle Station.

A posse of Vopos (People's Police) moved along the corridor demanding identity documents. "You're on the wrong train," I was told.

"Doesn't this train go to Leipzig?"

"Yes," came the reply, "but this one is not for foreigners."

I could understand why, for the condition of the vehicle was disgraceful and military music vied with Karl Marx quotations blasted from loudspeakers in each shabby compartment. However, I was permitted to remain aboard.

By teatime we reached the flag-bedecked walls of Leipzig Main, a railway station showpiece to the world. The authorities had deemed it prudent to repair this particular building in view of the influx of foreign visitors but, even so, much of the glass roof remained entirely missing.

My first objective was the foreign visitors' centre at the *Neues Rathaus* which, architecturally, is not a patch on the old one. The centre of the city was conspicuously signposted, the shops uncommonly well "dressed" for the benefit of visitors, the trams had been freshly painted and the streets tidied. Leipzig citizens gave the game away by crowding, awe-struck, around the abruptly filled shop windows and gazing at items they couldn't buy. Remaining war ruins were hidden behind giant red political hoardings.

Before reporting to the visitors' centre, I dropped in for a beer at a small *Gasthaus* at the corner of the market place. As I emptied my glass I remembered I had no Ostmarks, the East German currency. The good-natured proprietor was in no way put out and, waving aside my offers of alternative currencies, came and joined me at the table. From his opening remarks I realised he was no fan of the regime under which he lived.

"See all this here," came a stentorian whisper accompanied by an arm waving towards the nearest shop window, "all those goodies we can't afford. They'll go the minute the show closes. They've piled up the shop windows and even brought in extra traffic; even *people* to fill the streets!" He almost exploded with indignation. "By next week the place'll be like any other down-at-heel town in our beloved country."

The *Neues Rathaus* turned out to be not all that new and had been transformed into a genteel version of an interrogation centre. At a series of booths, visitors were being documented, tagged and classified under the stern gaze of President Wilhelm Pieck, the current compulsory pin-up in any official GDR building. A bevy of girls wearing uniforms and fixed smiles slotted me into "Heavy Engineering" and entered my particulars in a flurry of forms. Every visitor received a printed welcome from the immigration authority which, in a quartet of languages, drooled, "Dear Fair Guest from Abroad", and went on to wish satisfactory dealings with the "peace industry" of the German Democratic Republic. The missive ended: "Should there be any necessity for you to travel further on to some other place in the republic in connection with your business, or perhaps, for private reasons, you have the opportunity of applying to the Ministry of Foreign

Affairs to have your visa extended. We beg you to be kind enough to observe these directions as your present visa is only valid for the fair town of Leipzig." The instruction might have been written just for me and I suspected that my "private reasons" for leaving the "fair town" would not endear me to the Ministry of Foreign Affairs.

Next, the *Deutsche Notenbank* proceeded to obtain its pound of flesh with a hard-currency exchange rate that caused the most affluent of guests to wince, and to rub salt into the wound, offered a slip of paper listing the penalties for an impressive variety of possible currency irregularities. Finally, an aloof young lady, seeing my chosen lowest-of-the-low "private house accommodation" category of lodging, proffered an address for a lodging for which I had to pay in advance. This done, I then had to return to the *Deutsche Notenbank* for further funds.

My accommodation card gave the name "Frau Lindener, Brandvorwerkstrasse 80/1". I asked how to reach the street and was directed to an information booth crowded with visitors making similar enquiries.

A number five tram, it transpired, would take me most of the way but I forgot to ask the direction and ended up at the wrong end of town, where conditions were decidedly less rapturous than in the centre. Completing a circuit of the Leipzig tramway system, I finally reached the Lindener residence, one of a block of terraced flats indistinguishable from others in the same street.

I took to the Lindeners at once. He was a thin, slightly lugubrious intellectual who played first violin in the famous Gewandhaus Orchestra and spoke excellent English. His wife, in her early 30s, was a friendly, capable woman who treated me as one of the family. A diminutive daughter, full of mischief, lost no time in making up for any deficiency in spoken English.

I was urged to eat supper with them, although it was not included in the private house accommodation tariff, and this made me wonder how much money such host families got for their services after the state had taken its cut. We sat around chatting well into the night but I was hesitant about mentioning anything relating to my mission. I guessed that people such as the Lindeners had been graded "politically reliable" or else they would never have been permitted to have a foreign visitor under their roof. Herr Lindener made no pretence about the love he had for his job; music was plainly his life-blood and I could see that no indiscretions would be tolerated on his part lest they jeopardise the advancement of his profession.

Next day I spent at the fair. Entering by the main gate I found myself amongst an unsavoury mix of politics and commercialism. The place of honour, as could be expected, went to the Soviet Union with its ungainly Palace of Industry topped by a blood-red star of massive dimensions. The GDR, as host nation, came a poor second, followed by the pagoda-like Chinese pavilion. The European socialist republics of Poland, Czechoslovakia, Romania, Hungary, Bulgaria and Albania, in a supporting role, defiantly attempted a flash of individualism with their own products, while further down the line came "neutral" India, Argentina, Chile, Turkey, Peru and the Arab republics. Crowded into a single small pavilion, the few exhibits of France, Belgium and Britain were tucked away in a corner, by accident or design, next door to the toilets.

To escape from Soviet tractors and East German turbines I made frequent forays to the main gate to scan the crowds in case, by some miracle, Anna had managed to make it to Leipzig. Back at the exhibition I continued to feign interest in bits of machinery and the prestigious produce of a multitude of nations. The Chinese pavilion was full of tea, carpets and Mao Tse-Tung, the GDR showed off a range of Leica photographic equipment, as did the West Germans. Yugoslavia displayed her prowess with plums, Czechoslovakia went to town on Pilsner beer, and India exhibited tea, carpets and Jawaharlal Nehru. But the biggest crowd-puller lay close to the lavatories where France, Belgium and Britain showed off tantalising glimpses of the fruits of capitalism.

Playing truant for part of the second day, I made my way into the city on a round of visits of a more specialised nature. At the office of the Czechoslovakian Legation, just for the hell of it, I trotted out my business "spiel" in support of a plea for an entry or transit visa for that country. It seemed worth a try but I needn't have bothered. "Come back in a week," advised a horrid little man in a loud suit. "We may have a reply from Prague then."

148

At the railway station I asked about tickets for travel to the Czechoslovakian border. "Have you a travel permit?" asked the booking clerk with narrowed eyes. I looked blankly at him as he recited the rules, parrot-fashion. "All *Ausländer* in the GDR must be in possession of a police permit to move further than 50 kilometres from their temporary place of residence. Furthermore, foreigners must be in possession of an endorsed visa to visit any part of the republic other than Leipzig. Is that understood?"

I nodded weakly. "Anything else?"

Warming to his subject, the man continued. "Only the matter of visiting a frontier district. This also requires a police permit, unless, of course, you are in direct transit to the Czechoslovak Republic."

"When I've got all these permits do I come back to you?"

The question was pondered briefly. "No, firstly, only the State Travel Bureau can issue such tickets, and secondly," the face behind the grille winked, "I'd have died of old age long before you'd collected half of them!"

Undaunted, I sought the office of the State Travel Bureau but found it closed. I wondered whether I should just get on a train south and obtain a ticket from its staff who hopefully wouldn't be aware of all the rules and regulations, particularly if I chose local trains. But with time on my hands I continued my quest in Leipzig.

Rebuffed at the State Travel Bureau, I made for the source of all power, the Main Police Station, and cornered a knowledgeable-looking officer. "A permit to move freely in the GDR, why? You wish to go to Prague? Then may I please see your Czechoslovakian visa? No visa, but one applied for? Well, come back when it's issued and we'll see what can be done."

I tried a different tack but they knew all the answers. "A visit to Bad Schandau? But that's a military zone and you'll require a permit from our People's Army." I got the point. The People's Army — even if I tracked down the correct department in the People's Defence Ministry or whatever — would only swing it all back to the People's Police. They had it all nicely buttoned up between them without having to lose face with an unconditional refusal.

The Travel Bureau was open when I got back there. I approached the clerk, putting on a stern countenance. "It's imperative that I go to Prague the day after tomorrow," I began in a no-nonsense tone.

The elderly assistant was apologetic. "We can issue tickets only as far as the border," he said.

"That'll do. I can get another at Děčín."

"You presumably have a special visa allowing the journey?"

"Of course." A brazen lie.

"May I see your passport please, sir, so that the required references can be entered on the ticket application form."

I handed over the book. The poor old boy peered at the jumble of defaced pages in bewilderment. "Which —?"

150

"That one," I hissed as haughtily as I could manage, hating myself as I jabbed the page containing the Russian hieroglyphics. The man cowed and wrote something down on a proforma.

"If you would be good enough to come back tomorrow morning, sir, your tickets will be ready."

I thanked him nonchalantly, retrieved my passport and swept out of the office. I fought the urge to dance a jig for having found a chink in the armour of state security but a note of caution dampened my sense of triumph. Better not get too excited until the ticket was in my hand.

But all went smoothly. Returning next morning, I was handed the ticket voucher together with detailed information regarding train times of departure and arrival, and change of trains at Dresden; details I already knew. Following a final hour at the fair I returned to the Lindeners who, bless them, laid on a special last-night supper in my honour.

Early next morning I boarded a Dresden-bound train. I pictured Anna likewise catching a train from Prague to Děčín. I thought that I must love her very much to do what I intended to do. I thought that she must love me very much to keep on risking the wrath of the authorities by meeting me at restricted border crossings. Maybe this meeting would not be in vain.

CHAPTER
TWELVE

They called Dresden the Florence of the Elbe until a day in February 1945 when Allied bombers turned it into a molten furnace. I first glimpsed the city in 1944 from the barred window of a prison-train wagon rolling across the great river towards the camps in the east. It was, at that time, numbered among the most aesthetic cities in Europe. Yet with fresh first-hand memories of unspeakable horrors perpetrated by Germans, I had, later, and from a distance, watched Dresden's destruction without a grain of pity. Now, in 1954, I was, albeit briefly, to look upon the city, now in the throes of reconstruction, for a third time.

With a couple of hours to spare between trains I walked to the old Augustusbrücke, separating the Prague-like Old Town from the new. The face of the city still wore its dreadful scars but new buildings, painstakingly copied from the old, were being recreated inside cradles of scaffolding. For the regime that followed Hitler's, the tragedy of the colossal triple air raid provided a telling propaganda weapon, and from the many billboards the anti-West invective soundlessly screamed its warped message.

My rail journey as far as Dresden had proved the worth of my Soviet visa. The train I had intentionally chosen had been no express. It had dawdled contentedly across undulating terrain to a refrain of thumping polka music from coach compartment speakers. Police checks both on the train and at Meissen station culminated in salutes and respectful heel-clicking. My fellow travellers gazed at me in awe. I basked in my good luck.

Returning to the station and giving a pair of Russian military policemen a wide berth — since I had doubts about my visa's magic under Russian scrutiny — I boarded the Berlin-Prague Express, which drew in five minutes early. A showpiece of a train, it was decked out in silver and black livery; even the lowest-class coaches were of the "soft" variety. Relaxed in the cushions, I watched the suburbs of Dresden fade from view as the train paced the river and entered the cliff-and tree-bordered valley that gradually narrowed to became a gorge of the so-called "Saxon Switzerland" that comprised the foothills of the Erzgebirge.

Within half an hour the train slowed at the approaches to Bad Schandau, but I made no attempt to leave. The town was three kilometres from the Czechoslovakian border and I felt it worth an attempt at bluffing my way through without trying to dodge the immigration and customs officials who, within seconds of stopping, were threading their way through the coaches.

I nearly got away with it too. The police inspector was plainly impressed with my collection of hieroglyphics but they still failed to add up, in his Teutonic mind, to a Czechoslovakian entry visa. Putting on my important businessman act, I growled annoyance for the seeming lack of desire to further commercial relations between my country and his, and almost succeeded in persuading him. But finally, with abject apologies, he showed me off the train and, in an effort to be helpful, led me to a waiting northbound train and saw me aboard. "You'll be able to obtain a visa at the Czechoslovakian Embassy in Berlin in no time at all," he purred. "Gute Reise." I smiled, cursing him under my breath.

Waiting for his departure, I scrambled off the new train and returned to the head of the platform where the Prague-bound express still stood, taking care to remain out of sight of my well-meaning persecutor. At the barrier I was asked for all the usual documentation but before everything could be properly examined, another officer, glimpsing my Soviet visa, decided to undertake his good deed for the day. Without further ado he propelled me towards the express. "Come quickly, it's due out in a few minutes," he exclaimed excitedly and hustled me into a first-class coach where I sank into the luxurious upholstery, astounded at the turn of events. By arriving late I had avoided the controls on the train, but the ticket inspector was quick to descend upon me with typical ardour.

The absence of an onward ticket seemingly made no insurmountable problem — the Czechoslovakian rail staff would deal with that — but I had inadvertently placed myself in a reserved portion of the coach and I was directed to move myself to the neighbouring coach. Unfortunately, doing this, I ran into the back of the passport-inspection brigade who was on the point of completing its task. There came a bellow of rage and I perceived the very police inspector who had been so helpfully unhelpful the first time round.

"What are you doing on this train again?"

"One of your men put me on it," I explained fatuously.

"Come with me." All his earlier politeness had evaporated.

Barely had we left the express for the second time when it slid smoothly out of the station. If only that confounded ticket inspector had confronted me just a few seconds later, I would have got away with a clear run to Děčín on Czechoslovakian territory where Anna would be waiting.

I cursed my ill-fortune and East Germans in general as I was conducted in a heavy-handed manner to the administrative section of the station. In an office, its walls adorned with a solitary portrait of Comrade Joseph Stalin heavily draped in black crêpe, I found myself before a handsome Russian army captain. He smiled in a friendly fashion as he listened to the indignant outpourings of my escort.

"It seems you're anxious to leave the German Democratic Republic," he declared in passable English, the smile still hovering around the corners of his mouth. "Perhaps I'd better have a look at your passport." I had the feeling he liked Germans no more than I did, as I reluctantly handed over the book.

One look at my magic visa and all was revealed.

"This is a permit valid just for the town of Leipzig," explained the captain, tapping the visa. "You are about 200 kilometres off course." He seemed to be quite amused.

"When foreigners come to the British Industries Fair they're not expected to remain tied to Birmingham," was my concluding comment.

"This isn't England," snapped the inspector, making "England" sound like a dirty word.

I said nothing.

The Russian and the German conferred and I managed to follow the gist of their exchange, which was a verbal skirmish around the matter of which authority — Soviet Army or German People's Police — was to be responsible for my immediate future. Neither man appeared keen to act as my host, but eventually it was decided that the police were lumbered with me.

At this point in negotiations I made a contribution towards a solution. "Can I go now?" I enquired brightly, but my efforts were rewarded with a growl from the increasingly annoyed police officer, who curtly informed me that I was going nowhere, since I was under arrest.

"Why? What crimes have I committed? Is this how you treat your business guests in the GDR?" My voice rose higher and higher in righteous indignation but was stolidly ignored.

Removed from the office I was handed over to four heavily armed Vopos and, back in the operational part of the station, was "invited" aboard a one-coach diesel train standing in a siding. It didn't seem to be a service train at all, rather a police special, and it stood at a side platform not used by the public. Once their officer had departed, the quartet became exceedingly friendly, one of the men handing me a bottle of lager, which I drank with gratitude since I'd consumed nothing all day. While I tipped the beer down my throat I took stock of the new situation. Left alone for a minute, maybe I would do a bunk, disappear into the countryside and follow the river to the border through a conveniently all-concealing terrain. Train-hopping was now clearly a non-starter since too many of the railway's denizens knew of me and my unusual activities. But a night-time trek to the border might achieve the desired result. The thought of Anna awaiting my arrival at Děčín, barely 15 kilometres distant, provided the incentive.

A while later the diesel train jerked into motion, moving out onto the main southbound line in the wake of the Prague Express. My spirits rose a little; at least we were going in the right direction and every metre covered would reduce the distance of my proposed hike. But hardly had the train gathered speed than it began slowing down to draw to a stop at a wayside halt shadowed by the eastern wall of the Elbe gorge. On the river a string of barges was moving downstream. I remembered the comments of my informant in the Wapping pub.

One of the policemen interrupted my thoughts. "Tschechoslowakei," he announced enthusiastically, pointing to a pier that projected into the water less than 500 metres away.

I scrutinised the rough wooden structure, taking in every detail, my heart thumping against my ribs at the realisation that now only eight kilometres lay between me and my immediate goal.

We stopped at a small, nameless platform and I was led across the tracks onto a well-worn path to the river's edge. It was a brilliant day, the sun warm in a cloudless sky. I felt light-headed, and my companions, young boys pressed into service, caught something of my mood. Only their military uniforms and the ugly hardware they carried marred the illusion of an afternoon stroll in idyllic countryside. I asked them where we were going and they pointed across the river, intimating that wherever it was would not take long.

From close at hand the river looked a lot less sluggish; the current was strong and the water whipped up little plumes of froth. A powerful police launch, pulling at its retaining rope, lay at a small quay half-hidden by the bank. With ill-concealed interest I watched a northbound barge heave to at the Czechoslovakian control point for, presumably, customs examination.

The five of us climbed awkwardly into the open launch and one of the youths slid into the driving seat. Opening up at full throttle, we cleaved a diagonal course across the water towards an identical quay on the opposite bank further upstream. My escort, noticing my interest in the surroundings, cheerfully pointed out various rock features in the granite walls of the gorge, as if we were on a Bank Holiday river outing. My eyes were continually drawn towards the tantalisingly close Czechoslovakian territory, but I also tried to look elsewhere, so as not to arouse suspicion.

Disembarking at the new jetty, we made our way along an extension of the footpath that led towards a distant hamlet — no more than a small cluster of houses lying at the base of a cliff. Though it veered away at this point, the Elbe remained in sight across a low-lying marshy meadow. A heron, unperturbed, flapped in monotonous circles above some willows, yellow in the bright afternoon sunshine. A breeze skimmed over the momentarily deserted river, causing more wavelets that collapsed clean and calm a moment later.

At first glance, the hamlet looked like a perfectly normal cluster of cottages but in fact it was only the carcass of a long-dead community. Although not quite of the ominous character of those unfortunate villages that lay athwart the East-West border, this one too had paid the price of proximity to a frontier and a forbidden zone. There was no sign of its one-time inhabitants. The houses were unkempt and shuttered; their windows boarded, some surrounded by rusting coils of barbed wire. Only the larger, once-prosperous villas were currently occupied by soldiers and police of the border details who, like the military everywhere, used their billets uncaringly. An air of the front line pervaded everything and I noticed that the unpaved main street of the hamlet ended abruptly, after 100 metres, in a tangle of wire and concrete dragon's teeth that marked the German border.

We entered one of the villas with peeling stucco walls and green, paint-starved shutters. I was ushered into a room, the bareness of which had been softened by cheap curtaining plainly put up by male hands, a scattering of easy chairs and a spread of matting on the floor. There I was offered a meal of liver sausage with a hunk of rye bread and a litre of weak beer, brought to me by an officer wearing the green epaulettes of a border guard unit. I couldn't make up my mind whether the conversation that ensued was a general chat or a mild form of interrogation.

The man was slight in build, with a large close-shaven head and enormous, dark, luminous eyes. He was quite pleasant and seemed to be questioning me more out of personal curiosity than any sense of duty. I told him all I deemed it necessary he should know and then asked a few questions of my own about my future.

The officer shrugged. "It's a police matter but I don't think you'll be delayed long," he told me with a marked lack of conviction. I asked casual questions about the border and the immediate environment, but he would not give me any information.

Then I had a brainwave. "I have a friend at Děčín. Do you think I might telephone her at the station there?" I asked innocently. At the very least it would be a way of assuring Anna that I was close at hand.

The man wanted to know who she was.

"Oh, just a business acquaintance I hoped to meet there had I been allowed to proceed to Czechoslovakia." I replied in the manner of the sailor who had a girl in every port.

"We'll see about it," came the answer but the tone implied he wouldn't.

My next visitor was the jovial Russian. We greeted one another like long-lost brothers, which impressed the German. He too bombarded me with questions but assuredly not of the sort inspired by his line of duty. It appeared that he was something to do with the military police and his liaison duties frequently took him to border posts well out of sight of higher authority. Again I asked about telephoning Anna. "We'll see about it" was the unconvincing reply.

Outside it began to rain, a light blustery shower from lowering clouds that blotted out the blue sky. Around teatime I was invited to attend a film show in the canteen along the corridor and for an hour or so I watched a gruelling Soviet epic chronicling the activities of a Hero of Labour and an over-taxed blast furnace. It was hardly gripping, but the tear-jerking finale raised frenetic applause which seemed to be solely for the benefit of the Russian captain who sat next to me.

Towards evening the rain let up and I asked permission to go for a walk. To my surprise this was granted. Accompanied by a young NCO barely out of his teens, I made a tour of the unnatural village. At the fence we came across a troop of East German armoured cars, their 20mm cannon aimed provocatively

161

at Czechoslovakia. This line of demarcation was not an insurmountable barrier and, 50 metres beyond it, no more than a line of posts marked the edge of that country. I asked some searching questions of my young guide but he pretended not to understand.

The dusk was heavy with mist as we returned to the villa. I was worrying about Anna. She'd be waiting, poor girl, wondering what had happened to me. "Hold on for me all day and maybe the next one too," I'd told her. I tried again with my request for the telephone and at last I obtained a firm answer: no. There was no telephone connection, they said. I didn't believe it but hesitated to push my guardians too far in case their decided to make their own enquiries about the girl at Děčín station.

The Russian captain, dolled up in breeches and polished jackboots, came to proffer his farewells prior to spending the subsequent evening at another frontier outpost. He also bore news concerning my impending fate. I was to be returned to Berlin some time tomorrow, he informed me, and he light-heartedly suggested I desist from antagonising his German associates by sneaking into the wrong trains.

I had not the slightest desire to be "returned to Berlin", for the city was not even on my way home. The longer I could remain close to the Czechoslovakian border the better the chance I stood of breaching it and reaching Anna — either at Děčín if she was still there or, if not, then at her home. Here I was within spitting distance of the border, and after weeks of planning, preparation and execution, I was not going to let everything go to waste without a further bid for success. Now that I was being watched and guarded until I was safely out of the GDR, my only hope lay in escaping my present "house arrest" or getting away from my escort en route back to Bad Schandau. Either way meant immediate pursuit but such was my desperation that I was prepared to accept the odds.

Another meal followed, and a bed was made up in the room. Throughout the evening pleasant young men drifted in for a chat and a smoke, although whenever I asked to go to the toilet one of them accompanied me. They even had a guard on duty outside my door who remained there all night.

In the morning, although I was allowed another walk, the guard watched me like a hawk; it seemed my guardians had got wind of what was in my mind. In a hamlet full of armed soldiers and police, even if I could evade my escort I would have stood no chance at all of complete escape.

At midday they came for me again — the same four troopers who had brought me from Bad Schandau. My resolve had now hardened and I was tensed for action. The final opportunity to reach the border and beyond was approaching and I simply had to take it, come what may.

We turned onto the path that led towards the river, joining the waterway and then running parallel to its eastern bank. It was another fine day but not warm enough to have dried the muddy track following yesterday's rain. I scanned the ridge of higher ground that rose behind us to the south and the belt of willows and undergrowth that lay to the rear of it. They would provide momentary cover from the inevitable bullets my fleeing figure was likely to draw.

I turned my attention to my companions. The NCO was ahead of me; he carried no more than a stick he had picked up, with which he was idly flicking at tufts of grass beside the path. An automatic pistol in a holster was at his belt with a thin strap over its butt. Also ahead were two of the others, taking little notice of me. One was throwing stones into the water and the others followed suit, attempting to make the pebbles skip along the surface. Only one man was behind me and he suddenly joined his companions in the stone-throwing game. Together with the other two juniors, he carried an AK47 machine carbine slung nonchalantly over his shoulder. It suddenly struck me that none of their weapons appeared to be loaded — unless there were a round in the chambers, which was unlikely — for no magazines were clamped to their breeches. It would have to be now or never.

I quickly estimated the delay from the moment of take-off before things got nasty: 11 seconds — three seconds for the men to recover from their surprise, eight seconds for them to unsling their weapons, clip on magazines and cock the mechanisms prior to opening fire. I thought I could be safely over the ridge inside of eight seconds. I knew the NCO might react faster, and I could only hope he was not a deft pistol shot.

Behind me the man bent down to pick up another pebble, moving closer to the water's edge as he did so. Taking a deep breath I hurled myself sideways and took

164

exactly four steps before my feet slid from under me on the wet, slippery ground. Winded, I lay prostrate staring fixedly at the muzzle of the nearest carbine inches from my face, the gun loaded and cocked. I had underestimated the reactions of my companions by at least five seconds.

My escorts, formerly so easy-going, were now outraged, and I could hardly blame them. Rising sheepishly to my feet I attempted to smooth the situation by babbling on about a lizard I had seen in the grass and tried to capture but, even if they had understood what I was saying, the story was unlikely to have been believed. The atmosphere was distinctly chilly as we returned across the river. I noticed the drawn pistol of the NCO and cradled carbines of the others. Miserably I looked back across the foaming wake of the launch towards the Czechoslovakian pier receding into the distance.

While we waited for a northbound train I was unceremoniously locked in a small, cupboard-like room of the border-post halt. Faded identity-silhouette posters of British and American tanks adorned the walls. "Know your enemy", read the caption. I knew mine.

Released from confinement I watched a signal light turn from green to red as a bell began to ring. "We're stopping it just for you," the NCO remarked acidly. He was referring to the Prague-Berlin Express, audibly approaching. He and his colleagues were making quite sure they got rid of me.

The surprised driver screeched the silver locomotive to a halt at the little platform. Heads peered from coach windows. I was ushered into a first-class compartment but only one guard came with me. I couldn't see the others as the train moved away.

My lone companion remained very much awake all the way to Berlin's *Ostbahnhof*, a near three-hour journey. We spoke little. My thoughts were with Anna whom, once again, I had cruelly let down. Nearing Berlin, the man demanded payment of the fare but I refused on the grounds that I never wanted to come to the German capital in the first place. When we drew into the big dreary station I insisted that the Vopo come with me to the ticket barrier to forestall any complications there; only then did I let him go. It was my one small victory in the whole sorry episode.

I left the station and caught a U-Bahn train to the Western sector of the city.

For Anna, as I learnt later, the waiting at Děčín station had been long and tedious. Railway stations are always draughty and this one was particularly so. She had experienced no difficulty in reaching the Bohemian town despite it being in a restricted border zone. In fact she had been doubly fortunate, for family relatives lived nearby, allowing her to spend some of the waiting hours, including much of the first night, with them. There were only about eight scheduled southbound international trains anyway so she had been able to also make occasional trips into the town to break the monotony of the waiting.

As the hours wore on her excitement and anticipation had risen and fallen. She had worn her maroon dress she knew I liked. Whether I'd be permitted to return to Prague with her she had no means of knowing; she would be thankful for the smallest concession. But whatever fate decreed she was determined to be appropriately dressed for it.

At least the weather had been dry and sunny for most of the time. Her dallying on the platform had not gone unnoticed and several members of the station staff had enquired the reason. She'd told them the truth; that she was waiting for a friend. With each train arrival her excitement increased as the sprinkling of passengers alighted. But mostly they were border people going about their tasks. The last train came through at some ungodly hour the second night, but she had stuck it out. She would never have forgiven herself had I arrived to find her missing. But nobody got off the train and, despondent, Anna returned to the home of her friends, hoping they'd kept the front door unlocked for her.

The man in a raincoat watching her from the ticket-office window turned up his collar against the cool of the night and hurried off into the darkness.

CHAPTER
THIRTEEN

By 1955 the iron grip on the captive peoples of Eastern Europe had begun to soften; not that it was very noticeable. Maybe the hard currency of the West trickling into East German coffers at the Leipzig Trade Fair had been the catalyst. Certainly it wasn't a humanitarian consideration. Hungary started things moving and gradually other sterling-starved Eastern Bloc republics began admitting a limited number of selected (i.e. socialist-sympathetic) Western visitors. The race was on for a share of the hard currency that could be milked from limited tourism.

My failed and near-lethal attempt at meeting Anna on the Elbe in the German Democratic Republic 10 months earlier had not stopped me from devising new methods to plan more reunions. But it was the appearance of a fresh gap in the Iron Curtain that gave me the extra encouragement I needed.

I had heard that visitors to Hungary were unvetted, even though the tours were highly controlled. A small London-based agency had been chosen to supply a maximum of 15 visitors per tour; I at once applied for participation and was fortunate enough to obtain a place. Hungary bordered Slovakia, the then third

Czechoslovakian province. Maybe there lay an entry point.

That summer I found myself in the jovial company of 14 companions, en route by train to Budapest. As we were ogling the Danube on the riverside stretch of line east of Gyor, I first set eyes on the bridge. There it was, a three-span affair, carrying a spur of the main Vienna-Budapest railway line into Slovakia. But what really caught my attention was the cradle of scaffolding that hung beneath the spans — a potential route into the forbidden land. Beneath it the wide river flowed strongly, forming the border between two countries. I suspected the banks were guarded or booby-trapped. My inspection of the bridge was no more than a glimpse or two between the foliage of trees and undergrowth but it was enough to set my pulse racing. The tour was to begin with two full days in the Hungarian capital, the second of which was free to be spent at our own devices. I would ensure I made good use of it.

The train slowed at the approaches to the town of Komárom, one-and-a-half kilometres downstream, and we stopped at its station for 10 minutes. Barely an hour from Budapest, I would be able to return here with ease if nobody stopped me. A small road appeared to follow the riverbank all the way from the station to the bridge.

Following arrival at Budapest's Keleti Station we were taken to the down-at-heel Astoria Hotel. Its rooms were large and high-ceilinged, but the velvet curtains were now threadbare and the intricately carved marble staircase no longer echoed with the sound of bourgeois gaiety. Instead, dull, earnest workers' and trade unionist delegations filled the corridors. The lift no longer worked, there was no hot water and the radio was dead.

Our sightseeing tour spanned most of the next day. Every capital has many faces and Budapest is no exception. Battered in World War Two (and soon to be battered again in the 1956 uprising), its landmarks continued to flaunt themselves in various degrees of dilapidation: Gellért Hill, defaced by the standardised communist-inspired Liberation Monument; the Fisherman's Bastion; Margaret's Island and the imposing parliament building based on the design of London's Palace of Westminster. I was soon to recognise Budapest's renowned spirit, a unique blend of *laissez-faire*, biting wit and self-deprecation, ribaldry and sentiment. The place, I found, held an astonishing capacity for puns and jokes even under a regime that was plainly despised. In spite of the blood-red star of communism that topped the historic palaces, the spirit of Lajo Kossuth could not be dimmed.

On the second morning, having left our Hungarian guide with the impression that I was going on a river trip (which in a way I was), I left early for the station. I half-expected difficulties in obtaining a ticket to Komárom, but all went smoothly. The train was a slow one but a couple of hours later it deposited me at Komárom station and from there I walked into the town. Reaching the bridge involved an initial trudge along the main Gyorbound road before I could cut across to the minor artery I had spied from the train.

170

For all I knew I was now in a border zone but could see little indication of it. There were obviously guards at both ends of the bridge but, otherwise, I could see no further military activity — although this was not to say my movements were unobserved.

Clumps of poplars lined the Hungarian bank of the river and from the cover of the undergrowth that had sprouted beneath the trees I scrutinised the structure. There were soldiers at each end of the parapet and scaffolding around the buttresses and beneath the spans. A framework of planks that formed a catwalk for the workmen attending to the ironwork seemed to continue unbroken right across to the opposite bank. The closest pier, rising from the trees, loomed close and I registered every detail, as far as I could, of the splints that encased it as well as the scalability of the timbers.

My initial reconnaissance completed, I returned to the town to refuel my stomach with sausage and sauerkraut at a canteen restaurant. I also bought bread rolls which I stuffed into my pockets as provisions for my journey once inside Czechoslovakian territory.

Komárom was an uninspiring town and I exhausted my interest in its few charms after less than an hour as I waited for the dusk. Only then would there be just enough illumination to see what one was doing without being spotted too easily by any observers. I wore rubber-soled shoes and my wallet contained pounds sterling, American dollars, Hungarian florints and a small amount of Czechoslovakian crowns; at least financially, I was ready for any eventuality.

A wind swept through the market square of the town, tossing the skirts of peasant women, tearing at awnings, and ruffling the shaggy bunches of dahlias in jam-jars on the flower stalls. A shaft of sunshine broke through the grey sky. It looked like it was going to be a fine evening, which I didn't want. The sun flickered over the heaps of corn-cobs, purple cabbages, shiny peppers, plaited baskets of bilberries, and mounds of crab-apples, plums and pears.

I felt very much the stranger in Komárom. In Budapest foreigners were given little attention, but here, even though I had thought I looked so Hungarian in my leather jacket and baggy trousers, shoppers' stares fell to my clothes, and my shoes — the great give-away. I moved away from the market, wishing I had a companion in my escapade. In the war, bumbling, courageous Gordon had always been there, but now, in the post-war years, I had to fight my battles alone.

My intentions once I successfully entered Slovakia were vague in the extreme. At a small station along the spur line I hoped to catch a train to Bratislava, the Slovak provincial capital, and, from there, find an express on the main line to Prague. A 20-mile local train ride would then deliver me to Anna's home town. It was doubtful that I held enough Czechoslovakian currency to pay for the whole journey but, with a thriving currency black market existing in Czechoslovakia, I predicted little difficulty in exchanging a few pounds or dollars.

As with all my schemes, I had concentrated solely on illegally entering the country. How I was to get out of it never featured strongly, although I hoped I could always just reverse the mechanics of how I got in. Whether this would work in Hungary I was unsure; perhaps by the time I returned to the river the scaffolding on the bridge could have been removed and the validity of my Hungarian visa expired. In a normal country, the penalty for illegal entry would be no more than extradition or a fine but, as I had already discovered, under a communist regime the nasty catch-all accusation of espionage increased the likelihood of severe punishment.

Returning to the Gyor road, I made my way once more towards the bridge. By the time I reached the base of the southern pier, dusk was well on its way to becoming night. Overhead, the girders offered indistinct and uninviting sanctuary. As I climbed the rough timber framework, hand over hand, I began to feel vulnerable, although the ascent was not difficult. I have a reasonable head for heights but in certain circumstances am affected by vertigo, particularly on man-made structures. Here, in the unnatural surroundings of what reminded me of a mammoth Meccano set, I at once felt the symptoms. From above came the hollow rumble of a train amplified and echoing amongst the rusty spars. I began to sweat, not so much from the exertion of the climb as from a sudden fearful awareness of what I was doing.

At the top of the pier I rested on a wooden platform, then began to climb a stubby ladder that led vertically upwards into the dark recesses of the iron girders. The short ascent almost defeated me — I found myself afraid more of the dark unknown above than the climb itself. Gritting my teeth, I crawled from the head of the ladder onto one of the heavily flanged main girders that made up part of the first span. Its solid bulk was reassuring after the frailty of the timber scaffolding and from it I was able to gaze around at the network of spars and tubular connecting rods. From here I also had a disconcerting view of the abyss below. The river seemed far, far below. Before me lay a catwalk of planking that effectively made an extension to the steel flanges of the girder. The precarious path, accompanied by a retinue of spars and tubular linchpins, led directly over the river. A foot or two above my head was the carriageway of the bridge.

On hands and knees I moved gingerly forward, using the spars as hand-holds and keeping as close as possible to the iron wall and away from the sheer drop on my other side.

Progress was painfully slow. Within minutes my hair, face, hands and clothes were smothered in rusty dust. I longed to rise and stretch. At intervals I took a breather, extending myself out along the planks to relax stiff muscles. Below me the shimmer of water was, incongruously, enticing. It would at least make a soft landing if I fell, and I'd prefer to drown than be dashed to pieces on hard ground.

The train took me by surprise. The hollow rumble I had heard before suddenly exploded into a great smash of sound above me. The railway track lay close above

174

my head and my eyrie of girders, spars and struts trembled as I flattened myself over the catwalk, clinging on for dear life. The locomotive's heavy wheels pounded within inches of my head in a thunderous cacophony. The wagons followed, beating a rhythmic tattoo. Their sound faded away and then there was a dead, unnatural silence.

Resuming my deliberate movements, hand-hold after hand-hold, one foot carefully placed before the other left its anchorage, I carried on doggedly, trying to estimate the distance I had come. In another 15 minutes I would be on the Slovak side of the bridge. Repeatedly I rubbed my eyes to get the rust out of them. Night had fallen now but a full moon diluted the darkness.

And then suddenly I ran out of catwalk. One moment I had firm timbers beneath me, the next they were gone; a yawning gap lay before me. The shock was intense. I looked ahead: the framework of scaffolding continued unbroken towards the further end of the span, but the catwalk did not reappear.

Desperately I cast about for alternative ways of advancing but there were none. I carefully lowered myself into the fretwork of wooden joists below the catwalk to search the up-river side of the bridge span for another catwalk. I was so engrossed in this that I failed to spot the string of barges approaching from the direction of Komárom. I had been half-aware of the throb of the towing vessel — a squat tug — but only when a shout cut through my thoughts did I hastily return to the catwalk, to spread-eagle myself upon it once more. But it was too late. Plainly my silhouette had shown momentarily against the lesser darkness of the night sky. Now, dimly outlined by the cabin lights, I could make out the tug and a figure on it gesticulating wildly. For a moment I thought he might be shouting at me, but from above came answering voices and I heard a clatter of feet running across metal plating.

The head of the barge train was almost directly beneath the bridge now and I could just see the man's face, a white blob in the gloom. He appeared to be staring straight up at me but his attention was directed at the guards on the parapet. I was puzzled, unable to accept at first that I was the cause of the excitement. If so, there was only one thing to do — retreat and retreat quickly.

I turned around, not without difficulty in the confined space, and, in a crouching stance I hadn't dared to use before, part-crawled, part-loped my way back, all caution flung aside. Below, the glimmering water gave way to indistinct dry land and the base foundations of the buttress. I shinned recklessly down the vertical ladder and swung down the scaffolding. Any parapet guard wishing to reach river level and cut off my line of retreat would first have to negotiate the bridge approach embankment and find a way down through the scrub from there. I knew this could prove my salvation and provide a few vital seconds to offset the other's ability to move faster and without hindrance.

At the foot of the buttress I paused for a moment to ensure nobody was already on the shingle to intercept

176

me from there. The pounding of running feet had ceased, which indicated that the Hungarian guards had moved off the bridge. Fresh shouts came from the bridge approaches. I had judged correctly. The guards, caught in the middle of the span, probably fraternising with their Slovak counterparts, had to detour away from me to reach river-level. Setting off at an angle, I lunged into the bushes, keen to reach the Gyor road by any route other than that of the predictable riverside track.

I came to a stubble meadow and crossed it, then skirted the outer edge of the next field, using the cover of an overgrown hedgerow. When I reached the main road, I brushed the worst of the rust out of my hair, slowed to a walk and proceeded calmly towards Komárom.

I headed straight to the railway station, thankful for the semidarkness that hid my dishevelled appearance. A military vehicle, its headlights blazing, drove by at speed and I wondered if it had anything to do with me. Back at the station I locked myself in a toilet and spent a cramped hour cleaning myself up with water from the cistern. I was in a frightful mess; my hair and hands were brown with rust. Then I boarded a late-night train back to Budapest. Nobody noticed that my day-return excursion ticket had expired.

The rest of the tour took in regions outside of the capital and, with no further illict projects in mind, I threw myself into being a good and obedient tourist. My deliverance from trouble at Komárom had softened the blow of another failure to add to my mounting score of failed meetings with Anna. This time, at least, I had not involved her in the risky and frustrating business of meeting in a frontier zone.

When I returned home, a wonderful surprise awaited me. Following Hungary's example, Czechoslovakia was opening its border to a small number of clients of a politically-biased tour agency whose director had been the unsuccessful communist candidate for Tottenham. The proposed tour was a one-off event out of which the Czechoslovakian regime was going to make propagandist capital by showing the carefully selected clients their utopian country. The tour was to be something of a junket, with official speeches of welcome, radio interviews and visits to factories and trade union organisations.

Before leaving for Hungary I had applied optimistically for participation in the new tour, whatever the shameful implications, presenting myself as a true believer in the Eastern European brand of socialism. By some wondrous quirk of fate I had been included in the final list. Seemingly the entry documentation was confined to a group entry visa held by the trusted tour leader, which might have explained how my name had slipped through the net. I intended to exploit my luck to the full.

CHAPTER
FOURTEEN

Here was the biggest break I'd been given so far in my self-imposed crusade. Nothing, not even the wrath of my father for taking a further "holiday" off work, as he would define it, was going to stop me in this new project.

So barely had I returned home from Hungary when I was off again, to plaintive cries from my mother and controlled fury from my father. The row I had with him was, I suppose, as understandable as it was repetitious. Wasn't I butting my head against a brick wall, making a fool of myself, bringing disrepute onto the family? I'd heard it all before. He had then tried a new tack. What sort of example was I setting my employees by taking these repeated holidays? Nothing I said would make him understand the fact that, although these *were* designated holiday tours, they offered the only means of reaching Anna.

"Why should you receive a monthly wage when others had to work for it?" was his final thrust.

"Dock me as much as you want for the extra time I'm taking off — as you do your employees without the inquisition," I shot back.

But rows with Father, violent though they occasionally were, cooled swiftly. With Mother it was different. With her, displeasure had a habit of flickering on for days. Although the bedroom she was decorating was to be our "love-nest", as she described it, she knew full well there was little likelihood of Anna ever succeeding in joining me in Britain. Yet she continued the charade of being the understanding mother, particularly at a time when Father was exhibiting blatant opposition to the relationship.

At London's Victoria Station I joined my new and larger group of fellow holidaymakers. I had yet to see a more traitorous bunch. I felt it initially expedient to sport my red peace badge with which I had been issued by the tour company for the introductory gathering of the group but thereafter it remained mostly hidden behind my jacket lapel.

Right from the start, and encouraged by their collective security, my companions enacted what was virtually a cartoon characterisation of the "fanatical Red", their astonishing tirades against imagined repressive Dickensian conditions prevalent in the United Kingdom becoming louder and wilder as we travelled further into the European continent.

The worst offender was a gimlet-eyed woman enveloped in a bright orange dress. Her shrill voice provoked me into heated denial on several occasions but, for the most part, I held my tongue, not wanting to be branded a "reactionary" before we had even entered Czechoslovakia.

Our route across Europe was, for me, the old familiar one, although I obtained smug satisfaction in not having to go through my usual evasive measures at Schirnding station or, later, with the Czechoslovakian border people. On the platform at Cheb station I glanced around for my SNB police officer but he was nowhere to be seen. It was strange to be back at this station that had figured so prominently as a backdrop to my destiny, and it was stranger still to be standing on one of its platforms without concern for authority. There was of course another, more vital omission. Anna was not awaiting my arrival. We had arranged for our meeting this time to take place further down the line at Mariánské Lázně, a spa resort where the tour was based.

Although Anna was not at Cheb station, there was a reception committee of another sort awaiting us. Self-conscious in their national costume, girls distributed flowers and stilted English words of welcome to this first party of tourists from the capitalist West to their country since the establishment of the New Order. It was drizzling and the "Peace" banners hung limp in the grey morning. A scruffy army band thumped out a polka and, as if to show nothing had really changed in spite of this largesse of toleration of outside visitors from the other world, the ring of border guards remained encircling the train.

My compatriots had a field day, treating the curious Czechs on the platform to a catalogue of the alleged miseries of life in Britain. The orange-clad woman dominated the proceedings, attempting to explain to a perplexed audience the depth of pleasure she felt to be breathing the free, untainted air of the New Czechoslovakia, purged of the monstrous tyranny of suppression and exploitation that the British people were now suffering at the hands of a wicked government held under the influence of the United States of America.

An hour and a half behind schedule the "Peace Express" pulled out of the station to a flutter of banners and flags. It dawdled through the granite outcrops and dark pinewoods of the Böhmerwald. I re-read my copy of the tour programme, wondering how it would be possible to skip some of the scheduled trade-union meetings, radio interviews, factory visits and selective sightseeing in Prague, Karlovy Vary and Plzen. Within an hour I would be with Anna — not just for a few stolen minutes, but for the eternity of a whole fortnight. I shook my head in disbelief. Within those 14 days we had won ourselves, we would sweep aside the ministerial barriers a truculent Interior Ministry department had set up. Yes, we would accompany the group to Prague, but only to go to the ministry and other governmental authorities. Together, we would overcome all obstacles. My heart thudded with excitement.

But I could not dispel all my doubts. What if Anna had not received my last missive or had been prevented by an ever-watchful SNB from coming to meet me at Mariánské Lázně? Could they stop her visiting a resort town in an unrestricted zone? I knew they could. At least I was in her country on a legal basis and, if the worst came to the worst, I would simply take off from the spa and make my way to her. I was deep in thought, planning how I would manage to escape unnoticed from the group, when the train began to brake at the outer suburbs of the town.

Brushing aside one of my compatriots I went to the open window, ready to scan the station platform. A goods train rattled by in the opposite direction and the line of trucks took an interminable time to pass. When they had, a sea of faces swept into view from the shadow of the platform canopy. A display of bunting heralded another reception extravaganza as the thump of a band took over the dying drum-beat of metal wheels.

The faces merged into each other as I searched wildly for the one that mattered. The train jerked to a standstill but I went on looking from my vantage point above the heads of the crowd. Last out of the coach, I passed in a daze through a gap that opened for us in the crowd of well-wishers. A bunch of flowers was thrust into my hands. Surprised, I turned to the donor, but saw only a stranger. Kind, friendly, simple faces pressed around, asking questions about a world they knew nothing of. They were clapping now, smiling and nodding. I tried to smile back but was haunted by a deepening dread. I had told Anna we were to be based at the Zapotocki Hotel in the town centre. Maybe she would be waiting for me there. With so many watchful minions of the state about, I knew I must not do anything premature like making my own way to her home. Anyway, it would be best to get through the business of registration at the hotel before I took off on my own. My mind was whirring and the people around me became a blur.

And then suddenly, she stood before me. For a moment I was unable to comprehend; my smile was superficial, my reaction slow and clumsy. I looked at her as if she were the last person on earth I expected to see. She was crying, her mouth an O of wonder. She began smiling and crying at the same time and the spell was broken. Clasped in my arms, her mouth found mine and, in the middle of a crowd of several hundred onlookers, we kissed.

The audience was delighted and roared their approval, showering us with flowers. Undoubtedly we gave the people a demonstration of Anglo-Czechoslovakian solidarity that no official delegation could ever hope to achieve. One of the guides arrived to see what the fuss was about and stood, perplexed and disapproving, as we completed our public, private greeting. Brusquely told to desist because we were delaying a speech of welcome, we reluctantly obliged and allowed ourselves to be herded into the official enclosure where local dignitaries declaimed the virtues of militant socialism and peaceful co-existence. Holding hands, we ignored all the speeches and gazed blissfully into each others' eyes, revelling in the joy of reunion.

As we found seats in the coach that was to take us to the hotel, Anna produced a bunch of carnations, somewhat wilted from their tight handling within a small, hot fist.

"I almost forgot these," she said laughing and pushed the flowers at me.

"I'll look like a mobile garden if I get any more," I replied, suddenly aware that we had spoken our first words to one another after two long years.

More crowds were pressed around the grandiose portals of the Zapotocki Hotel and yet another band played boisterously beneath a slogan-laden banner stretched across the road. But the hotel's cold, old-fashioned reception hall was more tranquil and, in a quiet corner away from the rest of the group, we experienced the euphoria of being alone with each other for the first time in our lives.

Dinner in the hotel restaurant was an occasion for more speeches but, with Anna by my side, this was no great ordeal. By unspoken consent she had been allowed to join the group for the meal, a tolerance we were able to stretch to allow her participation in the full range of activities covered by the tour. She had arranged her own accommodation at a more modest nearby hotel, not being permitted a room at the Zapotocki, let alone to share my own. That evening we escaped from the inane conversation of my countrymen and the inquisitive stares of the Czechs, and walked through the ill-lit streets of the town like just another couple haunting the shadows.

Mariánské Lázně is one of the most beautiful spas in Europe, with graceful architecture surrounded by a plethora of exquisite parks, an environment surely planned and formed over the decades with lovers' strolls in mind. It was dark in the glades and there were pine-needles underfoot. Copper beeches and maples grew amongst the pines. The cool damp grass beneath them reflected a greenish light onto the domed thermal buildings that pushed up, like huge mushrooms, between the trees.

Back at the hotel, in the seclusion of my room, we delayed, joyously, our final goodnights. Anna stood by the bed and I lay back, gazing at her. The excitement was palpable. She looked like someone who had waited for something for a long time; someone who had prayed for this very moment. Somehow, unbelievably, there was finally fulfilment in this dangerous devotion.

I stretched out my arms and clasped her to me, my hands encircling her body, running softly across her breasts. I couldn't speak. I felt only, with my whole being, the bright and serious calmness of her young face. She seemed in fact younger than I'd remembered before, her youth fresh and brilliant, her eyes still full of the almost shocking assurance that I had noticed in them earlier. I had nothing to say; she did not speak either. She gave me one short smile, putting her face against mine. Her skin was very soft and warm. She let her head lie lightly against mine and I put my hand on her neck and kissed her, pulling her even closer beside me.

Later, abiding by the restrictions, she returned to her own hotel for what remained of the night.

CHAPTER
FIFTEEN

The running of the Czechoslovakian tour bore little resemblance to that of the earlier Hungarian one. The composition and attitude of the participants was the first contrast. Those on the Hungarian tour had been straightforward tourists with no political agenda. On the Czechoslovakian tour, they were not tourists but political activists. In Hungary, the sightseeing and leisure activities had been dictated by purely historical, geographical and general interest; here every visitation and activity held political overtones. In Hungary the excursions were voluntary; here they were compulsory. The only similarity lay in the leadership of the groups. The Hungarian state tourist office had taken over from the British courier within the country's border; here in Czechoslovakia the state tourism authority Čedok became our guide. But our Hungarian propagandist had been a bungling and not unlovable amateur compared with the four unsmiling "interpreters" of Čedok. Only two could speak English, a fact that raised no comment, although their real purpose as state "watchdogs" was obvious from the start.

Throughout the whole fortnight we were based at Mariánské Lázně and driven by coach to the assorted cultural and industrial establishments where we were subjected to heavy doses of propaganda. Although some of the destinations were not without interest, the very nature of the visits was alien to the traditional British notion of carefree holiday-making. We were encouraged to spend our "off-duty" evenings in Mariánské Lázně's Hall of Culture, there to fraternise with visiting guests of other socialist republics.

Anna and I were swept by circumstance into this maelstrom of pseudo-solidarity, political glorification and organised spontaneity. We barely left one another's side and Anna became an accepted member of the British group, a fact that surprised me considerably given the nature of the tour. We remained in the background, although our plight gradually began to dawn on some of the less blinkered and militant participants, generating a growing and genuine sympathy.

However, we were not content to while away our days together without devoting some of our time to the quest for our dual return to Britain. Here, on Czechoslovakian soil, was an opportunity to promote our cause. On the fourth day of the tour, we left with the group for the scheduled excursion to Prague. Here was our opportunity for an assault on the bastions of authority.

"Zlata Praha" (Golden Prague) and "Prague of the Hundred Spires" are just two of many epithets belonging to the Czechoslovakian capital. Poets and artists, royalty and commoners down the centuries have praised the regal beauty of Prague. Like Rome, it is

188

built upon seven hills, and it spans the River Vltava. Its blend of stunning natural setting and architecture offers an enchantment that few, if any, other cities in the world can match.

Playing truant from the group as they gaped obediently at the carvings in the city's Jan Hus Bethlehem Chapel, Anna and I made our way across the fairytale Charles Bridge and through the Old Town stone buildings to the British Embassy.

At the gates labelled by a polish-worn brass plate, we entered this fragment of Britain. The blue-uniformed policeman saluted smartly, recognising me as British. Inside the massive walls this Englishman's Bohemian castle, in contrast to the surrounding aura of totalitarianism, had become almost a cynical exaggeration of the British way of life, an expression of displeasure at the manner in which the rest of the world lived.

From a battered leather armchair, the pipe-smoking consul listened without interruption to my tale of woe. He was aware of the gist of the situation anyway, having already heard it from Anna, but I wanted him to know every facet and detail from me. When my two weeks in the country had elapsed, he alone could represent my interests and pursue any developments. For an hour we discussed ways and means of persuading a communist government to relinquish one of its subjects.

It was a depressing discussion, as I expected it to be. With Anna's first application to marry a foreigner (and, by implication, to emigrate) rejected by the state, the consul himself had, within the limits of diplomatic procedure, taken up the matter with the Czechoslovakian authorities. Results had been meagre in the extreme, the only positive "success" being a negative reply at the third prompting, the other two having not been replied to at all. But he promised that he would do everything he could, which was all we could hope for anyway.

The consul was interested in the composition of the group of "holidaymakers" I was with and asked if he might join, incognito, the Radio Prague recording session arranged for that evening in a trade union hotel. British-born wives of Czechs living in Prague had been invited to attend and, en masse, dispute the lies of a capitalist press ignorant enough to doubt their well-being in a people's paradise. This aspect of the session intrigued him, as it did me, so I readily agreed.

The central headquarters of the Ministry of the Interior were our next destination and together Anna and I stormed the thick plate-glass doors guarded by a squad of heavily armed police.

"We've come to the wrong place," I observed, turning around. "This is the Ministry of War."

Anna stopped me. "They're all like this," she whispered.

We gave my passport and Anna's identity card to a weasel-faced corporal. Both seemingly made substantial reading for the soldier.

"We want the emigration department," Anna stated simply.

The corporal continued his reading.

"Why?" he asked suddenly.

Anna explained briefly.

190

This produced one grunt and two forms. The forms demanded, in a manner not much less brusque than the grunt, the reasons why we should want to do business with the emigration department. The composition of a constructive reply took some time but, armed with a résumé of our combined life histories, we climbed a flight of stairs. On a landing a civilian sat behind a desk. He looked at us enquiringly.

"The emigration department, please," said Anna.

The official read the forms with deliberation and with a certain amount of puzzlement, as if he had never heard of an emigration department existing. But at length he asked, "Who do you wish to see?"

"The Minister." Anna's reply held a ring of challenge. Like me, she believed in starting things from the top and, if necessary, working downwards.

"The Minister," he repeated, as if in doubt of his hearing. "Have you an appointment?"

"No, but we want to make one."

The official was on safer ground now. "You must go away and write an application for an interview."

Anna was not to be fobbed off like that. "Why can't we apply here and now?" she asked and, before the wretched man could form a non-committal reply, launched into a lengthy verbal tirade. Up to this moment I had been able to follow the exchange but gave up as the flow of Czech poured over the wilting clerk.

"What was that all about?" I asked in the pause that followed.

"I told him you were here for only 10 days," she explained, "and that we had to see him within that time on a matter of great importance."

He reached for the telephone. I could read his mind better than I could understand what he said into the mouthpiece. The fawning respect to which he was so accustomed from visitors was alarmingly absent from this forceful girl who stood before him. *And* she had an Englishman in tow; a rare combination of circumstances. Although his employers hurled insults at Britain there undoubtedly existed a certain level of respect for the Anglo-Saxons.

"The Minister's secretary will see you," he whispered with a kind of reverence, "but you'll have to wait a few minutes if you don't mind."

We waited for 40 minutes before a suave young man appeared. Anna and I rose expectantly from the hard chairs we were sitting on.

"Sorry you've been kept waiting," he apologised in passable English. He was not the Minister's secretary; that worthy would see us in the other building. He gave Anna the details. We returned down the stairs, collecting our identity documents from the combat group in the vestibule.

After a snack lunch at a stand-up beer and sausage emporium, we headed for the "other building". It was an ugly concrete-faced structure liberally endowed with red emblems and SNB men, situated in the Dejvice district.

The whole wretched business started again. "We wish to see the Minister's secretary," began Anna.

The new soldier opened his mouth to ask why but Anna preempted him. "We have an appointment."

Instead he said, "Passports."

As he scrutinised them, we filled out more forms. For a change, I completed mine in English on the assumption that nobody would read them anyway. After a series of grunts into the phone, we were directed to the first floor, Room 15.

The door had a notice on it saying "Zaklepejte a Pockejte" which I took to be the equivalent of "Knock and Wait". We knocked, but nothing happened. A girl came out of number 14 and said it was number 16 we wanted. The notice on this door read "Knock and Enter", so we did. We passed through two rooms, in the second of which a girl smiled at us; the first smile received since entering ministry buildings. "The Minister's secretary will see you now," she purred, and indicated a third chamber.

The mild, middle-aged character to whom we presented ourselves did not inspire confidence. Nor was he the Minister's secretary, but only *one* of his secretaries, probably from the third division. Having shaken hands and acquainted himself with the facts of the case from a massive dossier, he relapsed into a long monologue which was part apology and part explanation for the manner in which his department was inconveniencing us. It was as good a piece of governmental clap-trap as I have heard and, in a long, devious manner, meant precisely nothing. Since Anna's marriage application had been rejected there could be no reason for the state to consider her emigration. It was as simple as that. We were ushered out, entirely dissatisfied with the interview, but not knowing how to constructively prolong it.

It was late afternoon before we got back to the hotel in time to attend the Radio Prague recording session at which my presence had been demanded. The session was behind schedule, owing to the absence of British-born wives of Czechoslovakian citizens with their verbal "proof" of idyllic conditions within the Czechoslovakian state. Only one had turned up and she was late. The British consul sat discreetly at the rear of the audience.

As the programme was due to be broadcast the following day, proceedings could not be delayed further and they began with the announcer asking different members of our group for their impressions of the visit. These were dutifully given. I noticed he had been well-briefed and picked only on the steadfastly "reliable" members of the group. Halfway through these preliminaries a panting second wife appeared on the scene, much to the relief of the programme producer.

"Sorry I'm late," she wheezed between gasps for breath. "Got stuck in one of those bloody meat queues the other end of town." The recording engineer made frantic efforts to erase several inches of tape. Someone sniggered in the audience.

The woman was then subjected to a sequence of mild questions on life in the People's Republic put to her by a carefully chosen few from the group but, to my

194

acute disappointment, failed to live up to her promisingly controversial start.

At the end of this miserable performance the group was herded out of the hotel and onto the waiting coach for the drive back to Mariánské Lázně. Our couriers were already in a bad mood because of the upset timetable and their tempers were not improved when I told them I intended remaining in Prague for the night as Anna and I had further business to attend to the next day. It was their first experience of open revolt within the group and I enjoyed their discomfiture.

"I shall return to Mariánské Lázně in due course," I finished. I wasn't even going to tell them that it would probably be tomorrow evening.

"But you can't stay on your own," the tour leader chimed in with growing concern.

"Why not?" Anna's voice lashed back. "I can look after him."

"But it's strictly forbidden," came the stock answer to anything that was not a stock question.

Anna was not to be deterred. "Why should a night in Prague be forbidden?"

The man was becoming impatient. He had steadfastly ignored Anna's unofficial involvement in the group, not even acknowledging her presence. "For you, no, but Mr Portway is a foreigner and he is registered in Mariánské Lázně. If he remains in Prague he will be in trouble."

"But he will register here in a hotel tonight."

A look of relief spread across the leader's face. "You mean he's not staying in a private house then?"

The man, mollified, returned to the waiting coach, content in the knowledge he had not been party to the sin of allowing an Englishman to spend a night under a private Czechoslovakian roof. But clearly he was far from happy and I guessed he would probably try to remove Anna from the group upon our return.

With a night alone in a city of repression, we tried to find laughter. We drank inferior vermouth at an inferior night club and danced on an overcrowded floor to a second-rate band. The pungent smell of cheap scent, vodka fumes and the local brand of cigarette pervaded everything. When we moved to the bar people made way for us, ceasing their conversation as they did so. Everywhere the buzz of talk stilled for a moment, then resumed. I looked at Anna but if she felt as uncomfortable as I did she gave no sign. Even so, although we were deeply content to be in each other's company, we found no laughter. And the man who stood near our table and followed us everywhere had little to laugh at either.

The hotel in which Anna had managed to get us a room was dingy, the beds hard and lumpy and the breakfast of ersatz coffee and stale rolls unappetising. But the sun was shining in a watery sky, transforming Prague's Gothic towers, Renaissance spires and Baroque cupolas into a city of magic. Alas, in Prague, dreams were all that was left of liberty. In the streets, red banners and placards proclaimed socialist development; loudspeakers attached to lamp posts blared out martial music and exhortation. The Party was ubiquitous, inescapable. Communist indoctrination began in nursery school at age three. There were party representatives in factories, offices, schools, newspaper editorial departments, apartment buildings, neighbourhoods. The Party duplicated all forms of management and government from the top down, matching Prime Minister with Party Secretary. About one in fifteen of the population belonged to the Party, the self-proclaimed "vanguard". Being a member helped in the everyday concerns of life like acquiring a reasonable job, a car, healthcare and better education for one's children. Not being a Party member meant putting up with second best, a sense of disenfranchisement and a submerged sort of existence.

The next task for Anna was a more ambitious one. We would take our case to the very top — to the President of the Republic. Stories were rife concerning Anton Zápotocký. Few were complimentary, though it was said that he played the accordion well when drunk. I'm also partial to accordion music, so at least he and I had one thing in common. As all kings and presidents should, Comrade Zápotocký ruled from a castle. His was the Castle of Hradčany, former home of Czech kings, situated high on the hill above the river. The sentries were no scarlet-clad warriors parading smartly between sentry boxes but merely a handful of peasant soldiers, clutching the usual ultra-lethal hardware, clustered around the main gate. We walked straight through, ignoring their presence. In turn they ignored ours.

A notice in the cobbled courtyard indicated an office. It only seemed to sell postcards but we decided it would do for a start. Anna asked the way to the presidential office and a hovering SNB man led the way up a flight of stone stairs, leaving us with instructions on how to find it.

"Is his lordship at home?" I asked Anna.

"The man said he was."

Marvelling at Anna's composure, I clattered after her, across a succession of reception halls, down an echoing corridor and up more granite steps. We eventually came to a door marked "Presidential Office. Appointments Only". The clean-shaven SNB officer standing in front of it wore a sharp crease in his trousers. We seemed to be getting somewhere.

Anna dazzled him with a smile and some well-chosen words of explanation which resulted in him opening the door for us. It was not, however, Mr Zápotocký, enthroned and crowned, who raised his head enquiringly at our arrival, only a mousy little man sitting in a high-backed chair. Again Anna explained our mission.

"Come back again this afternoon," she was told. "Two o'clock until four o'clock is the time for applying for presidential interviews."

The clock on the wall said five to twelve. Anna explained that I was a British visitor with limited time to spare.

At this the little man displayed a spark of interest and transferred his gaze to me, slowly appraising me in the manner of a farmer calculating the worth of a stallion. He retreated into an inner room. Together we waited in hushed expectation.

198

The man reappeared. "The President's secretary will see you," he announced and ushered us into a chamber of almost palatial quality. A Persian carpet graced the floor and soft light diffused out from exquisite cut-glass chandeliers. A young man in a dark suit rose from behind a giant mahogany desk to shake us by the hand. Anna spoke her party piece.

The secretary was sympathetic. He wrote copious notes on a pad. He even called for a stenographer, who wrote some more. But he couldn't produce the President. No, he told us, nobody could actually *meet* the President; not just like that. But he would be made personally aware of the facts of our case. The President was a very busy person indeed. Affairs of state, you know. But the secretary could promise one thing. Anna could make another marriage application and he himself would see that the President gave it personal consideration. And the President, as all Czechoslovakia knew so well, was a kind and considerate man.

With such benign words sounding hollow in our ears, we withdrew. The busiest people around here, I thought, were secretaries acting as buffers and apologists for their respective masters. Yet wasn't a people's government supposed to have been elected so that it could be made available to the people? I glared at a lounging youth trying not to look like a security man.

Because it was a stone unturned, we went back to the presidential office in the afternoon, intent upon making the promised second marriage application there and then, but the room was full of people craving interviews with a president they would never see. We gave up.

In the evening we returned by train to Mariánské Lázně. The sum total of our accomplishments over the two days had been the granting of permission for Anna to make another marriage application which, at least, was something. If that failed we were left with only one course of action. The Elbe below Bad Schandau, the rolling hills near Horní Dvořiště, the bridge at Komárom, and the as yet unattempted crossing of the Tatra Mountains into Poland, all pointed a way out. But as our train sped through the soft Bohemian landscape I became uncomfortably aware of the bitter truth, that Anna's escape would endanger her sisters and aged parents who remained behind. Darkness enveloped us as the train plunged into a tunnel. Our hands met and clasped tightly.

The weather, for the remaining days, did its best to shatter the illusion of carefree abandon as we flung ourselves into the assorted activities of the group. It rained each time we set out for the nearby swimming pool. It rained at Baron Skoda's castle-turned holiday centre near Plzen, and it rained for the "spontaneous" football match arranged between a team from Mariánské Lázně and the more sporty members of the British group. But at least the rain held off for the day out in Karlovy Vary, where we rubber-necked amongst the health palaces and colonnades, the *Kurhaus* and the *Kaiserbad*, and the sanatoria of this unique spa town favoured by an English king. The spa knew its golden days during the 19th century when it became the resort of royalty from all over Europe. Sadly, the present regime had allowed Karlovy Vary to age and decay. Only once did the sun manage to burst out of a reproachful sky to shine brilliantly upon the precious afternoon when Anna and I strolled up into the pine-clad hills to sit among the damp, steaming alpine-like meadows. High over the villas of Mariánské Lázně we looked out across the quiet valleys of the Tepelske Vrichy, listening to the singing of the birds in the woods around us. Here in our secret eyrie we spoke of our hopes and fears for the future, and in each other's arms, found solace in the present.

Mostly, however, we felt it prudent to remain with the group — a prudence encouraged by the indiscreet presence of the secret police who seldom left us to our own devices. They invariably dogged our footsteps, listening and watching. Even the members of the group made better company than these silent, faceless shadows. I noticed, amongst members of the group, the increasing sympathy and indignation towards our plight. The courier watchdogs were quick to recognise the change of attitude of some of the members, yet still no effort was made to banish Anna from the alien ranks — perhaps wary that this might have provoked even more sympathy for us.

Their minds blinkered to think of protest in terms of demonstrations and petitions, several tour members did in fact turn upon our Czechoslovakian hosts, threatening to march upon some vague authority that existed only in their imagination. It all petered out of course, but even this show of embryo resistance comforted Anna and me a little.

In the meantime the group programme wore on: we toured the underground tunnels of the famed Pilsner Urquell brewery in Plzen, and were dragged on a pilgrimage to Lidice. Having seen the war-ravaged village not long after its destruction and the murder of its population by the SS in 1943, I found its transformation into a shrine to communism particularly nauseating. Anna and I strolled down the avenues of wilted "peace roses" donated, mostly, by left-wing organisations of various countries.

On the last day of the tour the rain stopped. Playing truant from a scheduled inspection of a glass factory, Anna and I spent the day walking in the stillness of the forest. The thought of the inevitable parting, now so close, lay heavily upon us as we meandered, hand in hand, along a winding path next to a swollen stream. A faint mist rose from the sodden undergrowth, accentuating the shafts of sunshine between the pines. We stopped at a lonely clearing where the stream had risen and receded, leaving the river-sand dry and white.

Anna turned to me and began to say something about wishing me luck back in Britain. I was struck by the sudden clarity of the triangle of her throat, so pale against the black edges of her jacket collar and the darkness of her hair. She ceased speaking and looked at me for a prolonged moment before coming closer.

"I don't ask for it. I'm not holding you to marrying me, you know," she said in a small voice.

"You mean you don't want to?" I replied in jest. Then I saw she was being deadly serious.

"It's not that," she said. "I mean I don't ask it of you unless you want it more than anything in the world. This situation we are in might continue for years and years, and I would not want to stand in the way of your happiness if another girl — a more attainable girl — came into your life." Her face was strained.

"Oh God," I exclaimed. I put my cheek against her shoulder. "I do want it. I *do* want it. I want it so much. You must believe it, please. More than anything else in the world."

She continued looking at me but in a different manner. Her eyes were bright with wonder.

"Then it shall not be otherwise." she responded simply.

"What made you offer to release me?" I asked after a pause, although I thought I already knew the answer.

She stared at the ground. "You once wrote to me that you would understand if I gave you up," came the barely audible reply. "I thought then that you might have found someone else."

A stab of shame passed through me. I had never realised quite how much I had hurt her with that letter, written shortly after I met Saimi. I had sent it in a moment of weakness and regretted it ever since.

There was nothing I could say that wouldn't sound trite and inadequate. Instead I embraced her tightly and passionately. "It can never be otherwise," I added finally, using her own words.

The next day, the fourteenth of the tour, I left Czechoslovakia with the rest of the group on the midday Orient Express.

CHAPTER
SIXTEEN

It was a bitterly cold winter evening. An icy wind blew little gusts of snow that whirled under the street lamps. Anna scowled at the snowy waste of the square, silent and deserted. *Somebody* was there, behind her; she was sure — she had heard the footsteps. Stopping abruptly, she caught the hollow thud of booted feet, muffled on the compressed snow. Then the sound ceased. Moving on, Anna reached the narrow lane that offered a short-cut to the station. In five minutes she would be among the comforting crowds and then onto the smoky, overheated train to Slaný. Her shopping day in Prague had not been a success and she would be glad to be home and rid of whoever was following her.

Then, quite close by, on the same side of the lane and in the shadow of a doorway, she heard the scrape of a match being struck. She checked behind her, but the lane was empty. She knew the lane well; it was not so far from the import-export agency where she used to work.

She slowed, hesitating for a moment, then quickened her pace again. Flattening herself against the grimy wall, she heard a low voice call and saw two male figures outlined at the end of the lane. Now more determined than ever to identify the men, Anna moved away from the wall. She could see their leather jackets, tight trousers and even the thin leers on their hard faces.

Now she knew who they were — the secret police. Secret! They showed a perverted glee in positively advertising their presence to anyone unfortunate enough to be on the "conditioning" list of the SNB. She had known for months she was under surveillance but this sort of harassment was new to her. There was no mistake — these antics were not just silly youngsters larking about.

She hurried across the top end of Wenceslas Square. It was nearly dark now and there was a smell of more snow in the air. The shop displays were already lit up. One of them, illuminated by a greenish-white glare, exhibited the rows of square-toed boots from the Bata factory, uniform and hideous. And they would be gone tomorrow, judging by the length of the queues shuffling forward. Then there would be no more boots for months; instead something else equally as uninspiring would take their place. The men at the end of the nearest queue blew on their mittened fingers, peered at their newspapers; the women stared straight ahead, brooding or muttering out of the corners of their mouths to the one in front, the one behind. It was always the same. Here, queues had become a way of life.

Nobody appeared to be following her as she entered the great mouth of the railway station. In another hour she would be home. There would be a delicious meal awaiting her, she knew. Her mother, an excellent cook, took considerable pleasure in delighting the family with special delicacies; it offered her the only excitement she ever found in that dull, parochial little town. Her father loved the place of course; he was forever dabbling in its museum, serving on the committee, taking photographs of old Slaný and delving into the town's uneventful history. Life with him had become very difficult. He was the most untidy man imaginable and sometimes the most insufferable. Having been waited on hand and foot all his life by servants, he found it impossible to adjust to the changed circumstances. With the infliction of communism on the country, the family had lost everything; their farm, their land, and — except for the few rooms in which they'd been permitted to live — their home. Even the residue of the family wealth, along with the nation's currency, had been devalued to the point of worthlessness.

The train was surprisingly empty and she found a compartment to herself. But as the Prague suburbs dissolved into a white countryside, the door slid open and the two youths she had seen earlier stumbled in. She had heard them opening and closing doors along the corridor as if looking for her compartment.

For a while they said nothing, simply sitting boorishly puffing on cigarettes and occasionally glancing in her direction. Then one turned and in an apathetic tone of voice asked where she lived. She replied, "Slaný." They probably knew already.

As if the exchange was proof of an acquaintanceship, the two brazenly asked if she would go out with them that evening. The request was couched almost as a demand and her refusal was equally brusque. They made it plain that her refusal didn't bother them at all. She then asked them why they were molesting her. Both denied having seen her before, although plainly they knew she had seen them and they weren't even making any attempt to hide this fact. Their loutish behaviour made no sense; it was clear the two men had been put up to it.

The intruders left the train at Kralupy. They probably caught another straight back to Prague. What would they report? She was at a complete loss to understand the reason behind this new strategy of cruelty. Perhaps the latest rejection of her second marriage application had triggered a new phase in the "art" of dissuasion. Whatever it was, the prospect of her future was as disagreeable as it was sinister.

The leaves on the old wych elm had turned toast brown and were falling when I learned of this second rejection. The great tree at the bottom of the garden had been my secret retreat ever since childhood. As a schoolboy I had built a simple wooden seat around the trunk and here I sat reading Anna's latest letter and its disheartening news.

The circumstances of her second marriage application had seemed so much more encouraging than those of the first. It had been made within the very heart of the regime and my hopes — in spite of my efforts to suppress them — had been high. Now they had been dashed. As if to rub salt in the wound, another missive

208

from the British Embassy in Prague confirmed the decision, while the Czechoslovakian Embassy in London added, for good measure, the directive that I was not to attempt to gain entry to their country again under any pretext whatsoever. It was the most multiple "no" I could possibly imagine.

Hoping that the pen might indeed be mightier than the sword, I spent the following months writing to a range of individuals and organisations. I contacted the Foreign Secretary, the Home Secretary and the Minister of State for Foreign Affairs, as well as a prominent Socialist Member of Parliament who had become something of a specialist in the reunion of families separated by the gulf of extreme politics. I organised interviews with officials of the Foreign and Home offices and officers of the Intelligence Departments of the Ministry of Defence. I requested intervention from the Chairman of the Council of Ministers of the USSR and Secretary of the Presidium of the Supreme Soviet on the occasion of a state visit they made to London (and was temporarily arrested for attempting to hand the two well-guarded leaders a copy of the petition). I applied to the Secretary General of the United Nations Organisation together with the Director of the United Nations' Division of Human Rights in New York to take up my case. I asked the advice of various writers, of Czech émigrés and refugees, of European refugee organisations, of foreign embassies, of the Press Association, of anyone who might be able to shed, wittingly or unwittingly, any light on the subject.

Despite all my efforts, results were at first meagre. The Foreign Office was aloof and coldly discouraging. The embassies remained diplomatically silent. I heard nothing from the two Soviet leaders, even though my petition had been reinforced by the Foreign Secretary who had drawn their attention to the matter. The fact that my own member of parliament and near neighbour, Mr (later, Lord) R. A. Butler, had become Home Secretary was a lucky break, although his ministry was hardly in a position to help at this stage. But he could and did — with constant respectful prodding from me — encourage those that were. However, only the Ministry of Defence, and in particular the faceless minions of Military Intelligence, were stirred to action, although, alas, not for my direct benefit. Having first labelled me as a "security risk", they now perceived distinct possibilities of my becoming useful to them.

A ponderous form of assistance did, however, materialise from the United Nations Organisation, which was persuaded to address the Czechoslovakian government on the subject at a meeting of the Human Rights Division in New York. However, nothing resulted beyond a sharp reprimand from Czechoslovakia for meddling in its internal affairs. Although desperately grateful for their intervention, ineffective though it was, I guessed that my case had become just another of thousands of unsolved minor international problems on their books.

It was the Honourable Member for Eton and Slough who was to offer the most significant contribution. I was happy to claim the honour of friendship with the late Mr (later, Lord) Fenner Brockway, a man whose integrity, understanding and untiring championship of the rights of man is well-known. Yet when I first requested his help, I neither knew him nor was a member of his constituency.

In the second part of his autobiography, *Outside the Right* (George Allen & Unwin, 1961), Fenner writes: "He [Christopher Portway] lived in Mr R. A. Butler's constituency but I was moved by his story and Mr Butler said he would be glad if I would help because, as a minister, he could not intervene with a foreign government." He goes on to narrate the circumstances of his initial visit to the Czechoslovakian ambassador in London and tells of the pessimism he felt after learning of my transgressions of Czechoslovakian law and wholly anti-communist attitude. It said much for this great socialist warrior and his faith in me that he still felt able to petition on my behalf.

Fenner took me with him on his next visit to the ambassador's comfortable residence in Hampstead. His Excellency Dr Jiří Hájek had been delayed at his embassy, an aide (who looked to me suspiciously like a butler) informed us, but could we wait? By the time Dr Hájek arrived, we had drunk a considerable quantity of his best brandy between us. The ensuing interview was friendly and I became convinced that, although the man before me was a senior diplomat of the "enemy" camp, his concern for my situation was sincere. He would, he told us, do whatever he could to bring the matter to a successful conclusion even though, as he put it with surprising candour, the situation in his country at present was "difficult". I left feeling that in the Czechoslovakian ambassador I had found, if not a friend, at least a compassionate family man. (The fact that, years later, Dr Jiří Hájek was to become his country's foreign minister during the brief, liberal-minded Dubček regime and then one of the chief dissidents of the underground Charter 77 was fitting confirmation of my opinion.)

After skirmishing with its representatives in London, Fenner was all set to confront the Czechoslovakian government in Prague. The ambassador, who thought he could manage the introductory work better himself on the next routine visit, dissuaded him from this.

I was made aware of these preliminary negotiations during a series of lunches I attended with Fenner at Westminster. Although it was intensely comforting to know that somebody was, at last, taking concrete steps on my behalf, my hopes were still tinged with cynicism. Unobtrusively, I continued to investigate the less orthodox means of gaining the same ends. Among the cosmopolitan population of London, I encountered many Poles, Czechs, Hungarians and East Germans who had voted with their feet by illegally emigrating Westwards. Many of these contacts had every reason to remain silent and many did so but, fact by fact, piece by piece, I gradually added to the store of knowledge accumulated years before when I was probing the defences of the Czechoslovakian border with West Germany.

212

In the meantime, letters from Anna reached me at infrequent intervals. Some got "lost" but most of those that survived the censor's eye were cheerful missives, full of optimism and confidence. In others, however, I detected a note of despair and, occasionally, fear.

It was this fear, more than my cynicism, that drove me forward. An early return to Czechoslovakia, either by legal means or "fog channel", seemed to me imperative — it was no good awaiting the well-meaning deliberations of a British member of parliament and a Czechoslovakian diplomat. Only in faraway Poland had a tiny spark of hope shone momentarily in the darkness; an uprising had taken place that June in the industrial city of Poznań. It had been swiftly and ruthlessly put down, but the very fact that discontent could expand into open revolution gave me hope.

As expected, a whole string of tour operators throughout Britain and Western Europe had now "discovered" Czechoslovakia and a few other East European states, encouraged no doubt by advantageous rates of exchange newly introduced by regimes starved of hard currency. Again the Czechoslovakian tours on offer were heavily controlled by Čedok, the state tourist authority, though they were less politicised. More to keep the Czechoslovakian consulate in London on their toes than anything else, I applied to participate in most of them though, one by one, the mystified tour operators were forced to cancel my booking with each denial of an entry visa for me.

Individual visits, group tours: both were now taboo. To the consulate in London, I was well and truly a marked man. But what about the other consulates scattered about the continent of Europe? By choosing to visit a country lying north, east or south of Czechoslovakia could I provide reason for the acquisition of a *transit* visa? These were less difficult to acquire since their validity was limited to 48 hours. I would need to find a consulate in Europe geographically placed so that a transit visa seemed plausible, and where I wasn't known. In normal circumstances, the decision to grant such a visa in this instance rested chiefly upon possession of a visa or proof of sojourn in the destination country, but it occurred to me that again presenting myself as a businessman anxious to promote trade with the Eastern Bloc might provide the extra incentive needed.

A study of the map of Europe immediately ruled out the West-to-East line of transit, for neither the Soviet Union nor Poland would allow lone travellers from the West. This effectively eliminated the Czechoslovakian consulates of Paris and the capitals of Central and Western Europe. As for Austria and Hungary in the south, the Vienna consulate had already got wind of me and consulates, like the secret police, have notoriously long memories. The consulate in Budapest had less reason to know me, but their decision regarding the issue of an entry visa for that country would surely depend upon the issue of a Czechoslovakian visa beforehand; a catch-22 situation so far as I was concerned.

Thus all that remained were the four northern capitals of Scandinavia. Of these, Copenhagen and

Oslo, though worth trying if Stockholm and Helsinki failed me, were unlikely candidates geographically, since to reach Austria, the obvious goal in the south (which required no visa), there was no real need to pass over Czechoslovakian territory at all. But the capitals of Sweden and Finland . . . with my head a whirl of airline routes and international rail networks, I formed my plans.

In the middle of July 1956, I went north to Helsinki.

CHAPTER
SEVENTEEN

Because it was my legitimate holiday period, I was able to escape my office without a row with Father for abusing the firm's holiday schedule. But I once more had the challenge of creating the subterfuge of an expanding business deal with the Czechoslovakian state import agencies in Prague. This again I had to foster and manage without the knowledge of my father or fellow directors of the company. Consequently, I had not only to carry out my dealings in secret, but also to ensure that nobody saw the replies from Czechoslovakia: not an easy task in a tight little commercial enterprise such as ours. Nevertheless, I managed to build up a file of correspondence that offered a plausible reason for re-entering Czechoslovakia and nourished the contacts I had made, to a point where, commercially, relatively big things were beginning to be expected of me. How I was to unravel myself from these absurd undertakings was going to be another problem, but could be resolved at a later date. I had also corresponded with various acquaintances and agencies in Vienna, to authenticate the charade of needing to proceed onwards to Austria after Prague. When I boarded the Holland- Scandinavia Express, I felt as prepared as I was ever likely to be.

With a day to spare in Stockholm, I decided to give my new business acumen a trial run at the Czechoslovakian consulate there. After arriving at the city's Central Station, I tracked down the embassy in a leafy suburb.

Impressed by my imposing documentation, the consul general spoke to me himself. The interview got off to such a brisk start that I thought I might not have to continue to Helsinki after all. Under the impression that I was responsible for untold sums of hard currency, he offered me wine and the comfort of his study while the formalities of entry to his country were put into motion. The smooth young man shrugged amiably. He deplored the need for formalities, he said, but, as I would surely understand, these things had to be carried out in this day and age.

"Do you have to ask Prague?" I enquired, adding that my time was precious.

"Er, yes," he replied, with a shrug and a wave of his hand. "But this is a mere ritual." Normally this would take 10 days but, in the present circumstances, for me, he would telephone the department directly. His assistant was in fact now doing so. But the assistant entered the study at that moment without knocking and whispered excitedly to his boss. The consul excused himself and the two hurriedly left the room.

When he returned, I barely recognised him — a scowl had replaced his ingratiating smile. My passport was thrust back into my hands and I was curtly informed that my presence was not required in the Czechoslovak Republic. It took no great powers of deduction to surmise that the consulate must have a little black book with the names of "undesirables" such as me. I turned to leave, wishing I'd drunk more of his wine.

So it would have to be Helsinki after all. With one of four consulates out for the count, the sights of Stockholm turned sour. Glowering at the fashion dummies parading in the prosperous Kungsgaten, I window-shopped till I could board the ferry to Finland. I began to wonder whether I wasn't wasting my time. If one embassy had my name marked, the odds were others had it too.

The ferry carried me through the myriad islets of the Stockholm archipelago and its Finnish counterpart to Turku. There I caught a rattling bus to Helsinki, 100 kilometres away.

Finland, as both a country and a nation, has always intrigued me. It is essentially a new country, a land of new forest clearings and new-looking towns and cities where new things are happening. The landscape itself, which is flat and never bald or hoary with mountains, looks younger still. Finnish history is peppered with suppression and attempted suppression, the last example being in 1939 when Stalin hurled his armies and air power against the little country, which promptly upped and hurled them back. The north was devastated, 85,000 people died and territories were lost to the Soviet Union. The Finns kept their courage and tenacity — a quality they call *sisu* — and this is matched by a certain aloofness of character that, like their language, keeps them apart from the nationalities around them.

Helsinki is as new a capital as the country it heads. Much of its centre is the work of the German architect Carl Ludvig Engel, whose harmonious Senate Square fronting his Lutheran cathedral is one of the finest squares in Europe. Many people regard the most Finnish edifice in the city as the red granite railway station, so heavy-looking that it gives the impression of having sunk several feet into the ground. On this visit, however, I had not come to delve into the uniqueness of the land or its peoples and architecture; my motive was a far narrower one. Still, having arrived at the start of a weekend, I could but wait, which at least gave me the opportunity to find my way about the city.

At 10 o'clock on the Monday morning, I stood on the mat before the Czechoslovakian consulate door. Clients were plainly a rarity, judging by the surprised expression on the face of the guardian who opened it — understandably perhaps, in a resolutely neutral country situated on the sharp edge of Soviet domination. The attaché to whom I was eventually introduced remained disconcertingly unimpressed by my commercial credentials but could offer no immediate reason why a transit visa should not be granted to facilitate my onward journey to Austria. My initial reception here was in direct contrast to that of the consulate in Stockholm and even at this juncture I felt the project was doomed.

"Come back in about two weeks," he advised upon my completion of a bundle of forms.

I was taken aback. "But I want to go at once. My time is limited. Surely it doesn't take 14 days to stamp a passport!"

The attaché wore a face devoid of interest, humour or even pathos. It was like talking to a robot. He explained patiently that my application had to go to Prague — as if I didn't know.

"Couldn't my application be telegraphed?" There was always the chance that someone in the Czechoslovakian capital would omit to check my true credentials if there was enough urgency behind the application.

"If you're willing to pay for the service, yes."

"I *am* willing to pay for the service."

"In that case," he replied, "it will only take four days. Call back on Friday."

I accepted this as the best deal I could get and left.

The intervening days passed pleasantly enough as I was determined they should, since, after all, I was on holiday. The first couple of days I spent in and around Hämeenlinna on the edge of the Tampere lake chain. A bright, somewhat clinical, market town, it lay within the great silence of a myriad of ethereally beautiful and lonely Finnish lakes. Lonely myself, I found it easy to appreciate how Sibelius had obtained inspiration for his haunting music.

Ever optimistic, I returned to the consulate on the Friday morning, again meeting the morose attaché.

"Good morning, Mr Portway," he began almost cheerfully and this alone made me wary. "Yes, we have news for you." As well as being relatively cheerful, he sounded surprised that Prague had acknowledged his remote existence.

I waited for the grand pronouncement.

The attaché cleared his throat. "I am to inform you," he intoned, "that the government of the People's Republic has carefully considered your application for a transit visa but regrets that it is unable to empower me to grant you this facility."

"You mean no," I said. It wasn't really a shock or a great disappointment. I think my chief emotion was annoyance that the man had got so much satisfaction out of imparting the rejection. I turned on my heel and left.

The next morning I took leave of the sparkling newness of Helsinki and the brooding silence of Finland to sail on the SS *Birgar Jarl* ferry bound for Stockholm. My spirits were at a low ebb. Sharing my cabin for the overnight voyage across the Gulf of Finland was an English-speaking Norwegian who treated me to a non-stop eulogy of the glories of his country. Even his snores, as we lay in opposite bunks, held a musical Peer Gynt quality that, along with my dejection, prevented me from sleeping. I lay staring up at the ventilation duct thinking of Anna. But the idea of going to Oslo, from where my cabin companion hailed, kept intruding. Although I was fast losing faith in consulate-baiting, I reasoned that, while in Scandinavia, I might as well visit the third Czechoslovakian consulate of the quartet. I had plenty of days left of my holiday so decided then to add Oslo to my itinerary. As the clear light of a Scandinavian dawn crept through the porthole I finally fell asleep.

We arrived in Stockholm on a warm Sunday. Most of the Stockholmians had escaped from the bustle of the city for the day. Being in no hurry, and to save the expense of a hotel, I joined the general exodus to Drottningholm Palace before catching the night train to Oslo.

Here modern ugly buildings jostle for prominence among older and mellower ones and the whole ungainly mixture is tempered with an aura of hospitality, charm and fish. A tram carried me, in fits and starts, from the station to Fridtjof Nansens Plass. By 10 o'clock on the Monday morning I was ringing the bell of the *Cesky Konsulat*.

As at the Stockholm embassy, the interview began wonderfully. Again my qualifications brought forth the consul general in person and within 10 minutes his desk was awash with the pamphlets, catalogues and letters of introduction I had taken from my briefcase. My spirits began to rise. The consul was older than his Swedish counterpart and exhibited even more of an enlightened flair for business. He read my letters from the Prague import agencies with genuine interest, asked a few pertinent questions and granted me a transit visa without reference to Prague or even — if the consulate had one — the "black book". Unbelieving, I stared, fascinated, at the new mauve stamp in my passport and almost ran out of the office before he could change his mind.

222

The rest of the day was a marathon of obtaining tickets and attempting to acquire a permit to cross East Germany, since the flights from both Oslo and Copenhagen bound for Prague made stops at Schönfeld Airport just outside communist East Berlin. I intended taking the night train to the Danish capital and flying to Prague from there.

Things came slightly unstuck at the Soviet Embassy, however. Armed with my flight ticket, I rapped on the iron-studied portals of the pretentious, palace-like edifice. My summons produced a young Russian who spoke only his native tongue. Several colleagues, between them, could manage Norwegian, Swedish, Bulgarian, Ukrainian and Kurdish — all incomprehensible to me. Finally a Norwegian cleaning woman who spoke English was pressed into service. In the end, though, my request for a transit visa for no other reason than to land and take off from Schönfeld produced no more than shrugs and "niets". I gathered from a garbled explanation that my request had nothing to do with the USSR, which wasn't in the business of interfering in the domestic affairs of the GDR. East Germany, however, was not represented in Norway, so I decided to leave things in the hands of providence. Finally, I sent a semi-coded telegram to Anna intimating my arrival, miracles permitting, at Prague's Ruzyne Airport the following day.

I spent a sleepless night on the night train to Copenhagen, worrying about my journey and the unknown hazard of arriving in Berlin with my non-existent transit visa for that city. I also thought about what I would do if I did reach Prague and reunite with Anna. I would have to attempt an immediate prolongation of my Czechoslovakian transit visa and, for this, a visit to various offices including that of Motokov, the State Importation Agency for Mechanical Appliances, with whom I had been corresponding, would have to be made. No doubt Anna would want me also to spend some of our stolen hours at her home where, in a "safe house", we would be able to discuss plans I was hatching for her eventual defection to the West, should the new diplomatic overtures fail.

I was still wide awake as the train crossed the Ore Sound between Norway and Denmark. I joined the hurrying office-bound throngs from Copenhagen's Central Station 40 minutes later.

Three hours more and I presented myself at Kastrup Airport. It became apparent that the CSA (Czechoslovakian State Airline) flight OK 432 was something of an enigma when the clerk at the ticket desk expressed surprise that anyone wanted to fly to Czechoslovakia. At the entry to the departure lounge, an emigration official twice checked my passport upon learning of my intended destination.

The airhostess gave me a strange look as I settled into my seat for the two-hour hop to Berlin. Only four other passengers joined the flight. They looked to me like minor diplomats.

Given the green light, the old aircraft lumbered into the air, clawing for height over the Baltic.

CHAPTER
EIGHTEEN

We had entered what airline captains euphemistically describe as a "pocket of turbulence" and the aircraft had begun to roll about the sky. I was feeling increasingly nauseous and tried holding my breath, counting sheep, pretending to sleep — anything to help me feel better, but nothing worked. I groped for the airsickness bag in the seat pocket before me but, this being Flight OK 432, of course, it wasn't there. I turned towards the hostess, racked with pain. She was talking to two of the other passengers at the rear and, even in my distress, I could tell they were discussing me. However, I was gratified to see her detach herself and come my way.

"Your passport, please," she demanded coldly.

I groped in my pocket and handed it to her. She studied the document carefully, turning page by page.

"But you have no transit visum for the Deutsche Demokratische Republik."

Barely managing to speak, I told her, "I'm going to Prague; not Germany."

"But we land at Berlin and you cannot land at Berlin," she argued.

There was no answer to this piece of logic and my nausea became intense. Instead of replying, I tried to warn her I was about to be sick, but it was too late. With my vomit dripping down her sleeve, the girl retreated at speed towards her cabin, all further argument at an end. I felt better.

The firm grass runway of Schönfeld and the fresh breeze that cut across the flight apron cleared my head in seconds. The hostess, cleaned and smiling once more, ushered her minuscule flock to the airport buildings.

Inside the spartan hall, depressingly furnished with plastic and chrome chairs designed for maximum discomfort, I was left to my own devices amongst a scattering of fellow "transitees", all unaccountably jittery. The plaster walls displayed the compelling features of Big Brother Walter Ulbricht and his henchmen inflated to double size, as well as smaller prints of East German industrial and agricultural scenes.

A hurried exodus greeted the announcement heralding the resumption of the Prague flight. We filed out of the building clutching passports and flight tickets which nobody looked at; a turn of events that was cause for some amazement. The same aeroplane awaited us and I was able to return to my original seat in spite of an increase in passengers. The hostess pointedly handed me a paper bag.

It was only a short hop to Prague. As the late afternoon sun plashed crimson on the rocks of Sarka below, I began to worry again. Had my cryptic telegram reached Anna? Had she understood it? Would my status as *persona non grata* be revealed before I could reach her? Could Anna herself be prevented from meeting me?

Inside the building, I searched the faces of the crowd watching the aircraft arrivals, but was unable to see hers. Inside the immigration bay, I surrendered my passport. There was the thump of a rubber stamp and I was relieved my transit visa had been accepted. I had moved away when he called me back.

Heart in mouth, I returned to his desk. The man gave me a hard look. "You know this is a transit visa," he said. "It requires you to remain within the district of Prague except while leaving the republic, which in any case you must do within 48 hours. Is that clear?"

I nodded.

"Furthermore, while in the capital, you will accommodate yourself at the Alcron Hotel," he finished.

"Oh no, nothing as ritzy as that," I responded lightly, missing the point entirely. The Alcron was the most expensive pad in town.

"You will stay at the Alcron," repeated the officer with emphasis and I realised he was telling me, not advising me of this.

"Okay," I affirmed meekly, without the slightest intention of doing so.

Changing some pounds sterling into Czechoslovakian crowns, I retrieved my bag and passed out of the arrivals hall, straight into the arms of Anna.

"Have a good flight?" she enquired, gazing at me with affectionate eagerness.

"I was sick." As ever, tender words escaped me.

In several ways we made a strange pair as we walked out of the airport and caught the coach to the city centre. We seemed to have nothing in common but sheer youth and a shyness that we were slowly overcoming. I was tall and clumsy in both gait and words; she was shorter than me by a head and, even in another language, more fluent and sophisticated, but it was clear we both shared the same determination to be united permanently.

It seemed I had been in Prague only days before. The shabby trams rattled by, the people looked despondent and the cobbles were all greasy with damp. Policemen on duty whistled at cars that jumped the lights. Even in the main streets, the shop windows made the same drab viewing, although some displays gave a better impression of abundance than they had before.

I explained the restrictions of my visit and Anna's face fell, but lifted again when I mentioned the possibility of an extension. "Then we'll stay in Prague tonight," she decided, "and tomorrow you go and get your business done and we'll see what time's left after that."

In all we tried nine hotels. Eight of them had vacant rooms but, upon learning my nationality, reluctantly found reasons for denying me a room. The ninth was the Alcron.

"They'd never let me in here if they knew I was Czech," explained Anna as we approached the desk.

"You book in and I'll join you. It's a foreigners-only hotel, you know."

I had guessed this. In fact it was the main reason I had intended shunning the place. At the reception desk I obtained a room with no trouble at all, exchanging the reservation chit for my passport.

The fading splendour of the Alcron reminded me a little of Budapest's Astoria where I had stayed earlier on my ill-fated Hungarian trip. A wide mahogany staircase wound up a central coil of outsize chocolate-brown banisters towards an amber skylight at the top. Hand in hand, we stumbled up the wide steps laughing slightly hysterically at the circumstances and the prospect of another stolen night together.

In the morning I took my gamble. Using three of our precious hours, I made a whistle-stop tour of the various commercial enterprises I had previously contacted. Anna guided me through the maze of streets, and I struck oil at the head office of Motokov, the state import agency for mechanical appliances, which had been the main target of my pseudo-business dealings. Anna waited for me outside while I, attired as I was in formal suit and tie, presented myself to the musty reception bureau within. I was introduced to a long, lean individual who, it transpired, had been a signatory to some of the correspondence I had received from the agency. I repeated the gist of all I had written on the subject of my company's oil-fired product to him and his interpreter, although actually the man himself understood and spoke a little English. I was

229

there and then rewarded with an official order for a sample appliance. That they would copy its design and mechanism, should they approve of its operation, I had not the slightest doubt, although I didn't think they'd get very far on Soviet-supplied oil. This matter, however, was of no importance to me; what I did get out of the interview that morning was the coveted prize for which I had been aiming: a signed statement of intent that, submitted to the right quarters, would prolong my stay in Czechoslovakia.

Returning in triumph to Anna, we spent a couple of hours in Prague police stations obtaining another stamp in my passport that doubled my permitted sojourn. Before us now lay an eternity of 80 hours together, more than three days and nights. I basked happily in this unexpected bonus.

Next, we broke the rules and arranged for a taxi to take us the 35 kilometres to Anna's home. Although a train would have been cheaper, the fewer people who saw us the better, especially outside the confines of the city. On the back seat of the Skoda saloon we held hands but spoke little, for we didn't want the driver to realise that I was English; too many of his kin were likely to have become police informers to bolster a pitifully small income. Only as we entered the small market town I had last seen as a prisoner in 1945 did my interest stray outside the vehicle. The central square had barely altered at all and the town hall remained exactly as I remembered it. I pointed to the base of the clock tower that rose above the building.

"That was the lock-up in my day," I told Anna.

"It still is," came her laconic reply.

We stopped outside the substantial house surrounded by the overgrown garden and that I likewise remembered so vividly.

"It's even larger than I remembered," I remarked as soon as the driver had been paid off and the taxi had departed.

"It's all state property now, as you know. We've only got the ground floor for the six of us. It's not really much." I detected bitterness in her voice.

We were met at the front door by the whole family, including Anna's eldest sister Miluska, her youngest sister Mary and Mary's husband Paul. Within seconds I was being hugged, kissed and bombarded with greetings in both Czech and English. Anna's father, still the severe-looking, elderly man wearing spectacles and an out-dated suit, did his best to lead the reception formalities but was pushed into the background by his irreverent charges. With his remaining hair streaked across his wide forehead he made a comically forlorn figure but took his debunking in good heart. I sensed he was used to it and even enjoyed it.

His wife was plainly the practical side of the pair. Small and delicate, she soon had us seated round a table in the dining-cum-living room in preparation for a surprisingly lavish meal. This was a milestone in celebrating our commitment to one another as well as the acceptance of me from her family. It was made absolutely clear that our happiness was paramount and that no sacrifice they could make was too great to bear in the fulfilment of this goal. I could not help comparing Anna's parents with my own. How different were our respective fathers. Mine would not even make a requested visit on my behalf to the Czechoslovakian Embassy in London for fear of sullying his image, yet here was a man and his family prepared to accept harsh treatment and possible confiscation of their remaining property for the sake of their daughter.

That evening, in the warm security of their home, Anna and I settled down to discuss our plans. With the attitude of her family made abundantly clear, I felt it time to reveal a long-dormant and rather bizarre scheme for sneaking Anna out of Czechoslovakia should all else fail.

Poland had recently entered the list of those that featured in my plans. The mountainous district of the Slovak-Polish border, I thought, just might hold a key to one of the closed doors that surrounded us. Moreover, Poland itself still seethed with the ferment of a broken revolution, resulting in a new liberalisation now sweeping the country. If we could reach Poland another barrier would be breached.

But what then? The Polish People's Republic was still communist territory and, what was more, was separated from the West by the gulf of a fanatical regime in East Germany. Arrival in Poland might ensure being among a mainly sympathetic population but in no way did it guarantee a safe onward transition to Western freedom. Something more was required. My plan therefore involved disguising Anna as me so that she could use my passport containing a Polish visa, which, currently, did not require endorsement on arrival.

Now that I had discovered a precarious loophole in the diplomatic net that might ensure my further return to Czechoslovakia, I could hold this asset in cold storage pending the collection of the necessary Polish visa and props for the disguise. In the meantime, following the acquisition of that visa, I would undertake a tourist visit to the Polish Tatra Mountains resort of Zakopane to locate an advantageous point for the border crossing. Then I would return to Prague and, together, we would put the scheme into operation.

Anna herself held some knowledge of the Tatra Mountains on the Slovakian side of the border, having camped in them with Mary and Paul, and, while waiting, she expressed a willingness to go again with the plan in mind; the more both of us knew about the region the better. She pointed out, however, that my assumption of being able to re-enter Czechoslovakia in order to escort her across the border was a dangerous one. The avenue would be closed soon enough, she thought, if it weren't already. So Paul offered his services as guide and companion on the rugged journey she would have to make from Czechoslovakia to Poland.

Once we had met on Polish territory, Anna would disguise herself as me, then take my passport and fly out of the country using the return portion of my flight ticket to Poland. I would bring over the necessary clothes and make-up with me from England.

Following Anna's departure on the London-bound flight, my own plans as a passportless foreigner in Poland were a little less certain. I contemplated various measures including secretly crossing the River Oder into East Germany and so to multi-power Berlin, or stowing myself away, at the Baltic ports of Gdansk or Gdynia, on one of many ships bound for Sweden. But the likelihood of getting caught and of causing another diplomatic incident was high. A less dramatic and probably more effective method would be to simply report to the British Embassy in Warsaw, tell them I had lost my passport and ticket and rely upon their help to get me home. It would involve delay and, no doubt, much hassle with the Polish police but, in the existing climate of unrest, I didn't think I'd be held up for long. Anyway, so far as I was concerned, nothing mattered except to get Anna out.

We discussed and argued well into the night. The "Polish Plan", as I had grandiosely labelled it, was to remain a true last resort. We would give the parliamentarians and diplomats one more year in view of the latest developments in London. Then, if by August 1957 nothing had materialised, the plan would go ahead.

Putting further deliberations firmly aside, Anna and I attempted to spend the next day more fittingly as an engaged couple. We walked in the garden, sat on the sofa together, and talked about our life together in England.

Around midday an excitable man rushed into the house to announce that he had some important news for the English visitor. So much for my "secret" visit to Slaný. However, the man, a good friend of the family, posed no direct threat himself. He wanted to tell me about his personal sighting of a Soviet missile unit deep in the forest around the village of Msec, some 10 kilometres distant. The report, if correct, was indeed important, for it was supposed in the West at the time that no Soviet military forces or hardware were based on Czechoslovakian soil. I must have shown my scepticism, because he invited me to go along with him into the woods to see things for myself, an action that was firmly vetoed by Anna and her parents. So I had to accept his word and take down the fullest possible technical details of the alleged missile launchers, promising to report the matter to the British military attaché in Prague before I left the country.

A second intrusion into our day was more ominous from our personal point of view. An afternoon telephone call summoned us to Slaný Police Headquarters. So they *had* known of my illegal excursion from Prague. I suppose it had been naive of me to imagine otherwise. Anna and I were required to report there without delay. At once the three daughters rounded on their unfortunate father, but he swore he had told nobody untrustworthy of my presence in the town and I was inclined to believe him.

At the police station we were taken before an officer. He waved us towards a hard wooden bench without looking up and Anna managed to whisper that he wasn't the SNB captain she'd met previously. Then a younger man in plain clothes entered, talked to the officer, turned to us, cleared his throat and said in English, "Sit down, please, Sir and Madam." This was hardly an auspicious start since we were already seated. I concluded that this man *was* from the SNB.

The officer, a lieutenant, took off his cap and, placing it with great deliberation on the table in front of him, began to speak softly in excruciatingly bad English, inclining his head towards the civilian as if seeking his approval of what he was saying. The monologue ceased and it was the civilian's turn to speak. He took a deep breath.

"Passport," he demanded of me, getting to the kernel of the matter.

I handed the document over the desk and the officer, with an expression of the frankest cynicism, studied it from cover to cover. He then talked lengthily again to the civilian.

"You are," said the latter, "presumably aware that you are outside the jurisdictional district of Prague to which the restrictive nature of your visa entitles you. What do you have to say about this infringement of the regulations?"

I looked blankly at him, not so much because I didn't understand him as for the simple reason that I was uncertain what to say. Anna, misinterpreting my reaction, tried to explain the question to me, but was told to keep quiet by the lieutenant. "To see my fiancée and her family," I finally replied.

I received a mirthless smile.

236

"Was that the object of your *business* visit to the Czechoslovak Socialist Republic?" he enquired with heavy sarcasm.

I replied that it wasn't but that, with my preliminary commercial appointments in Prague carried out, I felt I could relax somewhat and take the opportunity to enjoy a little pleasure. The fact that this took me a few kilometres outside the capital's statutory limits was surely — the civilian interrupted my excuse.

"So you *knew* you were contravening the regulations."

I raised my hand in an expansive gesture. "Come on, it's only a few kilometres outside the limit," I said. "How am I to know exactly where the boundary runs? But I'm sorry if I've offended anyone; it was not intended. I'll go back to Prague tomorrow."

"No, you'll go back today."

He spoke once more with his uniformed colleague, presumably translating the exchange. The lieutenant nodded and replaced his cap. The interview was at an end.

All things considered, I felt I was lucky; things could have been much worse. But I still couldn't quite understand the situation. Even had their consulate in Oslo made an error in issuing me with a transit visa, surely, in a state such as this, I could have been ejected from the country as soon as I had arrived at Prague airport. If they knew, as they must, that I was an undesirable alien, why issue me with no more than a ticking off for exceeding my limits of movement, instead of taking more positive action such as immediate expulsion? The workings of a top-heavy bureaucracy made no sense whatever to me, although I was thankful for the fact that one authority did not appear to have a clue as to what the other was doing.

Repacking our bags and bidding farewell to Anna's delightful family, we returned, by train, to Prague, and to the Alcron Hotel. The third morning was spent, not entirely fruitlessly, at the British Embassy. The consul was the one I had met before and he was surprised to see me again. He greeted me courteously enough and was suitably sympathetic concerning my long-standing predicament. He wanted to know how I had managed to gain entry to the country with my "record", as he put it, and was vastly amused when I explained the ruse I had used. He also asked about Anna, who had prudently remained outside, and I gave him a run-down of developments which had occurred in the meantime. In return, he told me that my case remained very much to the fore in the embassy files and that, at suitable intervals, it was brought out for an airing. The fact that a few notables in the UK were now being brought to bear on the Czechoslovakian authorities was indeed good news, he said, as it would prevent Anna from being "silenced".

The subsequent interview with the military attaché was, in contrast, pure farce. I found myself standing before a civilian-suited colonel wearing the regimental tie of my sister regiment and was about to open my mouth to speak my piece about the Soviet rocket battery when, with a finger to his lips, the colonel silenced me. He then wrote on a scrap of paper, "This

238

room is bugged. I know who you are so make small talk and write down the gist of what you've come to tell me about." He pushed a notepad at me.

So scribbling away madly, I attempted to grapple with the technicalities of military rocket systems while also chatting about the vagaries of Czechoslovakian weather. Every now and again, the two subjects merged, both in the written report and my speech. I doubt that either made sense to anyone.

Signing the former with a flourish, and adding my military rank and number for good measure, I was taken out into the embassy courtyard by the colonel who, away from eavesdropping microphones, gave me the reason for the extraordinary charade — although I had guessed it already. It seemed he found it convenient to have known eavesdroppers listening to any snippets of false information that he was able to give them.

For the remainder of our time together, Anna and I tried to relax and ignore the hands of the clock inexorably creeping towards the hour of another parting. As we strolled past the flower-bedecked windows of the Mala Strana, the Little Town, we spoke of the direction our lives might take after our ultimate reunion. It was a subject we had discussed only superficially before, mainly on account of the dim prospects of ever achieving it. But now I discussed in more detail starting life together in the self-contained flat my mother was enthusiastically forming within our large house. My mother had, I explained, ulterior motives. Throughout the war, she had pluckily maintained the 20-roomed house and kept the substantial garden in order, for the sake of her husband and two sons. Now she planned to hive off portions of the house and keep me within her sphere of influence. It hadn't worked with my brother Michael, who had initially begun his married life in another portion of the rambling house, likewise painstakingly transformed into a self-contained flat. After a short time, and a lot of tension, he and his wife moved away. Now my mother was trying again, knowing that I was more pliable. I was not at all convinced that it would work any better with us, but was prepared to give it a try if my bride agreed. Anna made no comment to my explanation. How could she? She had never met my parents so was unable to judge the situation for herself.

The lengthening shadows of St Nicholas Church fell across us as we reached Malostranske Namesti, the heart of the Little Town, and the loveliest square in the city.

We both shivered in the cool of evening. The striking of the church clock above reverberated around the square then, one after another, all the different church chimes rang out, echoed through the streets, and died away. It was time to leave each other again. With the validity of my visa already exhausted, we headed reluctantly back to the hotel to collect our bags. I tried to dissuade Anna from accompanying me to the station as railway platform partings were becoming all too regular and painful events in our lives, but she insisted.

Standing on the platform, Anna attempted to smile but her eyes were moist. I kissed her goodbye light-heartedly as if I were going away for no more than a weekend. She held me tightly. "Next time, I'll be coming with you," she whispered.

The train moved away, crawling out from the great dome of the station, before entering the adjoining tunnel. I could still see her from its darkness.

CHAPTER
NINETEEN

I had been back in Britain for less than a month when Fenner Brockway invited me again to Westminster. Over a cup of tea and a bun in the Members' canteen, I listened in incredulous silence to a catalogue of "proven misdeeds" attributed to my fiancée over the past couple of years. In short, Anna was alleged to be two-timing me.

The accusations, still fresh from the lips of the ambassador of the Czechoslovak Socialist Republic, and repeated now in a neutral voice by a highly respected member of the British Parliament, astounded me. It seemed absurd that senior governmental officials and high-ranking diplomats were devoting their time to reports on the gossip of a small country town. Fenner was embarrassed to be the messenger of this news and was more distressed than I.

Even if I had no immediate explanation for some of Anna's "indiscretions", the accusations were ludicrous and clumsily substantiated. This clumsiness surprised me, for the Czechs were capable of cleverer deceptions. In addition, I knew my Anna. Our physical acquaintanceship over four years might only have been measured in days but together we had touched the depths and heights of human emotion.

Upon deeper investigation, the flimsiness of the charges was revealed. "Your fiancée's dresses", they said, "are fashionable and expensive; only obtainable in the most exclusive of Prague salons." How could she afford such outfits when she was no longer working? What they did not trouble to learn, however, was that I had brought her the material from Britain; nor did they know of Anna's considerable dressmaking skills. Unfortunately I could hardly explain to them the reason for her "holiday" in the Tatra Mountains in the summer following my brief visit, which they also suggested as being beyond the means of a non-working girl.

A skiing session in the company of some soldiers from the Czechoslovakian army could produce no immediate explanation from me, but I wasn't concerned about this either. I did know of Anna's enthusiasm for the sport and of the fact that the only local slopes around Slaný adjoined the town's barracks. But the most laughable charge concerned the alleged late-night debauchery of Anna and an unknown tall, fair young man in a Prague cabaret hall. Looking at the dates and details they had supplied, it was all too clear that I was the secret admirer!

I treated other less specific instances of Anna's apparent infidelity with the contempt they deserved. Fenner was as pleased as I was when their allegations were finally revoked.

243

Meanwhile, the British press came to my aid with a barrage of lurid headlines in their inner pages, such as REDS HOLD FIANCEE or IRON CURTAIN ROMANCE FRUSTRATED BY RED GOVERNMENT. Appreciating both the value of press support and the harm it could inflict by blatant misreporting — particularly in view of the Czechoslovakian ambassador's insinuation that his help was conditional upon no press intervention — I tried to shake off the reporters. I spent two consecutive nights in the clamorous offices of a couple of London newspapers attempting, unsuccessfully, to persuade them to tone the story down.

Even quicker off the mark was the Ministry of Defence, who had summoned me to their offices as soon as I returned from Prague to glean further details about the Soviet rocket battery. Later, a Czech working for British Intelligence came to see me at home, concerned about my vulnerability to blackmail. His inventory of horror stories about British patriots being forced into betraying their country was no news to me, and wasn't particularly disturbing. Indeed, it was a comfort to know that the faceless employees of my *own* security services were watching my every move. Come August 1957 it might be good to have them around.

Sensing the ever-increasing danger to Anna, I lost no time in getting to work on preliminaries for the "Polish Plan". Should I fail to reach Czechoslovakia again, I would instead go straight to Poland, and meet her at a pre-arranged point on the Polish side of the mountainous border. I intended to visit Poland beforehand anyway, to locate a suitable crossing point and observe for myself the degree of governmental control in the country. But first I had less exacting tasks to perform.

There was the small matter of a doctored passport under a different name — one I could use, if need be, for my final attempt to enter Czechoslovakia, as I could not depend on the Scandinavian "loophole" being still available to me. I owned a batch of expired passports, returned by the Foreign Office who had cut off the corners and stamped "cancelled" across each page. I also had a somewhat flamboyant friend from my soldiering days, whose artistic talents ranged from interior decoration and oil painting to the "touching up" of legal documents. I went to see Tom at his rambling old ruin of a home in Suffolk, but he wasn't able to revalidate any of my passports. Or so he said, but I had a sneaking feeling he had self-righteously decided to "go straight". I also visited another old school friend, Trevor, who slightly resembled me facially. I told him he would be doing me a great favour if he could apply in his own name for a Czechoslovakian entry visa at the consulate in London. This he promised to do and, furthermore, he agreed to let me use his passport if successful. The identity photograph would need only a slight "blurring", a simple enough task for the capable, if reformed, Tom. I continued to nurture the idea of using the "unofficial" passport for my final entry to Czechoslovakia and to use my own, adorned with a Polish entry visa, for the

Polish venture. There were nonetheless shortcomings to this arrangement that made sense of Anna's offer to make her own way, with Paul, across Slovakian territory and over the Polish border.

Next on the agenda was an initial discussion with a well-known Haymarket firm of wigmakers and theatre make-up specialists. Since I had no intention of revealing the real reason for transforming a dark, five-foot-two girl into a fair, near six-foot man, the salesman must have thought I was either mad or a terrorist. I made a number of visits to the emporium in Panton Street, finally coming away with an assortment of facial creams, "ageing" lotions, a blonde wig and a great deal of advice on the sort of clothes best suited to hiding the female figure.

Then, on 22 October 1956, there was a full-scale revolt against communism in Budapest. Along with millions of others in Britain and Western Europe, I listened, spellbound, to the details of the savage acts of retribution being performed. When Budapest Radio broadcast an impassioned plea for help as Soviet tanks began quelling the rebellion with equal savagery, my admiration turned to shame. In my case it was not only a nationally-held shame but also a personal one, for here was an opportunity to use the chaos of war to my own advantage. It surely would not be impossible to arrange for Anna's transfer to Hungarian soil and out to neutral Austria across a temporarily unguarded Eastern European frontier, but it would need to be done quickly, before the border crossings into Hungary were closed. However, fettered by indecision, I waited inert while the grim drama unfolded.

Only when a communication arrived from a London University student organisation did I snap out of inertia. It asked in a matter-of-fact tone whether I would be prepared, with my wartime evasion experience and a more recent knowledge of conditions in Hungary, to put these assets at the disposal of the patriots in the shrapnel-scarred streets of Budapest.

This was the spur I needed and I went to see the organising secretary, a dangerously dedicated young man. With vague misgivings, I volunteered my services and was appointed to the "advisory committee" where, with an ex-paratrooper major and a ruffian who had "dabbled" in demolition, I found myself saddled with a multitude of potential projects, one of which involved dynamiting sections of the Hungarian State Railway.

My suspicions about the whole affair crystallised a few days later when a series of messages reached me announcing weekend training hikes on Dartmoor, while, in direct contradiction, two midnight telephone calls instructed me to report without delay to an address in Vienna. Fortunately I delayed my departure long enough to receive the cancellation message for the Vienna rendezvous and, while the embryo freedom-fighters might or might not have been frolicking in the heather, the tragedy in Hungary drew to its inevitable finale.

Soon after the Budapest uprising, I found the opportunity to make a brief visit to Poland. The Polish Consulate in London's Langham Place had granted me a visa with disconcerting ease and I was determined not to waste it.

Zakopane is the chief resort in the Polish Tatras and it lies about 100 kilometres south of Cracow. From a tourist's perspective I found the small town a disappointment, but its setting in the Carpathian High Tatra range gave it an air of undeserved grandeur. Following a night in a hotel, I hired a car and drove up the valley away from the cluster of chalets, passing the cold silent waters of the lake of Kuźnice. The road ended once the gradient became too steep, and here I left the vehicle to continue on foot. Above me towered the peak Kasprowy Wierch, the southern flank of which is in Slovakia. A cable-car ride to its summit served to show that border guards were very few in a region where nature provided its own barrier. Patrols, I was told, went out in the known tourist haunts, mainly to head off over-enthusiastic hikers, but otherwise there was little in the way of a guarded frontier, at least on the Polish side.

Later I drove another route around the massif of Kasprowy Wierch to little Javorina, the Polish — Slovak village border post. Most of the houses were huddled around the single-lane bridge. To gauge reaction, I made my way across it. The Polish soldier waved me through without a murmur and the Czech guard, unsure of himself, would have caused no fuss either had his officer not emerged from the guardroom just at the wrong moment. I was politely informed that I could go no further without permission, but the incident proved to me the degree of laxity existing here.

Continuing along a road that remained in Polish territory, I came to Lake Morske Oko, a favourite attraction in the summer months. Now its sombre waters were undisturbed and deserted, enclosed by granite walls that formed the saucer in which it lay. A muddy footpath led towards another sector of the border, upward past a second but smaller lake called Czarny Stan and, within half an hour, I was standing beside a stone marking the division between the two countries. I waited, resting in the rock-studded undergrowth for more than an hour, during which I neither saw nor heard a single border guard. Here, surely, was our passage out of Czechoslovakia. It didn't have to be this exact spot, but the terrain a few hundred metres either side offered good exit and entry points. I took some photographs, made a few notes, carefully marked my large-scale map and left.

The enclave of Polish soil — subsequently known as the Tatra National Park — jutting into Slovakia is quite small and within a couple of days I had virtually explored it all, but I found no better site than the one above Czarny Stan. The border, of course, continued for hundreds of kilometres in both directions but here, in the Zakopane region, were the highest and wildest peaks. Furthermore, in the high season there would be plenty of tourists on both sides, so that our proximity to the border would be unremarkable.

Within my allotted 10 days of holiday, I was home again. I was radiant with optimism. Border conditions were far less strict than I could possibly have imagined and the trek through the mountains into Poland would be a piece of cake.

I learned from Trevor that his application for a Czechoslovakian visa had been rejected, which ruled out the ruse of the alternative passport. However, I was still determined to meet Anna before she set out for the mountains so that I could brief her thoroughly about my findings in Zakopane — this could hardly be trusted to a letter. Additionally, it would give me the opportunity to experiment with some of the props of disguise I had bought. So, with this in mind, I journeyed north once more to spend a long weekend in Copenhagen, to see whether a top-heavy Czechoslovakian bureaucracy was, by chance, still working for me.

CHAPTER
TWENTY

Webers Hotel was an unpretentious but comfortable establishment in the Vesterbrogade, close to the centre of Copenhagen. Its warm, friendly fug welcomed me as I came in from the snow-swept street outside. With numb, fumbling fingers I signed the register and climbed the single flight of stairs to my room. A bottle of red wine and a bowl of fruit, compliments of the management, stood on my bedside table.

It was December 1956, and I had made Copenhagen my destination simply because it had not yet featured in my campaign for a transit visa. I had carefully paved the way again, and in this particular deception a Danish girl called Christine had been very helpful.

I had met her on the train while returning from Hungary 18 months previously and, finding her to be of sympathetic nature, had told her something of my situation. She expressed an eagerness to help and when we parted I made a mental note of the offer. Only following my subsequent earlier Scandinavian escapades did I remember her offer and I decided to follow it up.

So Christine willingly became my "post office" in her native Denmark and, through her, I was able to represent myself to the Czechoslovakian Consulate in

Copenhagen as a British businessman temporarily domiciled in Denmark. In my re-posted letters and brochures I had given such a good account of myself and the firm I represented that the commercial attaché had actually invited me to his office for a discussion on the possibility of his *persuading* me to visit Prague. My supposed commercial prowess had even reached the ears of Webers Hotel that Christine had recommended, hence the welcoming wine and fruit. Christine herself, alas, was out of town, so I was unable to thank her for her astuteness.

Sipping the wine, I slowly unpacked my suitcase. I was carrying more then usual this time. On the bed I laid out an expensive blonde wig, trousers and a jacket several sizes too small for me, and numerous pots of mysterious creams. If I *did* manage to reach Prague, then I'd at least ensure Anna had a proper dress rehearsal for her escape. Were the customs people to search my suitcase at Prague airport, they were going to think they had a very odd customer indeed!

On a cold but clear and sunny morning, I arrived at the Czechoslovakian Consulate in a select district called Svanemollevij. The commercial attaché was even warmer to me than his Oslo colleague. His face shone with enthusiasm as we discussed the Czechoslovakian iron industry, about which I knew very little. I had decided to switch from the oil-fired central heating appliance section of the family business to the iron-founding side, partly on account of the fact that I was basically involved with the subject in my day-to-day job, but also because I didn't want the attaché to check

252

with Motokov in Prague and discover I'd already visited the organisation. Within minutes, the man was discussing the possibility of my visit to the locomotive plant at Ostrava. With some misgivings, I allowed him to dictate to his secretary a letter of introduction to some industrial enterprise in Prague as a preliminary. I was then invited to complete the usual visa application form for an entry visa no less, allowing me an almost unrestricted stay in the country. The attaché bustled about, unearthing reams of technical reports and sheets of production figures from a huge roll-top desk.

Left alone for a few moments, I did my best to compose myself enough to hide my incredulity at the way things were going. In a moment, I thought, he'd come across my name in the little black book and return with a stormy face. But no, in he swept again and there, on the last page of my battered, ink-stained passport was another mauve stamp. He hadn't even seemed to have noticed the cancelled transit visa on an earlier page. After a double aquavit and a flurry of fond farewells, I headed straight to the airways terminal in the city centre.

By midday I had booked a seat on my old friend, Flight OK 432 of CSA, departing that very afternoon for Berlin and Prague. The Czechoslovakian attaché had assured me that East German immigration officials were now taking a more relaxed view of passengers passing through the airport. I caught the coach to Kastrup airport, hoping he was right.

On board the familiar aircraft, there were five other passengers, and a careworn version of the previous stewardess. The green light came on, engines surged and we were away, the old Ilyushin almost grazing the fence at the end of the runway before the Zeeland coast receded behind the starboard propeller. Again the Baltic below was grey and muted, merging with the sky.

The distant spires of Straslund and the German mainland riding into view made me glow with anticipation. The world was suddenly a joyful place. So rapidly had everything been organised, I had not had the opportunity to send Anna a cable, but it was safer not to in any case. She did know that I was going to Denmark and had probably guessed the reason why. I had dreamed of making a surprise arrival at her home and now, through no planning on my part, this dream was likely to come true. I lay back in my seat, imagining the first delicious moments as I walked unannounced into the midst of the household.

"Your passport, please." I was back in a world of practicalities. The hostess hovered over me.

I fumbled in my jacket pocket and waited for the expected outburst at my lack of East German visa.

"You go to Prague, yes?

I nodded. She returned my passport without a word and walked away.

After our descent, we rolled to a standstill and, being in no hurry, I watched my flight companions collect their briefcases and leave the aircraft. I was about to follow when the stewardess stopped me. I waited, impatient and on edge. The pilot and crew filed out of the cockpit and I was alone on the aeroplane. Had they forgotten me? Would I still be here when they came to service the aircraft? A babble of voices relaxed me: here was the new intake of Prague-bound passengers; all was well. I started back towards my seat.

But no new passengers appeared. Instead, through the door, came a police officer followed by two of his men. They made directly for me and I began worrying again.

The officer gave me a perfunctory salute.

"You are Herr Portvy, I think?"

I replied that I was, more or less.

"Then please, I must ask you to come with me."

"May I ask why?" I enquired politely.

"A matter concerning your visa," he said. "We won't keep you long, I assure you. Please be so kind."

In a neon-lit office I was introduced to a bad-tempered civilian who turned out to be a representative of the Czechoslovakian Embassy in Berlin.

He came straight to the point.

"Mr Portway, you not go to Prague. You go back. You understand, yes?"

"No," I said, understanding too well.

The sour-faced minor diplomat explained. It appeared that the granting of my visa in Copenhagen had been an error that had been discovered too late for me to be stopped at Kastrup. A message had therefore been flashed to the Berlin embassy that had resulted in him being sent, on his afternoon off, to a draughty airfield to rectify a mistake that wasn't his. To emphasise his displeasure, the man proceeded to stamp indelible cancellation marks across the offending visa in my passport.

Still clinging to my well-tried business theme, I launched into a torrent of invective directed at the wretched little secretary. He stared at me owlishly through thick-lensed spectacles, probably understanding few of the words but assuredly aware of the murder in my eyes. When, finally, he got in a few words of his own they didn't help.

"This is not a commercial matter," he explained in a tone that intimated he was dealing with a fractious child. "That is not the responsibility of my department."

Departments, formalities, entry visas, transit visas, double transit visas, exit permits, marriage permits. Frustration at all the ridiculous machinery of delay welled up inside me and in a neon-lit office near the terminal building, I exploded.

"All you bloody government lackeys are the same," I roared. "All locked up in your stupid little departments not caring a tuppenny damn what happens so long as your own fat arses are comfortably seated in your departmental chairs!" During the course of my recital the clatter of office typewriters had ceased and there was a heavy silence.

An English-speaking police officer laid a hand on my shoulder to restrain any further outbursts, but I'd said my piece. I noticed the typists were enjoying the situation; the Czech noticed it too and diplomatically withdrew. He plainly saw no purpose in hanging around.

256

But for me the ordeal was not over. The officer, attempting to pour oil on troubled water, purred in my ear something about an aircraft departing for Copenhagen. My flight would be gratis; courtesy of CSA.

Resigned to the inevitable I told him that, my plans ruined, I'd return to Britain by the direct route from one of the Western airports in Berlin, if he didn't mind.

The chap avoided my eye. "There's the little matter of the transit visa," he said quietly.

"Yes, but as I'm virtually in Berlin I can fly direct to London from there, so shan't need . . ." I began, then faded into silence at the realisation of what he was trying to tell me.

"You mean I've got to fly hundreds of miles northwards, then hundreds of miles south just because I'm not permitted to cross a couple of miles of your precious German Democratic bloody Republic?" The policeman pretended not to hear.

The detention room of Schönfeld Airport was a stark barred-windowed chamber containing a scattering of benches and hardback chair. I waited there for hours. I heard, or thought I heard, the departure of Flight OK 432 on the final leg of its journey to Prague. Even though I had prepared myself for the likelihood of failure when I set out from Britain, my hopes had risen with the luck I had had in Copenhagen. One small grain of comfort I clung to was the knowledge that Anna had not known of my journey, so would not have to share my despondency. And there was a tiny new flame of hope too. Although I had to go back to

Copenhagen, I would ensure the detour wasn't entirely wasted. From the Danish capital I would contact the Oslo consulate to gauge the reaction to a repeat of my earlier visa success there. Maybe, just maybe, they had not been made aware of their original mistake. Thus there was a slender chance that I could be back on the Copenhagen-Berlin-Prague flight within a couple of days, and it really did seem that the GDR people weren't too fussy about transit visas on through flights.

When I was eventually led out of the room I thought it would be to the departing aircraft. Instead I found myself before the same police officer. He sat, upright and unsmiling, at a desk behind a large-scale map of Berlin.

"Mr Portway," he began, getting my name right this time, "you seem to be in the habit of crossing GDR territory without the necessary permission. It has been brought to my attention that you made a similar transitory journey not many months ago."

I digested this for a moment.

"Yes, I was on my way to Prague like I was on this occasion."

The officer twiddled a pencil between his thumb and forefinger.

"Well, you won't do it again. It seems Prague doesn't want your presence. Nor do we. You are, it seems, something of a troublemaker."

I stoutly denied the allegation. "On the other occasion, as well as this one, I was granted a Czechoslovakian visa. I can't help it if they saw fit on this occasion to revoke it halfway through my journey.

I'm a businessman plain and simple. Why should I want to cause anyone trouble?"

The officer plainly didn't believe me. Perhaps it was only the fact that it was a Czechoslovakian matter, and not an East German one, that prevented him from pursuing that line of enquiry any further.

"What sort of business do you carry out in Prague?" he asked, turning to my suitcase.

My heart skipped a beat. I really didn't want him looking through my belongings; his discovery of the items of disguise, especially the wig and the creams, would arouse real suspicion.

"Oh, just the importation of central-heating equipment," I replied airily and then remembered the current commercial reason I'd given the Czechoslovakian consulate in Copenhagen. To deflect the chap from this line of questioning and possible interest in the contents of my case I asked when I would be able to return to Copenhagen.

He made no reply and, instead, put his hand on the suitcase, reading the labels. In a moment he'd have the thing open.

An airport official entered the room and spoke briefly. The officer abruptly lost interest.

"Your flight's ready now. You can go," came the curt instruction. I needed no second bidding. Grabbing my case, I was on my way. On the grass runway stood a familiar Ilyushin aeroplane.

My earlier anger had entirely subsided, leaving me drained of emotion. Even the new spark of hope arising from the slight chance of the Oslo loophole being still open had dimmed as a result of the warning I'd received at Schönfeld. But on wider issues there were no doubts. The "Polish Plan" remained undiminished. It would go ahead, sustained by other means. It would entail getting the information through to Anna by some secret method and there would be no chance of a pre-departure dress disguise rehearsal. I would have to go straight to Poland to meet her in the mountains. The current setback was simply one more to chalk up to experience.

A late arrival in Copenhagen, a short night in a modest hotel near the station and, next morning, just for the hell of it, I telephoned the Czechoslovakian Consulate in Oslo. I asked to speak to the commercial attaché.

"He's not available," said a cold voice.

Without giving my name, I enquired of the chances of obtaining a transit visa for Czechoslovakia in the light of urgent business I found necessary to transact with some Prague import agencies.

"Why don't you apply in Copenhagen?" He retorted. I wondered how he knew I was in Denmark but I was ready with a reply. "Following my business here," I explained, "I have to continue to Norway, and so it is from Oslo I would want to go to Prague."

The voice told me to wait a minute.

"All visa applications have to be referred to Prague," came a familiar refrain from a new voice.

"Even transit visas?"

"All visas."

I was reluctant to terminate the exchange. "But you granted me one without delay last year."

This time the pause was pregnant.

"Your name. Is it Mr Portway?" asked the same voice, now thin with suspicion. I saw no point in denying it.

"Yes, but I —"

An amplified click sounded and I was talking to myself.

CHAPTER
TWENTY-ONE

My reaction to Fenner Brockway's abruptly announced intention of going to Prague to intercede directly on my behalf was strange indeed. I felt only a chary disappointment in that Fenner's mission might mean postponing or abandoning the "Polish Plan", so firmly had this project established itself in my mind.

Following my return from Denmark, I had resumed the secret correspondence with Anna, attempting to explain, in a mixture of code and phrases that I hoped were unintelligible to anyone but her, the next moves in the plan. We had got as far as making tentative dates for our meeting on the Polish border and I had made a preliminary application for another Polish visa. While these exchanges were taking place, Fenner was making further futile representations to the Czechoslovakian ambassador in London. But then one day, over lunch at Westminster, Fenner told me his decision to take up the matter directly with the Prague regime.

Suddenly, from a very different quarter, there came a new and much more startling development. My first reaction was simple disbelief. Worn down at last by incessant clamour, the Czechoslovakian authorities had instigated, it seemed, the ponderous process of expelling Anna from her homeland.

Over 1000 kilometres away to the east, Anna gazed with incredulity at the typed letter in her hand. It had arrived that morning from the Ministry of the Interior in Prague. If she was prepared to complete the following formalities divesting her of certain rights, it read, she would be permitted to emigrate from the country. A list of certificates to be obtained from various sources terminated the brief communication.

Hardly daring to believe it, Anna showed the letter to her father. Equally incredulous, he was able only to strengthen her own conviction that the whole thing was a trap, a concoction of the SNB. Her mother and other members of the family were reluctantly of the same opinion.

Still in a daze, Anna went to the family solicitor to obtain a more professional opinion. In the drab surroundings of his office she listened in mounting excitement as he assured her that the statement appeared to be no trick and advised her on obtaining the seven certificates that stood between her and the miraculous exit permit.

It was not going to be simple, as there were several Catch-22 situations involved. The National Bank could issue a nil-liability certificate if the State Customs authority would supply a counter certificate to the effect that no property was being removed from the country. The District National Committee (equivalent to a county council in Great Britain) needed confirmation that she would be in a position to obtain registration as a British subject — but this assurance could not be given until she was in a position to obtain registration. Čedok, the state tourism bureau, could not supply an air ticket to any Western European destination without payment in sterling or US dollars, while a train ticket paid in Czechoslovakian crowns was valid only to the state border. In turn, the consulates of West Germany, France, Belgium or Holland, through which she might require to pass if she travelled by rail, would be unable to consider the granting of a transit visa if the subject became stateless — even temporarily — as would indeed be the case. These and other technical and legal hurdles rose to become a whirl of confusion in Anna's mind. Yet they offered a more attractive proposition than the much-vaunted "Polish Plan", instructions about which she had been receiving complicated undercover letters from me for weeks.

Her mind flew off at a tangent as it always did when new difficulties arose. So enthusiastic had I been that she wondered, not for the first time, whether I was primarily motivated by the challenge involved. She didn't think I loved her purely for her unavailability, but it was certainly an added attraction. I would never admit it, of course, but she could read me like a book. She hoped she could live up to my expectations once we were married and settled down to an unadventurous life together.

There was no doubt about my obsession with this "Polish Plan". Plainly I meant every word I wrote to her about it. My enthusiasm was almost infectious. She herself had dutifully revisited the Slovak Tatras at my bidding. But the idea of sneaking around in those hostile mountains, the illegal crossing of borders and, worst of all, disguising herself as a man, gave her nightmares.

And another thing. My plan encompassed her transfer to Western Europe but took no account of the consequences to myself. The scheme of giving myself up to the Polish authorities, even with the knowledge of the British Embassy in Warsaw, was precarious. The story about the lost or stolen passport and air ticket sounded ridiculously thin to her, as it would to them. Heaven knows how long they'd hold me while they investigated, and when the ruse was revealed — as it surely would be — I'd be imprisoned for years. What a situation to be in; our roles reversed with her probably a refugee in a Western European camp and me east of the border in jail!

As a result of these horrific premonitions, Anna bent her thoughts more constructively to leaving her homeland in the legal, less lethal and, thankfully, less dramatic manner.

Frantic for further details, facts and confirmation of the tidings that had reached me secondhand via Fenner and the Czechoslovakian ambassador, I bombarded Anna with uncoded letters. My parents became aware that I might have succeeded after all in a quest they had long deemed hopeless. For my mother, this was more of a shock than a source of pleasure, but my father became abruptly paternal, confiding in me the less joyous moments of his own married life as if to warn me of my awesome responsibilities.

My enthusiasm for the "Polish Plan" faded with the first revelation of the new development. Here, at last, on the passive front was something tangible. There was no doubt about it; a legal departure would be so much more satisfactory. It would ensure continued contact with and possible visits to Anna's family in the years to come as the East-West thaw increased. Nor would the state have reason to inflict any form of punishment on her family, as could so easily be the case were she to leave illegally. But although Anna kept me adequately informed of progress at her end, waiting was hell.

By the end of the first two months Anna had a total of four certificates, but some of these were soon going to expire. I had sent her a formal letter to show the authorities, assuring them that I would purchase the air tickets and pay in sterling any other expenses.

Another month passed and one of the certificates expired. Unconvinced by the intentions of the Czechoslovakian authorities, I dredged up the "Polish Plan" again as Anna's letters, full of frustration, drove me towards desperation. They spoke of procrastination and inertia on the part of the local and national administration, and each letter sent me into another outburst of feverish but useless activity. I don't know what crazed measures I would have taken had not the Czechoslovakian Ministry of the Interior finally produced the blessed document irrevocably divesting her of Czechoslovakian nationality.

Stateless, penniless and jobless, the state could find no further reason for holding her. But there was still a final hurdle. On account of her new statelessness, no passport could be issued and with no passport how could an exit visa be furnished? To overcome this problem of its own making, the Ministry had two choices. One was to pass a new law and the other was to issue a stateless person's travel document, not universally recognised. The second and easier solution was, of course, chosen and Anna was awarded a travel document to which could be affixed the necessary seals and stamps of an exit permit. The Ministry showed itself in no mood to compromise. As long as it could get rid of her across the state border what did it care about outside consequences? But the British embassy in Prague embellished the document with a one-way British entry visa in spite of its near invalidity, and for this I have to thank the consul, Mr Bedford, for his by-passing of official regulations.

The first news of her triumph over the forces of bureaucracy came from Anna herself, but I remained sceptical, sure that it was all a trick. A telegram from the House of Commons followed. It read "Permit granted conditional renounce Czech nationality" and it was signed "Fenner Brockway". In the following days there were further messages confirming the impending departure of Anna from her homeland: coldly official statements from the Foreign Office, chatty letters from the Committee of Human Rights, a hand-written note from Mr R. A. Butler, who had since become Chancellor of the Exchequer, and a request from

Independent Television to cover the impending wedding.

My suspicious mind was finally put at rest, although I continued to live in a fever of excitement. Finally the cable I had been waiting for arrived. Sent by Anna it read simply: "Arriving Orly Sunday seventeenth twenty twenty."

On Saturday, March 16, at Victoria Station, I boarded the night express for Paris.

Back in Slaný, Anna said goodbye to her family, not knowing when she would be able to see them again. The final parting was, for her, both joyful and extremely sad. For her mother, father, Miluska, Mary and Paul, it must also have produced tangled emotions. On Sunday, March 17, 1957, at Prague's Ruzyne Airport, Anna boarded an Air France Viscount for a one-way flight to Paris.

The French capital lay under a damp blanket of mist. Hands deep in my pockets, I strolled towards the Étoile, trying to pass the hours until Anna's flight arrived. Not until twenty minutes past eight that evening would the near five years of waiting, scheming, planning, frustration and heartbreak be over.

Sleep had been impossible on the ferry. At Gare St Lazare I had checked the time of the return service and confirmed my reservation of a double sleeper for our London-bound journey 36 hours later. From the station I had made my way to a luxury hotel in the Madeleine area and booked one of its best rooms for our first night of freedom together. Washed and shaved,

I stretched out on the bed and attempted to relax, picturing the airport arrival hall and the small figure of Anna as she detached herself from the other travellers and fell into my arms. I lay there, quivering with anticipation, inhaling the imagined perfume of her hair, my heart bursting with happiness.

The picture faded as I mused on the more prosaic possibilities of a short break in the French capital. Anna would be tired, possibly a little confused, so I mustn't let my eagerness to show her the sights run away with me. Perhaps then, we would have an intimate meal together in one of the expensive restaurants on the Boulevard Haussmann close by the hotel. Afterwards, a short stroll, gazing into the windows of shops, unlike anything she would have seen before. The next day we would sleep late, then wander about Paris, where I would show her the glories of Notre Dame, Sacré Coeur and the Arc de Triomphe. We would amble, arm in arm, along the banks of the Seine to the Louvre, the Tuileries and the white-stoned Palais de Chaillot. We would gaze down upon the magnificence of the city from the summit of the Eiffel Tower and descend for an aperitif and a meal in one of the snug restaurants of Montmartre . . .

I still had a few more long hours to while away, so I went to a cinema, trying, without success, to make sense of an American psychological thriller which would have probably been incomprehensible even had it been in English. After another stroll through the city, and fully half an hour before I intended, I found myself at the air terminal in the Place des Invalides, where I took a coach to Orly Airport.

Once there, I spent another hour pacing up and down its crowded concourse, too impatient to sit down. I was having my usual eleventh-hour doubts: would she be aboard the aircraft? Could anything have gone wrong in Prague? What if she hadn't been allowed to leave the country after all?

The announcement of her flight arrival finally came. I glued my eyes to the double doors through which the arrivals had to pass. A hush fell on the waiting crowd around me and I noted that others too were waiting to be reunited with the arriving passengers.

After what seemed like hours the double doors pushed open and everyone tensed. Those with relations and friends to meet crowded towards the rope barrier, watching every traveller who came through the open doors. A small man in an overcoat was the first to come through. He stood blinking uncertainly in the neon light, then, with nobody claiming him as their own, scuttled into the body of the audience and was gone. Next, a middle-aged couple walked through and was mobbed by a bevy of relatives, hugging and chattering. As the flow of newcomers increased, the waiting crowd shrank. I found myself, suddenly alarmed and frightened, one of a small forlorn group of onlookers.

I moved to a position from where I could see through the doors as they opened again to allow passengers from another flight to pass through into a re-expanding crowd. A handful of officials, a gendarme and part of a customs bench were all that was visible. I couldn't see Anna anywhere. What could have happened?

I strode through the doors and was forcibly stopped by the gendarme. I shouted at him to let me pass so that I could speak to an immigration officer and demand assurance that all passengers had been accounted for from the Prague flight. The man gripped my arm and started to push me back. Suddenly, in speechless wonder, I saw Anna arguing with a gesticulating official. She was on the far side of the customs bay but I could hear her voice, raised in exasperation. Brushing aside the indignant gendarme who was by now reaching for his pistol, I leaped towards her and was by her side within seconds.

"She's my fiancée," I explained loudly, as if this gave me the right to contravene the regulations. "Why is she being held back?" My voice was strident with anger.

"You are English?" enquired the immigration officer as if that explained everything.

I nodded.

"Just a moment please, wait here." The man walked over to a presumably more senior officer and spoke to him. Both of them now returned to us and the senior of the two made a great show of examining Anna's papers.

He spoke perfect English in a soft, competent manner. "I'm afraid this lady does not have a proper passport or documentation enabling her to enter this country," he told me. "I regret she will have to return to Prague."

I was shocked and speechless. Then, after a moment, holding Anna firmly by the hand, I turned to face both men.

"She goes back to Prague over my dead body. Anyway, what's wrong with her passport?"

The senior officer explained that Anna's papers in no way constituted a passport or in fact a legal travel document. Neither did she have a French visa of any description.

I retorted that, being stateless, there was no way she could hold a proper passport, and that whatever shortcomings might exist so far as the document was concerned, it held a legal and valid British entry visa. The official admitted that the British visa did seem to be genuine. But this was France, and —

"Well, if she can't remain in France," I interrupted, "why can't she be put on the next aeroplane to England? Why send her back when, with no more trouble, she can be sent forward?" The conversation was becoming painfully similar to others I could remember with airport officials.

I wasn't angry any more; I was simply incredulous. For the best part of five years we had been fighting to be together. Now, on the threshold of victory, a Frenchman, a citizen of a country in which love and romance were revered, wanted to destroy everything. I demanded time to contact the Chancellor of the Exchequer in London, the Foreign Minister, the Prime Minister, the United Nations, even the —

The man saw I meant business. "I'll make further enquiries," he promised. "Wait here. Sit down if you wish." He indicated some chairs on the other side of the customs bench and walked away. Over by the double doors the gendarme watched us scornfully.

Turning to Anna, as we sat down, I saw a great sadness cloud her face.

"Hello," I said weakly. I realised I hadn't even had the chance to greet her properly. At least I could put that right now. I swept her into my arms in a fierce hug. "It'll be all right, just you see. I won't let them send you back, I promise."

The senior officer returned with two colleagues. The English-speaking official smiled weakly. "I think things will be fine," he affirmed, "but she's not to leave the airport."

We were escorted to a large room that turned out to be the airport detention lounge, where we spent half the night sharing a big overstuffed sofa until we were told that she would be put aboard the earliest possible morning flight to Heathrow. I could go with her if there was a seat to spare, but I'd need tickets. Our train and ferry reservations and sleeper vouchers were now useless, but my main worry was the lack of time available to collect my baggage from the hotel and book the necessary flights. The first coach back to the terminal left Orly about four in the morning and I planned to catch that. A wave of fatigue engulfed me; the paltry details didn't seem important any more. Anna's head was on my shoulder and I could feel the steady beating of her heart. The ordeal of five years was sliding away from me. I was very, very happy.

It was still dark when I returned in an empty coach to the Invalides. Back in the airways coach terminal I bought two flight tickets for London from a sleepy-eyed booking clerk. Final check-in was at half past six and the coach that served the flight left an hour earlier. With barely 55 minutes to spare, I dashed back to the hotel, grabbed my bags and bullied a grumpy night porter into letting me check out at such an early hour.

I made it back to the coach terminal with four minutes to spare. Somehow Paris had lost its allure. On the way back to the airport, all I could think about was Anna, tired, bewildered and trusting, anxiously awaiting my return in a bleak detention room.

I found her there amidst the clamour of an awakening airport. Arm in arm we joined the queue for customs clearance. We had spoken very little since we'd met, and we had so much to say. It didn't matter now; a lifetime together stretched before us. As we walked towards the aeroplane, a pale sun broke through the early morning sky.

Epilogue

Anna and I were married on the 5 April 1957, twelve years after we had first set eyes upon one another. Among the guests were members of parliament and other distinguished people who had been directly or indirectly involved in our struggle. The ceremony took place under the bright stare of television cameras, such had been the media interest generated by our battle and final victory. Alas, none of Anna's relatives were permitted by their own government to attend the ceremonies.

For years immediately after Anna's departure from her homeland we were both excommunicated from Czechoslovakia. We had been willing to accept this penalty, despite Anna's enforced separation from her family. Following the births of our children, Alice and Paul, however, a gradual relaxation of restrictions enabled us to make occasional and permitted return visits to Anna's parents, who were delighted to see their grandchildren growing up.

The British intelligence services made use of my permitted visits to Czechoslovakia, and for a time I assisted them in gathering a mass of information about the country, most of it relating to the economy, but some to military matters. I was actually more interested in using my knowledge and experience to help Anna's sister Mary, and her husband Paul, whose lives had become a misery at the hands of the Czechoslovakian authorities. As a consequence of his past misdemeanours and known disharmony with the regime, Paul was under constant surveillance, which made it very difficult for him to escape. After yet another drawn-out saga in which I was heavily involved — secret schemes, illegal border crossings, and pleas to the authorities — Paul and Mary were eventually able to come and live in England. Anna and I were, of course, overjoyed.

We settled in the picturesque village of Gosfield, where our two children, Alice and Paul, grew up and flourished. Both are now happily married, Paul, to our delight, following in his father's footsteps by falling in love with a Czech woman, with whom he now lives in Prague. I never lost the urge to travel, and even on restricted fortnight holidays found my way to far-flung destinations. When the firm was taken over by a larger company, I jumped at the chance to make a precarious living as a freelance travel writer. Sadly, Anna passed away a few months before the publication of this book. Through our many years of marriage, she continued to let me seek out adventure all over the world, including Eastern Europe where, today, the borders are open wide to everyone.

Veterans' Voices

Caroline Freeman-Cuerden

"One thing I shall never forget is standing on a pile of bricks that had been my home. Sometimes I found familiar items lying torn and scattered around me."

The story of Coventry's war is one that has often been told: the apparently endless bombing that reduced the city centre to piles of rubble and destroyed the cathedral. The stories of 23 Coventry men and women are recounted here in their own words. We hear from all theatres of the war — fighter pilots and RAF ground crew, a sailor who served in the Arctic, a soldier at Dunkirk and men taken prisoner of war in Germany. There are also first-hand accounts of D-Day, fighting in the jungles of Burma and Sumatra, and serving as a dispatch rider at El Alamein. We also discover what it was like to return to a devastated Coventry at the end of the war.

ISBN 978-0-7531-9420-1 (hb)
ISBN 978-0-7531-9421-8 (pb)

Men of the Bombers

Ralph Barker

"He had no way of knowing that his entire crew had baled out. The awful loneliness he had felt for the last six hours had become reality".

What sustained the morale of the Men of the Bombers in their titanic struggle against the forces arrayed against them? A vastly superior enemy, technological inferiority, policy blunders, target distance and the weather, all brought continual frustration and heavy losses. Was it belief in themselves, or in their leaders? Was it personal pride? How did they manage to sustain their much-maligned campaign?

The secret lay in crew bonding. Once a member of a bomber crew, posted to a squadron, one couldn't let the other blokes down. This is the quality that shines through all these stories, from the 55-year-old gunner lost over Dunkirk to the fierce loyalty of surviving crewmen who championed awards for lost comrades.

ISBN 978-0-7531-9418-8 (hb)
ISBN 978-0-7531-9419-5 (pb)

Lie in the Dark and Listen

Wing Commander Ken Rees
with Karen Arrandale

"If the war hadn't intervened, instead of the stuff of films I suppose my life could have been the stuff of television. Are You Being Served say, rather than The Great Escape."

Often quoted as the model for the Steve McQueen character in *The Great Escape*, Ken Rees had already had an eventful life by the age of 21. He had trained to be a pilot officer, flown 56 hair-raising bomber missions by night over Germany, taken part in the siege of Malta, got married, been shot down into a remote Nowegian lake and been captured, interrogated and sent to Stalag Luft III. He took part in and survived the Great Escape and the forced march to Bremen. Truly a real-life adventure story, written with accuracy, pace and drama.

ISBN 978-0-7531-9400-3 (hb)
ISBN 978-0-7531-9401-0 (pb)

Blind to Misfortune

Bill Griffiths with Hugh Popham

"Somewhere within me I knew that, during these years as a prisoner, I had been in a sense sheltered from reality."

Bill Griffiths lost both hands and both eyes when he was a prisoner of the Japanese in Java in 1942. But Bill had no intention of allowing himself to become an object of pity and it was not long after his return to civilian life that he began to make it clear that, even if he had no hands and no eyes, he still had his own two feet and he certainly intended to stand on them. Inevitably, life has not been without its ups and downs, and certainly Bill could not have got where was without the care and devotion of his wife Alice. Their story is one of remarkable courage, told with no trace of bitterness and a generous helping of laughter.

ISBN 978-0-7531-9374-7 **(hb)**
ISBN 978-0-7531-9375-4 **(pb)**

The Long Way Home

John McCallum

"Not many POWs had the good fortune to have a big brother to look after them in such circumstances, and to think he was there because of me made me feel terribly guilty at times."

At the age of 19, Glasgow-born John McCallum signed up as a Supplementary Reservist. By the middle of September 1939, he was in France, working frantically to set up communication lines after the outbreak of war. Wounded and captured, he was sent to the notorious Stalag VIIIB prison camp, together with his brother, Jimmy, and friend Joe Harkin.

The three men set about planning their escape. With the help of a local girl, they put their plan into action. In an astonishing coincidence, they passed through the town of Sagan, around which the 76 airmen of the "Great Escape" were being pursued and caught. However, unlike most of these other escapers, John, Jimmy and Joe eventually made it to freedom.

ISBN 978-0-7531-9370-9 (hb)
ISBN 978-0-7531-9371-6 (pb)